To everyone who needs a second chance, you deserve it, a difficult time, bad choice or a mistake does not define you for life. Dust yourself off and press on.

For anyone who needs a reminder to take the shot they've been afraid to- it's worth it.

For anyone who needs a reminder of what a beautiful gift it is to live and to love.

Slapshots & Second Chances

Silverwood Snipers Book One

Ashley Malinowski

ISBN: 979-8-9950138-0-8

Author's Note

This story includes themes that may be difficult for some readers.

Content elements include:

Grief, loss, and emotional trauma; death of a romantic partner (not FMC); pregnancy loss (implied, off-page); references to an abusive relationship; stalking behavior; fire trauma; kidnapping; threats of violence; pregnancy; alcohol use; strong language; and sexual content.

Acknowledgments

This book would not have been possible without the help of many people.

Above all else, I am thankful to my Lord and Savior, Jesus Christ, for allowing me to live with the desire and talent of writing.

Thank you to my editors Kate Seger and Krysten Meissner for their countless hours of helping to edit this book and being immersed in Silverwood, Maine with me.

Thank you to my incredible PA ladies, Megan Ashley Smith, and Zena Vaughn.

To the team at Artscandare for the beautiful cover design.

Chapter One

Silverwood, Maine

The biting cold seeped through the fabric of the Silverwood Snipers hockey jersey, tingling against his skin. Slade Fisher's breath curled into the sharp scent of ice—fresh rink, damp gear, and a trace of winter. He flexed his fingers around his stick, the familiar weight resting comfortably in his hands as he lined up his shot.

"You ready for this, man?" their left defender, Hunter, asked, tapping his stick against the ice. "Big night ahead. How's your shoulder from that hit earlier?"

Slade sighed. "Yeah, I'm ready. Shoulder's fine."

"You sure? You got crushed into the boards earlier," added his twin brother and Snipers' center, Stryker, eyeing him with concern.

"I'm good," Slade lied, rubbing his sore shoulder as the dull ache radiated through the joint.

He would have to make an appointment with Talulla Murphy, the Snipers' new physical therapist. She also happened to be his cousin. That would have to wait, though, because tonight he was proposing to his girlfriend, Jessica, at the Winter Walk. They had been high school sweethearts since sophomore year and some of the best six years of his life so far thanks to her.

Christmas was still a week away but he just couldn't wait any longer. Each year, their sleepy little town of Silverwood, which was nestled along Maine's coastline just south of Portland, would light up nearly every inch of its downtown square with festive lights for the month-long event and he and Jess never missed it.

Slade locked his eyes on the net, coiled his body, and with a whip-like motion, his stick met the puck with a *crack* that echoed through the arena. It shot through the air like a firework, sailing at blistering speed before burying itself deep in the corner of the goal, leaving their goalie, Gunner, stupefied.

A perfect slapshot.

All of his teammates whistled, clapping their sticks against the ice.

"Damn, captain, if that's not a sign you're ready, I don't know what is," Jayden laughed. He was the Snipers' right defender.

Slade grinned, shaking out his arms, adrenaline buzzing through his veins. "Yeah. Tonight's going to be unforgettable."

Slade pushed open the doors of the Silverwood Hockey Arena, letting them slam shut behind him. The adrenaline from practice had faded, leaving him tired and ready for the next few days off.

His breath fogged the air as the cold December wind hit him like a smack to the face while he crossed the parking lot toward his black pickup truck. Still, he welcomed it.

Wearing his favorite gray hoodie with the Silverwood Snipers logo, sweatpants, and a black beanie, he glanced down at his watch. He had enough time to go home, shower and change, then head to the town square.

As Slade yanked the truck door open with more force than necessary, he felt the small velvet box in his pocket and pictured the princess-cut solitaire diamond ring inside.

Slamming the door shut, he smiled, imagining the look on Jessica's face when he proposed. She was going to be so happy; snow had always been their thing, and Christmas was their favorite holiday.

He gripped the steering wheel, then let go, wiping his palms on his sweatpants. His heart was speeding stupid fast—all he could think about was her laugh and the way she tucked her hair behind her ear when she was nervous.

Slade put the truck into gear, the tires spinning briefly on the icy pavement before catching traction as he pulled onto the main road toward his apartment.

After pulling into the lot, he jumped out and headed inside, letting the door swing closed behind him.

The modest, organized living space greeted him. Normally after practice, Slade would flop onto the worn but comfortable black leather couch and watch the 65-inch TV. As he moved toward the kitchen, he passed the shelves filled with trophies and photos of his family, friends, and team—the Silverwood Snipers, the professional hockey team he'd played for since graduating high school. They were his second family.

Grabbing a water bottle from the fridge and taking a long sip, he checked the clock on the stove and felt his pulse quicken.

He didn't have much time.

He shrugged off his practice sweatshirt, wincing slightly at the tug on his shoulder, and headed for the bathroom. After a quick shower, Slade stared into the closet like it might blink first.

The navy suit was the obvious choice—clean lines, tailored shoulders, perfect for galas and banquets. He held it up to himself and frowned. Too formal. Too press conference. Tonight wasn't about headlines.

The team hoodie caught his eye. He knew Jessica loved wearing this hoodie of his—soft, worn, faintly carrying a hint of the locker room. He chuckled. Definitely not for this occasion. He wanted her to say yes, not ask if he needed a shower. He would take it with him though so she could wear it after the ring was on her finger.

He tried a black button-down next. Sleek. Confident. But under the bathroom light, it made him look tired. Onto the bed it went, landing beside the hoodie.

The pile grew: light jeans that felt too casual, a blazer that was too stiff, a sweater that reminded him of losing a game in overtime last winter in Boston. Nothing felt right. Nothing felt like *Jess*.

Finally, he settled on his best jeans and a white dress shirt, spraying himself with Jessica's favorite cologne. He paired the outfit with the leather jacket she claimed made him look like trouble.

Before heading out, he paused at the full-length mirror. He adjusted the collar on his shirt, running a hand through his hair to smooth it down. Not perfect, but real. Like him—like *them*.

His gaze flicked to the photo on the dresser—him and Jessica at last year's Winter Walk, smiling in front of the Christmas lights.

He whispered to the empty room, "Let's do this."

Slade grabbed his Snipers hoodie—Jessica loved to wear it and was always cold—and headed back out to his truck.

He gripped the wheel tightly as he drove through town.

The warm glow of the twinkling lights wrapped around snow-dusted trees reminded him why he had chosen this time of year and this place to propose. The holiday magic and the festive spirit of Winter Walk filled the town square all December long.

Couples walked hand in hand, their laughter blending with the squeals of children chasing each other through the freshly fallen snow. It was perfect.

His nerves kicked in at that moment and he welcomed the distraction of other people to calm him. Noise always centered him.

Slade slowed the truck as he reached the event parking lot. He pulled into a spot and rolled down the window, letting in a gush of crisp winter air along with the scent of roasted chestnuts and hot cocoa. Holiday melodies flowed softly from nearby speakers. Turning off the engine, he closed his eyes briefly, letting the noise wash over him.

His phone buzzed in his pocket. He fished it out, noticing several missed calls and texts. There was a voicemail.

Slade hesitated, then pressed play. The phone speaker crackled to life as Jessica's voice filled the truck cab.

"Hey, it's me." Her voice trembled.

She was crying. Why was she crying?

"There's a f-fire at the h-house. I- I can't get out, Slade. The s-smoke is t-thick. S-Slade, I'm s-scared. I'm trying to find a way out, but..." Her voice broke and the sound of her coughing and struggling to catch her breath reached his ears. "P-pl-please, if you get this, I need you to…"

Jessica stopped mid-sentence and let out a piercing scream.

The line went silent.

Fire? Jessica's house is on fire. Is she alone? Where are her parents? Where is her brother? How did the fire start?

His mind raced with questions as he tried to make sense of what was happening. Just then his phone pinged as more messages came in. He glanced at the screen, his thumb hovering over the notifications before he finally tapped it open.

JESSICA:

I'm inside.

JESSICA:

I love you.

His body locked up, fingers numb around the phone, his heart hammering so violently it was painful. Slade pressed his hand to his heart.

She sent that because she doesn't think she's going to make it out alive —I'm coming, Jess. I will get you out of there.

His skin burned, cold sweat prickled down his spine. His stomach churned at the thought of her hurt and alone.

He was Slade Fisher—star left wing for the Silverwood Snipers. Known for his killer slap shots. Feared on the ice. Always controlled and unshakable. He wasn't supposed to feel this deeply; wasn't supposed to let emotions consume him.

But when it came to Jessica, everything was different.

His hands trembled wildly, nearly dropping his phone as he fumbled with shaking fingers to pull up her number and struggled to press call.

Straight to voicemail.

His vision tunneled as panic crashed over him like a brutal, unstoppable force.

No, no, no, no, no. NO!

He redialed Jessica's number. Voicemail again.

His phone began vibrating as text messages flooded in. He looked at his screen through blurred vision. It was the team group chat:

JAYDEN:

> Just heard there's a fire on Crestview Drive.
> Let us know if you need anything.

MIGUEL:

> Slade, there's a fire on Crestview Drive.
> That's Jess's street, right? Have you heard
> from her?

TALULLA:

> Slade, we heard about the fire. Is Jess okay?
> Have you talked to her? Are you okay after
> that hard hit into the boards earlier? Call me.

HUNTER:

> Hey man, everything alright?

GARRETT:

> Hey man, you and Jess okay? We heard
> about the fire.

GUNNER:

> I know your phone is probably blowing up
> with texts but just worried about the news of
> the fire. Lemme know you and Jess are
> okay.

Slade took a shaky breath and opened the text thread he had with his family.

CALLAHAN:

Has anyone heard from Slade or Jess? Are
they safe?

SCARLETT:

Slade and Stryker had practice tonight. He
was supposed to go to Jess's after. It's their
big night.

STRYKER:

He left right after practice. He was going
home to shower and then to meet Jess.

MOM:

Slade, call me when you see this. Let me
know you and Jessica are okay.

DAD:

Son, please call me. Scarlett saw something
about a fire on Crestview Drive where
Jessica lives.

JULIETTE:

I just got a frantic call from mom about a fire.
What's happening? Do we need to be
worried?

BENNETT:

Hey bro, really worried about you guys.
Please answer.

Slade barely registered the words. All he could think about was
Jessica.

*Please be okay, Jess. Damn it, I should have gone straight there from
practice and picked her up.*

He started the truck and the engine roared to life.

Silverwood blurred past him, festive lights streaking across the windshield as he raced to Jessica's house. Slade's mind filled with the terrifying image of her trapped in the burning inferno of her house.

Why wasn't she able to get out of the house? What was stopping her?

She was scared and crying when she called him and left that message. He could clearly hear the fear in her voice. The way she struggled to breathe, the sound of her cough—and that gut-wrenching scream she let out at the end followed by the utter silence as the line went dead echoed through his brain, making him fear for the worst.

Muscles coiled so tightly, he could barely breathe, Slade leaned forward with his eyes locked on the road, willing the truck to get to her faster.

"Damn it!" he roared, slamming his palm against the dashboard.

Howling wind and snow hammered the windshield making visibility nearly impossible. Snowflakes blurred against the headlights. His foot pressed the gas pedal nearly to the floor, the tires skidding over the snow-packed road. He knew he was going too fast, knew the roads were slick, knew that one wrong move could send him careening into a ditch —but he didn't care.

He had to get to her. He had to save her.

His phone buzzed again and the screen lit up with a call from Stryker.

Hoping his twin could somehow help with this nightmare, Slade quickly answered, "Stryk—something happened to Jess," he said, voice quivering.

"Yeah, her street—" Stryker began, but Slade cut him off impatiently.

"No, no, Stryk, she called me. She left a voicemail. She's trapped inside the house. She-she said she can't get out. I-I should have been there," Slade choked out. "I'm heading there now."

"I'm leaving the arena with Hunter and Gunner. We'll meet you there," Stryker said, his tone leaving no room for argument.

Chapter Two

The night sky glowed orange as Slade rounded the corner onto Crestview Drive. Emergency vehicles were parked on the street with lights flashing. They had blocked the road off and were not letting anyone drive down it.

Firefighters struggled to control the crackling fury of the blaze that consumed the once-beautiful blue house. Bright orange flames scorched the walls, blackening them as smoke billowed upward. Sections of the roof sagged under the relentless inferno, threatening to collapse at any moment.

Slade slammed on his brakes at the end of the street, tires squealing. He jammed it into park, threw open the door without cutting the motor, and bounded out running as fast as he could down the street toward Jessica's house, scanning the crowd of emergency personnel and neighbors, hoping to see her.

His heart felt like it was in a vice, his breaths coming in short, panicked gasps.

"Jessica!" The name tore from his throat, swallowed by the chaos ahead.

Red and blue lights sliced through the haze of smoke billowing out of her house, illuminating faces that weren't hers. Neighbors huddled in stunned clusters. Firefighters shouted commands. Ambulance doors stood open, waiting.

Slade shoved past a police barrier, ignoring the officer's protest. His lungs burned, though whether from panic or smoke, he couldn't tell. The message on his phone screen flashed in his mind: *I'm inside.*

He scanned each face. *Not her. Not her. Not her.*

"Is anyone still in there?" Slade demanded, racing to the nearest fire-fighter. "I'm looking for the girl who lives here, my girlfriend, Jessica. Have you seen her?"

"Stand back. We're doing everything we can, sir," the firefighter replied, his voice muffled by his mask.

Another firefighter nearby shouted to a colleague, "Looks like a short in the Christmas lights—seen it happen before. Probably sparked in the walls."

Slade barely registered the words.

"To hell with this! Screw all of you just standing here! Cowards! I'll get her myself! Jessica!" Slade yelled as he dashed toward the house.

If they won't find her, I will.

He lunged toward the house and slammed into a wall of bodies. Three firefighters grabbed him, hauling him back as he fought like an animal.

"You can't go in there, son, it's too dangerous," one barked.

Slade thrashed like a man possessed. "Try and stop me! That's my girl in there. I'm not leaving her to die," Slade yelled, finally breaking free.

He was halfway across the yard when the lead firefighter yelled, "Victim confirmed inside! We're sending a team in—nobody else goes near that structure!"

Without a second thought, Slade ignored the command and sprinted the rest of the way toward the burning house, outrunning and ignoring the protests of the firefighters behind him.

Slade kicked through the remnants of the house's front door.

The flames licked the walls, burning everything around him.

"Jessica!" he called out over the roar of the fire.

The blistering heat curled around him, pressing in, suffocating, relentless, swallowing every breath before it could fully reach his lungs. Sweat trickled down his face, evaporating almost instantly as the temperature climbed. His clothes clung to his body, damp with sweat and singed at the edges.

The flames surged, growing bigger, closer.

The smoke thickened.

His eyes stung, and his lungs felt more scorched with each breath. The acrid smell of burning wood made him gag.

The floor creaked dangerously with each step he took.

"Jess!" he called out, his voice hoarse. "Where are you?"

His eyes darted around, searching for any sign of his girlfriend.

A beam overhead groaned, the heat and pressure of the fire weakening it.

Crack.

It gave way under the pressure and snapped free, striking Slade. A sharp, searing sensation exploded through his shoulder.

Nausea rolled over him as he tried to breathe through the pain. He squeezed his eyes shut, fighting the urge to throw up.

There was no time to focus on himself right now. His mind was on one thing: finding Jessica.

Slade raced through the living room where the remains of the Christmas tree stood engulfed.

He scanned the room, eyes darting wildly, but there was no sign of her.

"Jessica! Damn it, where are you?" he yelled as he kicked his way through the pile of charred debris, cradling his arm against him to keep it from moving as he made his way further into the house.

His stomach dropped as his eyes landed on the sight of her slumped, motionless form on the floor of the hallway that led to her bedroom, a beam pinning her down.

"Jessica!" He dashed toward her, his shoulder screaming in protest with every movement.

He shoved the beam aside and rolled her over. Her face was pale and smudged with soot. Her eyes were closed but she seemed to be breathing.

He dropped to his knees, feeling the heat scorch through his jeans.

"Jessica, wake up," Slade yelled, shaking her. "We're getting out of here, Jess," he continued as he scooped her into his arms, trying his best to shield her from the flames and smoke.

He made his way back the way he had come, through the house where he had spent a lot of time over his six years of being with Jessica. It was hard to believe this would be the last image he had of it. He went through the hallway into the living room, dodging more debris.

He could see the exit ahead, blurred by the smoke, with the flames closing in, almost blocking the chance of escape.

He ran toward what was once the front door, his feet crunching over scattered rubble, every muscle in his body screaming in protest.

His legs trembled.

His shoulder throbbed.

He pushed through the pain.

He didn't stop, couldn't stop.

Getting her to safety was the only option.

Slade stumbled into the night air, his face streaked with soot and sweat.

"Help!" he called out, collapsing to his knees with Jessica still in his arms. His vision blurred at the edges.

I have to keep going. Just a little bit more. I can't pass out now, but fuck this pain. Just get Jessica to the first responders so they can help her. It's about Jess.

He couldn't let go of her—not yet.

He struggled through the chaos of the flashing lights and commanding voices of first responders. Amidst the whirlwind of the adrenaline rushing through him, Slade glanced down at Jessica and saw that her Bible was still clutched in her hands. The edges were singed, and the purple leather cover was smudged with soot. Even unconscious and after climbing over the fallen debris, through the flames and smoke, she held onto it.

"I've got her," a paramedic said, taking Jessica from his arms and heading for a stretcher waiting nearby.

Slade instantly felt the relief of her unconscious body being lifted from him.

I did what I had to do. My shoulder will heal. Jessica has to heal, too.

Two other medics rushed over to assist, one checking Jessica's vitals and the other grabbing an oxygen mask and slipping it over her face.

She has to wake up. She has to breathe.

"Take it easy, son. You did good, but you're bleeding. Let's get you taken care of," a nearby paramedic said, placing a reassuring hand on Slade's arm and guiding him away from the flames and smoke.

Slade looked down, noticing for the first time his torn shirt and a deep gash where blood was trickling down his arm.

He nodded faintly, his eyes still fixed on Jess. "Worry about her. She's all that matters."

A violent cough wracked his body along with a wave of pain. He clenched his jaw as his shoulder burned, and he suppressed a groan that threatened to escape, trying to focus his breathing enough to get through the pain.

"Get him on oxygen!" one paramedic shouted while another placed an oxygen mask over Slade's face.

Slade sat on the curb, cool, clean air flooding his lungs.

He glanced up to see his twin brother, Stryker, racing toward him, Hunter and Gunner, two of their best friends and teammates, following close behind.

"Slade, what the hell were you thinking?" Stryker's eyes burned, wild with something caught between fury and fear as he looked at his brother. "You could've gotten yourself killed running in there like that!"

Slade pulled the mask away, taking a deep breath. "I had to, Stryk. Jess was in there. I couldn't just stand by and do nothing."

Stryker shook his head, kneeling to look Slade in the eye. "I know how much you love Jess, man. But..." His voice was choked with emotion.

"'But' nothing, Stryker!" Slade snapped, hopping to his feet. His fists clenched at his sides, shoulders tight.

"You should have let the firefighters do their job, Slade. They are the ones trained to run into burning buildings like that. You are trained for hockey," Stryker shot back.

Slade took a step forward, but the movement sent a sharp jolt of pain through his body. His stomach twisted. He gritted his teeth, praying he would stay conscious long enough to know Jessica was okay. His fingers twitched at his side—a nervous habit he knew his brother would likely pick up on.

When another cough wracked Slade's body, Stryker's expression shifted to one of alarm. Slade tried to hide how much pain he was in, but he couldn't help but cringe as agony wracked his body with the force of his cough.

Stryker didn't miss it. "Slade, you're hurt."

"I'm fine." Slade shifted his weight, rolling his injured shoulder, attempting to prove to Stryker he was okay, but he winced.

"You can barely stand," Stryker said, wrapping a strong arm around him and grounding him. "Is it your shoulder? What happened in there?"

Slade exhaled shakily as he leaned into his brother, "J-Jess. I have to see her. We can worry about me after."

"Fine, but you're getting checked at the hospital."

They made their way to where Jessica lay motionless on a stretcher, surrounded by paramedics.

Her face was pale, smudged with soot and ash. Her long, dark brown hair, braided off to the side, was tangled and singed at the ends, along with the festive Christmas bow she had added. Her favorite red dress, which she had worn in anticipation of their night, was burned and torn.

Slade's heart pounded as he approached, his breath catching in his throat.

He leaned closer, "J-Jess," his voice trembled, "B-baby, it's me. It's Slade. You said you needed me. I'm here. I got to you, Jess. You have to wake up. You have to be okay. I have a surprise for you," he whispered, tears threatening to shatter his tough exterior.

The paramedics worked quickly as they prepared to move her to the ambulance.

"Is she going to be okay?" Slade asked desperately, his voice trembling, his hand touching her face.

"We're doing everything we can." The paramedic's serious tone told Slade things were worse than he had initially thought.

"Jessica," he whispered, his voice breaking. "Please, wake up, stay with me. Please. I love you so much."

The paramedic's voice cut in, "We have to get her to the hospital."

Slade nodded, his grip tightening on Jessica's hand. "I'm not leaving her."

The paramedic looked up. "Are you family?"

He knelt beside her, heart pounding, and gently took her hand.

"I'm her husband," he said, slipping the ring onto her finger.

The paramedic paused, seeming to decide if he should let the obvious white lie slide or not but quickly nodded in understanding sympathy. "Alright. Get in."

Stryker placed a reassuring hand on Slade's shoulder. "Give me the keys to your truck. I'll bring it so you have it when this is over. We'll be right behind you, Slade."

At that moment, Slade realized half his hockey team was standing there. Word sure did spread fast in this small town.

"Thanks, Stryk," Slade said, tossing Stryker the keys to his truck.

"Of course. I'll call mom and dad on the way and tell them to meet us at the hospital."

As they loaded Jessica into the ambulance, Slade climbed in beside her.

The doors closed, and the sirens wailed as they sped through the icy streets of Silverwood and toward the hospital.

Slade sat on the edge of the bench inside the dimly lit ambulance, the harsh overhead bulb flickering ominously like it couldn't decide whether to stay alive. The scent of smoke clung to him—his clothes, his hair, even his skin—as if the fire had left its fingerprints behind. Oxygen tanks hissed softly in the corner. A paramedic said something to him, but Slade barely registered it.

His eyes were locked on Jessica.

Unmoving. Pale.

Every beep from the monitor felt like it struck bone.

Then her eyelids fluttered, and a small gasp escaped her lips.

She struggled to focus.

"S-Sl-Slade."

"Jess? Jess, baby," he whispered, leaning closer, his voice a desperate plea.

Jessica's lips trembled, and she struggled to talk, "I-I- l-lo-ov-ve y-you."

Tears welled in Slade's eyes. "I love you, too, Jess. Stay with me. Please. We are going to get you help. I promise."

But as quickly as she had awakened, her vitals began to drop. The machines blared alarms, and the paramedics sprang into action.

"She's crashing! Heart rate below 40 bpm. Oxygen saturation is falling!" the lead paramedic announced, his voice raw.

Slade staggered backward, shoved aside by trained hands and the blur of controlled chaos.

He could only watch as the woman he loved slipped further from reach—her fingers twitching, her eyes fluttering—and pray with all his heart and soul that someone, anyone, could pull her back.

Chapter Three

The ambulance screeched to a halt outside Silverwood General Hospital.

"Let's move!" a paramedic barked as they yanked the stretcher out, Jessica strapped down and ghostly pale beneath a thin blanket, an oxygen mask fogging with shallow breaths.

"BP's 70 over 40 and falling—O2's at 72!" one of them shouted as they rushed through the emergency room doors, wheels rattling across tile.

Slade stumbled after them, soot-streaked and limping, his breath coming in harsh gasps. Pain tore down his arm from where the beam had caught him, but he barely felt it.

He couldn't breathe right until he knew she still could.

The ER buzzed around him—voices, footsteps, beeping monitors—but it all blurred until he heard—

"Slade?"

He turned, blinking against the unforgiving lights.

Dr. Callahan Fisher. His older brother. Dressed in scrubs, clipboard in his hand.

Slade had forgotten he was on shift tonight.

Callahan's eyes swept over him—ash-covered, shaking, empty-handed—then beyond him toward the trauma doors.

Slade saw the moment realization hit Callahan like a gut punch, and he knew.

Jessica.

"Female patient, early twenties, found unconscious in a residential fire. Heavy smoke inhalation. Unresponsive."

Callahan's face hardened instantly. "Get her to Trauma Room 3. Now. Prep for intubation."

The stretcher disappeared behind swinging doors.

"Slade, what happened?" Callahan asked.

"T-there was a fire at her house. I had to get her out. I..." He started to explain, but Stryker cut him off.

"Slade, you need to be looked at, too," Stryker said, walking up to where Slade stood with the doctors.

"I'm fine," Slade said, trying to push past, the adrenaline still coursing through him. "Worry about Jessica."

"You're not fine. You hurt your shoulder at practice earlier, and then you ran into a burning building, damn it. You should get looked at," Stryker said.

Slade hesitated. "It's nothing, Talulla can look at it later."

"Slade, stop being so stubborn, man. Nothing can turn into something real quick," Gunner said.

Slade's fists clenched. "I'm f-f-fine," he choked out as a coughing fit took over.

"Slade, look at your arm. You're bleeding, man. Get checked out. You're no good to Jess if you collapse," Hunter spoke up for the first time.

Why is everyone so concerned about my shoulder? The focus should be on Jessica, not on me right now.

Slade's eyes bore into Callahan's, a storm of emotions swirling within. "She's the love of my life, damn it! I was going to ask her to be my wife tonight. I need to be with her."

Callahan didn't answer, but Slade caught the shift in his posture as he took in his soot-streaked face, his torn shirt, and the way he favored his bloodied arm.

His brother's eyes narrowed as he looked behind Slade. "Get him to X-ray," he commanded the nurses.

Slade exhaled, tension coiling in his shoulders, "Jessica—"

"I'm going to check on her," Callahan cut him off. "Dr. Patel is with her now. You're not going near her until you get checked out, Slade."

"What the hell? No! You can't keep me from her, Cal!" Slade yelled, frustration bubbling.

"Slade, you won't do Jessica any good unless you take care of yourself. Go get your shoulder looked at. You can be mad at me, but this is best for you both. I will stay with Jessica and update you as soon as I know more." Callahan's tone made it clear he was giving that order not just as Slade's brother but also as a doctor in the emergency room.

Before he could argue further, a nurse around his age with pink scrubs, brown hair pulled back in a ponytail, and bright green eyes approached him.

"Hi, Slade, I'm Willow. I'll be your nurse tonight. Let's get you to X-rays so you can get back to Jessica," she said softly.

Slade followed her, too tired to fight anymore.

The pain in his shoulder intensified with every step, but he tried not to let on how much.

"Try to relax," Willow said softly, her touch careful but firm. "We need to make sure there's no serious damage. We can't have the star player of the Silverwood Snipers out for too long with an injury."

"Y-You follow hockey?" Slade asked.

"Yeah, a bit. Plus, your brother talks about you." Willow smiled.

The nurse explained the process as the x-ray technician positioned him beneath the machine, but Slade's mind was on Jessica. He didn't even know if she was alive. He would relax when he knew she was okay.

"You took a pretty hard hit," the technician said, adjusting the scanner.

When the X-rays were finished, Slade sat in the room waiting for the results. He bounced his good leg, then stood, then sat again. The walls felt too close, the silence too heavy. He checked the clock. Twice.

By the time the door finally opened, it felt like a lifetime had passed. Another doctor stepped in, holding the scan of his shoulder like a verdict.

"You have a dislocated shoulder, which we will reset here. We are going to put your arm in a sling, let it heal, and you will need physical therapy."

Slade forced himself to listen. The medication they had given him was starting to take effect, and now at least he didn't feel like he was going to throw up from the pain.

With his shoulder reset, resting in a sling along with the medicine in his system and a prescription to fill as well as strict orders to take it easy for the next few weeks, Slade ran down the hall toward the trauma rooms.

He peered through the windows of each room until he spotted Jessica laying motionless on a hospital bed. Black soot stained the stark white of the hospital bedding and pillows. Tubes and wires snaked across her body, connecting her to monitors that screamed in protest with relentless beeping and the sharp whine of alarms.

"We're losing her again. Get me the crash cart," Callahan called out.

Slade's breath caught in his throat as he heard his brother say those words.

Losing her? Crash cart?

His body was moving before he could fully process what was happening and burst through the door as the paddles pressed against Jessica's chest, the room crackling with electricity.

"Clear!" Callahan's command sliced through the noise.

The line remained flat.

"Jessica!" Slade yelled as he tried to fight his way into the room. "Jessica! No!"

"Sir, you can't be in here—"

"Like hell, I can't. She needs me!" Slade shouted back.

"SLADE, OUT NOW!" Callahan shot Slade a warning look. "Let me do my job."

Slade stumbled backward as an orderly pulled him from the room, being mindful of Slade's injured arm. He stood, his face pressed against the frosted glass of the window, numb with horror, as his brother did everything in his power to bring Jessica back to him.

"Clear!" Callahan called out as he pressed the paddles to Jessica's chest again.

Slade flinched when her body jolted.

She didn't move again.

"We're not losing her. Charge to 300," Callahan called out through gritted teeth.

Slade's fists clenched at his sides, nails digging into his palms. He could see the nurse adjusting the settings. See the sweat on Callahan's brow. See the stillness in Jessica's body.

Then another jolt. Harder this time.

Jessica's body jerked as the shock hit, muscles seizing beneath the paddles. For one desperate moment, Slade let himself hope.

Her chest rose sharply, then fell, the monitor beeping out its flat rhythm as they prepared to try again.

"Jessica, damn it!" Callahan shouted into the room.

Slade's whole body leaned toward the glass, silently willing her to fight.

"This isn't how it ends," he whispered. "You don't leave me like this."

"Last chance! Clear!" Callahan's voice was rough with urgency as he pressed the paddles to Jessica's chest one final time.

Her body arched against the table as the current surged through her, then collapsed, motionless.

All eyes snapped to the monitor.

Slade held his breath. Time froze.

A beat.

Another.

Silence.

The flatline stretched, sharp and unforgiving.

Jessica's heart remained still.

Callahan's hands hovered in the air, trembling. Willow muttered a curse under her breath.

And still—the line stayed flat.

Still—nothing.

"Time of death: 10:47 pm," Callahan said, his voice raw, removing his gloves in defeat.

Slade didn't hear the rest.

Didn't feel the pain in his arm anymore.

Didn't notice the blood on his shirt or the ache in his ribs.

He just stood there, staring through the glass, watching the woman he loved leave him forever.

Chapter Four

The door swung open, and Callahan stepped into the hallway. Slade rushed toward him, knocking over a chair with a crash, flanked by Stryker, Scarlett, and a handful of teammates who'd followed the ambulance, their faces tight with worry.

"Cal," Slade said, looking into his brother's eyes, his voice shaky. "Please, tell me she isn't—"

Slade dropped off when he saw the lump rise in Callahan's throat. His brother was trying to be strong, for his sake but Slade's heart sank when he saw the expression on his face.

"We tried everything," Callahan said quietly, stepping closer. "The team did everything they could, Slade."

Slade shook his head, backing a step. "No. No, I've seen—I've seen you bring people back before. I talked to her in the ambulance. She was conscious."

Callahan reached out but stopped short of touching him. "She coded three times. We got her back twice. But that last one... her body just couldn't come back from it."

Slade's fists clenched at his sides. "You're saying she fought. And you let her lose."

"No," Callahan said gently, voice cracking. "She didn't lose, Slade. She held on longer than most people could have. But her heart—her lungs—she was too far gone. She didn't suffer. She wasn't alone."

The words settled like ash in Slade's chest.

A silence stretched between them.

Slade stared at his brother. At the trauma bay door behind him.

He blinked. "No."

Callahan stepped forward, reaching out instinctively. "Slade—"

Slade felt as if the ground had been pulled out from under him. His knees buckled, his vision blurred, and a wave of nausea washed over him.

"You're lying! Tell me you're lying!"

Callahan only shook his head sadly.

"No!" he roared, staggering backward, clutching his head with both hands.

His fists slammed into the wall beside him, knuckles splitting, but he barely noticed. The pain inside him roared louder than any physical wound.

"No, no, no, NO!" he screamed, his voice raw and broken, echoing off the walls.

"Slade!" Stryker lunged forward, catching him just before he could punch again.

Slade fought him off blindly, flailing, tears streaming. "Let me GO! I need her—I need her back—just let me go!"

Hunter rushed in from the side, grabbing Slade's other arm, dragging him away from the wall, before he could hurt himself more. Together, the two men tried to restrain the spiraling chaos.

"Stop, Slade, just stop!" Hunter growled, the tremble in his voice betraying the pain beneath the command. "You're gonna tear yourself apart!"

"She needed me—I should've gotten there faster—I should've—"

"You did everything you could and so did Cal. Nothing more could have been done. You loved her, man," Stryker said softly. "She knew that. She knew."

Slade collapsed forward, chest heaving, sobs ripping through him like lightning.

Jessica, the love of his life, was *gone.*

Slade sat in the same spot on the floor of the waiting room, trying to process his new reality. Time didn't feel real but he thought maybe he'd be rooted there forever. He couldn't see a way of going forward.

"Slade, let's go home. There is nothing else we can do here," Stryker said gently, placing a hand on his shoulder.

He wiped his eyes on his shirt, still smelling the smoke from the fire.

We were supposed to have forever. Now I have to say goodbye to her.

Grief surged up, but it wasn't clean. It burned.

One second, he wanted to collapse into his brother's arms, the next, he wanted to punch the wall again and scream until something broke.

Everything had changed in minutes. And the world just kept turning—like it didn't even notice she was gone.

"I need to see her," he said, looking up at his brother as he fought another wave of emotion, "I need to say goodbye."

Stryker nodded in understanding as he helped Slade up from the floor.

Once at her room, Slade took a deep breath, trying to steady himself and control his emotions before pushing open the door.

Inside, the room was eerily quiet.

His eyes fell on Jessica's still form. She looked as if she were sleeping peacefully.

He walked slowly toward the bed, then reached out and gently brushed a strand of hair from her forehead.

"Hey Jess," he whispered, his voice breaking. "It's me, baby. It's Slade."

He sank into the chair beside her bed, his eyes never leaving her face. "I can't believe you're gone," he said, his voice barely above a whisper. "I don't know what I am going to do without you. It's been you and me for six years. W-We w-were supposed to go to the W-Winter W-Walk t-tonight. I-I was going t-to ask you to be my w-wife." He struggled to get his words out as emotion took over. Tears filled his eyes, but he didn't bother to wipe them away.

"I wanted to tell you so many things. I wanted to tell you how much I loved you. I wanted to spend the rest of my life with you as my wife. Now... now it is too late."

As his gaze wandered around the room, it landed on her Bible on the table beside her bed.

How did her Bible get in here? Slade wondered, remembering Jessica had it when he carried her out of the house. *Who put it here? Did Callahan? Why didn't he give it to me?*

He lifted it off the table and pressed it to his chest.

When he opened it, a small piece of paper fluttered out and landed on the floor. With trembling hands, Slade picked up the paper and turned it over. It was a sonogram image.

He looked at the top and saw Jessica's name and date of birth. The words "Surprise Daddy" were written in her beautiful script, like calligraphy, next to the image. Jessica had highlighted Psalm 127:3 in the Bible, which said, "Children are an inheritance from the Lord."

His heart clenched as he realized what he was looking at.

Jessica was pregnant.

"No, no, no," he whispered, his voice choked with emotion. "Jess... you were carrying our child." His heart ached with a new kind of pain as he looked at the image of their unborn baby. "Our baby, another life lost... I didn't know."

He took her hand in his, feeling the coolness of her skin. "I wish I could hear your voice one more time, Jess. I wish you could have told me the news about our child. I wish I could have shared how happy that would have made me to be a father, something I didn't even know I wanted until this moment. I wish I could hear you laugh one more time. I wish I could see you smile one more time. I wish I could tell you how you changed my life."

He leaned over and kissed her forehead. "Goodbye, Jess. I'll miss you every single day. I'll always love you. Thank you for some of the best years of my life," he said, his voice choked with emotion.

The waiting room was still packed when Slade walked out of the double doors. Jessica's family had come earlier, gripped in deep despair for their daughter, but he could hardly look at them. They had said their good-byes to Jess and were gone now, probably to find a hotel until they could figure out a new living situation in this nightmare of destruction and loss.

His teammates, Hunter Montgomery, Gunner Steele, Jayden Powell, Garrett Foley, and Miguel Diaz, were gathered near the vending machine, quiet and tense. Stryker stood with them, arms crossed, gaze flicking toward the door every few seconds.

By the window, Callahan had changed out of his station uniform and now wore a hoodie and jeans, staring blankly out at the parking lot as if trying to make sense of everything beyond the glass. Willow, the nurse from earlier in the night, sat in a chair still in her scrubs from her shift with a sweatshirt he recognized as Stryker's.

Slade's mother, Genevieve, sat in the far corner, beneath a faded watercolor print of a lighthouse on the Maine coast. She was still dressed in her clothes from her shift at the Portland Head Light Museum. Her eyes were closed, her hands folded, and her head bowed in prayer. Her own old, worn Bible sat on her lap.

His father, Daniel, sat beside her, elbows on his knees, weathered hands clasped tight. He still wore his work jacket from the lighthouse, his name stitched in red thread over his heart. His Red Sox cap was off, resting on his thigh.

His nineteen year old sister Scarlett, normally happy and witty, sat silently in one of the stiff plastic chairs, her leg bouncing with nervous energy. Beside her was their youngest brother, Bennett, a senior in high school, sitting slouched with his head in his hands.

On the other side of Scarlett was her friend who he learned was also Willow's sister, Violet, quiet and pale, her eyes scanning every face as if waiting for one of them to say the nightmare was over.

Miguel's girlfriend, Samantha Romano, newly hired to handle media for the Snipers, sat beside them wrapped in Miguel's Snipers sweatshirt, her tablet on her lap. Talulla and her three brothers, Killian, Jameson and Rowan, filled the remaining seats in the room looking ashen.

No one spoke.

Slade barely acknowledged them, his eyes drawn to the brightly lit Christmas tree in the corner of the room. The twinkling lights and cheerful ornaments reminded him of what a happy time it should be. Jessica had loved Christmas, and the sight of the tree brought a fresh wave of pain crashing over him.

I need to do something, anything, to make this pain stop, he thought desperately.

"Why?!" he shouted, his voice raw with pain. "Why did this have to happen?"

His jaw clenched, breath shallow, rage and grief churning just beneath his skin. He ripped his sling off without thinking, throwing it on the floor. The pain in his shoulder was nothing compared to the pain in his heart right now. He lunged at the tree, his hands tearing at the lights. The bulbs shattered under his grip, the ornaments crashing to the ground.

"She's gone! She's gone because of this! I couldn't save her! I failed her!" Slade screamed as he knocked the tree over, the sound of breaking glass echoing through the hospital hallways. The twinkling lights flickered and died.

Strong arms wrapped around him, pulling him back. "Slade, stop!" Stryker yelled, struggling to hold him.

"Let me go!" Slade roared, thrashing against Stryker's grip.

Stryker tightened his hold, his own eyes glistening with unshed tears.

Their father stepped into his line of sight then, placing his hands on Slade's face gently. "I know, son. I know. But destroying this won't bring her back."

Slade's entire body trembled with fury. "You don't understand!" he screamed, his voice cracking. "She was everything to me! Everything!"

Slade suddenly stopped struggling. His breaths came in ragged gasps as he reached into his pocket and pulled out the sonogram. "She was pregnant," he said, his voice cracking, barely holding together. "She was carrying our child. I just found out... she didn't tell me. I found this in her Bible. The verse about children being a blessing was highlighted."

The room fell silent as Slade held up the sonogram for them to see. Tears streamed down his face as he choked out, "I've lost them both... Jess and our baby."

Slade's strength finally gave out, and he collapsed to his knees once more, sobbing.

Chapter Five

Slade walked out of the hospital doors into the cold night air and the sight of a fresh coat of snow. His brothers and teammates had shown up for him today, and he doubted they would leave him alone at any point in the next few days or weeks. They were all heading back to his apartment across town.

Stryker had insisted on driving because Slade was in no condition to do so. Slade normally didn't allow anyone to drive his truck but tonight he no longer cared about anything. Now Jessica was gone, and nothing would ever be the same. Slade was reeling in pain and grief. He didn't care who drove—he just wanted to get out of this hospital and never step foot in there again.

He slid into the passenger seat without a word. He didn't want to talk.

He didn't want to think.

He didn't want to feel.

The drive back to his apartment was a blur.

Rain began to mix with the snow, pattering against the windshield in a rhythm that matched Slade's stilted breathing.

Every few minutes, Stryker would look over at his brother. "I'm here, man," he said quietly.

Slade didn't respond, his gaze fixed on the sonogram in his hands.

Walking into his apartment, he felt like a completely different man from the one who left earlier that night. He had been filled with excitement when he left to meet Jessica, and now, in only a few hours, everything had been ripped away from him.

Slade's fists clenched, his whole body shaking as he struggled to contain his emotions that were rising again, his mind a whirlwind of conflicting feelings, but the pain and anger were too overwhelming.

With a sudden, violent outburst, he flung the Bible across the room, its pages fluttering in the air before landing with a thud. "Why? Why did this have to happen?" he shouted, his voice echoing through the house.

Slade's rage boiled over. He stormed into the living room, vision swimming with tears. A photo of him and Jessica on prom night sat on the mantel, smiling like nothing could ever touch them. He grabbed it and smashed it to the floor—glass exploding across the hardwood.

Graduation night. Another frame. Gone in a heartbeat.

The small table beside the couch was next. He slammed his fists into it, splintering wood, sending a lamp crashing to the floor.

Another photo—signing day. Jessica had surprised him with a custom jersey and a kiss that made the cameras blush. He didn't hesitate. He hurled it across the room, then stomped on the broken frame, breathing like a wild animal.

His shoulder screamed as he tore at the lights on the Christmas tree, ripping the strands free with shaking hands.

He didn't want to think. Didn't want to breathe.

Didn't want to *be* in a world where she wasn't.

Slade barely registered the other guys in the room, but he heard the footsteps—Stryker's first, then Hunter, Gunner, and the rest of the team behind him. Their presence pressed in around him, silent and stunned. He could feel their eyes on him, feel the weight of their shock. Stryker stepped closer, hesitation in every movement.

"Slade, you have to stop," Stryker said, his voice firm yet compassionate. "Destroying everything isn't going to bring them back."

Slade whirled around to face his twin, his eyes wild with anger and grief. "You think I don't know that? Who cares if I destroy it all? None of it matters," he shouted, his voice cracking. "I lost her! I lost our child! I lost everything!"

He collapsed, curling in a ball amidst the wreckage, sobs wracking his body.

Chapter Six

Slade stood in the empty locker room, the familiar scent of sweat and ice filling the air. The last time he had been here had been the night Jessica died. It seemed like a different lifetime, even though it had only been three months ago.

The cold days of winter were giving way to early signs of spring. Life around him was moving forward, but he was still stuck in that night. He felt like he couldn't go on, at least not in Silverwood. He hadn't left his place since he returned after Jessica's funeral. He didn't want anyone's pity.

His apartment was littered with take-out containers because he had no desire to cook. He had hired a cleaning service to come in once a week to help him keep the place clean. Stryker, Hunter, and Gunner would stop by to check on him; the first month after the fire, they would take turns spending the night, hoping to help him. Slade figured it was to make sure he didn't harm himself, although they never outright said it to him.

Scarlett would stop in usually once a week to check on him. His parents also came by a few times a week to be sure he was eating, and both tried to convince him to stay at the family home instead of his apartment, but he refused. They wanted him to talk with a counselor and try to get through the pain and live life again, but Slade didn't want to burden anyone else with his problems. In Slade's opinion, counselors were for people in far worse situations than he was.

The decision to leave Silverwood and the Snipers was one of the hardest he had made in his twenty-one years.

He was there to clear out his locker.

He had missed every practice and game since the night of the fire.

He pulled his jersey from its hook, tracing the Silverwood Snipers logo and his number, 21, with his fingers. He folded it and placed it in his duffel bag with his skates, gloves, and a photo of him and Jessica that he kept taped in his locker. He reached up and grabbed his nameplate from above his stall, the letters spelling out FISHER engraved into its golden face, and put it in his bag. Finally, he grabbed his stick and put his bag over his shoulder

It's just a break.

That's what he told himself, his parents, his siblings, his teammates, his coaches, and the Snipers' owners, who also happened to be his Uncle Seamus and Aunt Catherine when he met with them. Playing for the Snipers professionally had been everything he ever wanted, a goal he had worked tirelessly to achieve.

But now, everything was different. Slade had thought he would grow old with Jessica, and they would raise their family here while he played his whole career for this team he loved. He longed to play hockey, to keep living his dream of playing for the Snipers, but the constant reminders of his loss made it unbearable.

Slade got in his truck with his duffel bag of clothes, his hockey gear, a photograph of Jessica, her Bible, the sonogram picture, and the silver locket she'd always worn.

Stryker was going to take over his apartment as well as his spot as Captain. The Snipers had their backup left wing to take his place on the team.

He was leaving Silverwood, and he didn't know if he would ever return.

Slade didn't have a destination in mind. The open road felt like the only solution to the restlessness gnawing at him. With the money he'd earned from playing for the Snipers safely tucked away, he could afford to take his time.

He planned to drive until the ache in his chest dulled, until he found a place where the memories of Jessica hurt a little less.

A place far from Silverwood, the memories, and the pain. Where people didn't know him, or about the fire, and everything he had lost that night.

A place where he could be more than just a star hockey player who now couldn't even show up for his team.

A place where he could start piecing himself back together.

He wasn't sure what he was looking for, but figured he'd know it when he found it.

Slade was about to turn onto the highway when he realized he couldn't leave without saying goodbye and turned the truck around in the gas station parking lot. He needed to visit Jessica's grave one last time before leaving.

Snow crunched under Slade's boots, too loud in the silence of the cemetery that made every thought echo. His breath curled white into the air as he moved between the headstones, each step slower than the last.

When he reached hers, he stopped. Jessica Anderson. The letters carved into granite looked too permanent, too final. A spray of flowers, bright against the frost, sat at the base. Her parents must have been by recently to visit her too. He felt awful for not spending more time with them after she was gone, but he just couldn't handle seeing his pain mirrored in their eyes. He knew they struggled with guilt for not being there that night either; they had already been at the Winter Walk in anticipation of witnessing Slade propose to their precious daughter, having no idea the peril she was in.

The pain of losing that moment sliced through him again. He crouched, his knees pressing into the cold earth, one hand braced against the stone as if it might steady him.

"Hey, Jess," he whispered, voice catching. "I don't even know where to start."

He turned the Bible over in his hands, the leather worn soft. The sonogram slipped free.

Slade's thumb traced the tiny image. "I didn't get to tell you I wanted it too. That I wanted all of it—you, the baby, the future we dreamed about." His throat tightened. He pressed the sonogram against the stone, then pulled it back to his chest. "Now I'm just here. Wishing for a do-over."

For a moment, his head dropped against the granite, the cold biting his skin. His shoulders trembled, breath uneven.

"I keep seeing you that night in the snow," he said, a cracked smile tugging briefly at his lips. "Chasing flakes with your tongue, laughing so hard you fell backward. Said the snow tasted like Christmas." His voice faltered. "Oh, Jess... you made everything lighter."

He paused, fingers brushing the carved letters of her name. The silence pressed in, broken only by the sound of his shaky breaths.

"I can't stay here anymore. Everywhere I look, it's you. The arena. Main Street. Even snow—" he stopped, swallowing hard, his thumb still on her name. "I can't breathe in it."

He kissed the granite, then rose, brushing snow from his knees. He set the Bible carefully against the flowers, his hand lingering there for a moment. Then he slid the sonogram into his jacket pocket, close to his heart.

And he walked away.

The SILVERWOOD SCOOP

Local Sports & Community News

Slade Fisher Walks Away from Hockey After Tragedy

Samantha Romano, Silverwood Snipers' Media Correspondent

In a shocking turn for local sports fans, Slade Fisher has officially stepped away from the ice. The Silverwood Snipers' star left-wing cleared out his locker earlier this week and quietly left town—three months after the devastating house fire on Crestview Drive claimed the life of his longtime girlfriend, Jessica Anderson.

Fisher, once considered a rising star in the pros, has not released a public statement. Sources close to the team say he's been "a ghost" since the tragedy, opting out of practice, press, and playoffs.

What's next for Silverwood's golden boy?

Only time will tell.

Stay tuned to *The Silverwood Scoop* for updates.

Chapter Seven

Crescent Bay, North Carolina, was a small coastal town where time moved slowly. The salty breeze and the crashing waves gave Slade a strange sense of comfort. He pulled into the parking lot of the small motel by the beach he had been staying at for the last week after searching for his escape over the past month.

The aged and weathered sign read *Seabreeze Lodge*. The owner was an older woman named Mary; she reminded Slade of his mother. Her warm smile and wise words made everyone feel at home.

She smiled as he entered the lobby to get to his room. "Hope the room is treating you well, honey. It's nothing fancy, but it's clean and quiet. You look like you could use some peace."

"Thank you, ma'am."

She hadn't seemed to recognize him, so he figured she didn't pay much attention to hockey. Or if she had, at least she had pretended not to know who he was, which he was grateful for.

The neon lights of *The Hollow* hummed dully through the cracked windows. The air was thick with the smell of stale beer, cigarette smoke ingrained deep in the wooden beams and leather from long before the ban on indoor smoking.

Music played from the old jukebox in the corner, which cast a dim glow on the floor.

Not the kind of place you found in travel guides, it was tucked away on a street a block away from his motel where the pavement fractured beneath the weight of years, and the smell of grease and regret clung to the air like a second skin.

Nobody asked questions here.

Nobody cared who you used to be.

Which was exactly why he stayed.

Slade sat in the back room, slumped against the cushions of the battered leather couch, his short-sleeved shirt exposing the ink etched into his skin.

He had been here long enough that the bartender, whom he recognized from the motel, had stopped asking him if he wanted another drink, but instead just slid them across the scarred wood of the bar top.

Slade took the glass without looking up, the burn steadying him.

A woman leaned against him. *What was her name?* He really didn't care.

She was saying something about how he looked like trouble, about how she liked that in a man. He nodded absently, trying not to be reminded of Jess, tipping his drink back and letting the burn lace through his veins. She leaned in closer and laughed, the sound grating against him like sandpaper.

She smelled of vanilla. Her dark hair spilled over one shoulder, deliberately tousled, the kind of mess that took effort. The curve of her cheekbones caught the dim light. Her lips were painted a deep red.

Her fingers traced his hockey tattoo, but he barely registered the touch.

The warmth of her skin against him sent a shiver down his spine, but he didn't pull away. He couldn't.

"So...What's your story?" she asked, her voice soft, almost reverent.

He didn't answer right away. His throat tightened, the words caught somewhere between the ache in his chest and the whiskey burning in his veins.

Her touch lingered, caressing the curve of the stick, the sharp edges of the numbers—intimate in a way that felt too close.

"It's nothing," he said finally, his voice rough. "Just a stupid tattoo."

She didn't believe him. He could see it in the way her eyes searched his, in the way her fingers paused over the numbers, but she didn't press. Instead, she leaned in, her lips brushing against his shoulder, her breath warm against his skin.

He let it happen.

He let everything happen.

The booze, the nights with women who whispered his name like it meant something.

It didn't.

Nothing did.

Not since Jessica.

At least that's what he told himself, but that was a lie.

So, he drowned his sorrows...in liquor. In lips he didn't care about. In the weight of a world that kept spinning, cruel and unrelenting, without his true love.

He squeezed his eyes shut, shaking the thought away before it could take shape. He wasn't doing this. He wasn't feeling anything tonight. He was here to disappear, to dissolve into the haze of bad decisions and a world that didn't ask questions. If he kept moving and numbing, it meant he didn't have to remember the way Jessica laughed or the way she fit against his side on cold nights. It meant he didn't have to relive that last moment when everything changed.

And when the bartender slid another drink his way, he took it. Because if he couldn't outrun the past, he sure as hell could numb it.

Another night, another woman, same bar.

A sequined top shimmered under the strobes, all careless confidence and sharp angles. She didn't smile—just tilted her head in invitation. He took it.

They moved together—locked in rhythm, though only one of them was really there. Slade's movements were loose, yet jarring, like his body hadn't caught up to his mind. The girl flowed with the beat, unbothered by the distance in his eyes.

Her hands brushed his shoulders. His grip tightened on her waist, like he was holding on to gravity itself. Their faces drew close. He wasn't looking at her—he was looking *through* her. Searching for a way out.

Then it happened.

He kissed her. Rough. Messy. Less connection, more collision. The girl, Marley, he thought her name was, startled—just a flicker—then he let himself go. In this place, nothing was real. No one asked questions.

They stumbled into the gloom across the street back to his motel room, behind curtains that dulled the sound and hid the truth. His jacket hit the floor. Her fingers found his jaw. His eyes fluttered shut— not from pleasure, but from the need to disappear.

Hands in hair. Lips pressed too hard.

Bodies speaking in a language neither of them understood anymore.

And for a moment, he forgot.

Forgot the rink.

Forgot the funeral.

Forgot the face that haunted him every time he closed his eyes.

But only for a moment.

The months were blurring together and before he knew it, a year had passed. He had missed Bennett's high school graduation and sending him off to college in New Mexico to become an architect. Mother's Day, Father's Day, an entire hockey season, Christmas, birthdays...shoot he had even missed his own birthday. He knew that had hurt Stryker deeply. He just couldn't make himself care.

Text after text–from his parents, siblings, teammates–were all left unanswered by him or if anything, they got one word responses just so they'd leave him alone about being alive.

He couldn't believe he was back here again.

Same haze. Same stench of stale liquor and sweat. Same throb of music pulsing through his skull like punishment.

He knew Jessica wouldn't want this—wouldn't want him like this.

But the ache never let up and this was the only thing that dulled it.

He slumped into a couch that sagged beneath him, surrounded by strangers chasing their own oblivion. Laughter echoed, sharp and hollow. Lights flickered overhead like they were trying to burn out.

A woman drifted into his orbit. Mid-twenties, too much eyeliner, just enough edge. She didn't ask his name. He didn't care to offer it.

He handed her the bottle. She took a slow sip. Their shoulders brushed. Her fingers slid down his arm—not tender, not curious. Just a habit.

He leaned in.

The kiss was a mess. Desperate. Muted by numbness on both sides. Breath tangled. Hands wandered. No words—just motion, just noise, just escape.

They didn't make it to a bedroom. No one here cared. The shadows took them in, the bass muting any shame.

She touched his face like she was trying to find him in there.

But he wasn't there.

He was on the ice, watching Jessica fall.

In the hospital, hearing the monitor flatline.

Standing in front of her casket with fists clenched and heart hollowed out.

She whispered something. Maybe it was his name.

He let his eyes close. Pretended to sleep.

Later, gray light crept through dirty blinds, harsh and indifferent. His shirt clung to his chest, the bottle still in his hand. Every muscle ached.

He blinked at the unfamiliar room. Motel curtains drawn. A single flickering bulb overhead.

This isn't my room. This isn't who I was.

In the bathroom, he caught his reflection. Red eyes. A cut lip he didn't know how he'd gotten. A number scribbled across his arm in red lipstick.

He stared. Nothing looked like him anymore.

The woman stirred in the next room. "Hey... you got a name?"

"Not one you need," he said.

He grabbed his hoodie and his wallet and walked out into the morning without another word.

The days continued to slip by without his notice or care. The concept of time had ceased to matter to him, nothing mattered—but deep down, he knew that wasn't right.

He had told himself he wouldn't go back to the bar. Told himself he'd pull himself together, figure out what he wanted.

It had been a lie. He'd been lying to himself more and more often lately. Lying that this was what he wanted. Lying that he could build any kind of life here.

And yet, here he was again.

The bar reeked of grease and stale beer, the kind of smell that didn't just cling. It sank into you if you let it. Slade hunched over a warm bottle, the bitter taste matching the sensation spreading inside him.

Around him, men sagged into their stools, faces dulled by too many nights just like this one. Their laughter was low and empty. He caught the thought unbidden: this is the finish line if I stay.

On the TV above the bar, the Snipers cut across the ice in a blur. Blades carving, shoulders slamming, cheers rising. His brother, Stryker, with the large captain's "C" on his jersey was being featured at the bottom of the screen. His reflection transposed itself over the spot where his brother was shown, a pale outline over the life he used to live.

For a heartbeat, he didn't recognize himself. *How had over two and a half years wasted away already? Had he really been gone that long–not just physically, but emotionally?*

Then—her laugh. Jessica's laugh. Sharp, teasing, a sound that once made him forget losses before the final buzzer. He could see her in the stands, grinning as she called out, "Don't pout, Slade. It's one dumb shot—take another."

His hand trembled on the bottle, knuckles whitening until he slammed it back on the bar.

The glass rang like a death knell. Heavy, useless. Dead weight.

The stool screeched as he shoved away from it. A couple of the regulars looked up, but he didn't care. Let them rot here. He wouldn't.

Outside, the cold hit him like a clean check to the ribs. Sharp, merciless, bracing. His lungs burned with it, but for the first time in months, he felt like they were doing their job.

He sucked in the night and tasted something alive.

Jessica hadn't loved a man who hid from the world. She had loved the one who skated until his legs gave out, who wanted the puck when the game was on the line. If he meant to honor her—if he meant to honor himself—then he had to stop dying and start playing again.

The SILVERWOOD SCOOP

Local Sports & Community News

Missing No More? Slade Fisher Spotted in North Carolina

Samantha Romano, Silverwood Snipers' Media Correspondent

It's been more than two years since former Silverwood Snipers star Slade Fisher vanished from the spotlight following the tragic death of long-time girlfriend Jessica Anderson. He left town without a word—no forwarding address, no official statement, and no clear sign of contact with family or friends still living in Silverwood.

But now, the hockey world may finally have a lead.

Sources say Fisher was recently spotted in Crescent Bay, North Carolina, at a local dive bar known as *The Hollow*. Witnesses reported seeing him later that night getting into a dark vehicle parked outside the bar.

Just days later, the same man—described as "worn down" and "not quite himself"—was seen stepping out of a car in front of *Seabreeze Lodge*, a quiet coastal motel on the edge of town.

Could the once-beloved hometown hero be laying low in Crescent Bay?

Photos haven't surfaced yet, but word is spreading—and those who've seen him say he's a far cry from the rising star who once lit up the ice.

What has Slade Fisher been doing all this time?

And more importantly... What brought him back into the open?

Stay tuned. *The Scoop* is watching.

Chapter Eight

One night in August, Slade sat alone in his room at *Seabreeze Lodge*, the flickering light from the television casting shadows on the walls that had become his makeshift home since running from his past.

The ocean breeze wafted through the open bay windows, along with the sound of the waves crashing on the beach outside.

The room was dark, but the memories were so vivid they took him right back to that day. The smell of smoke, the crackling flames, the searing pain in his shoulder as that beam hit him taking his breath away, the sound of the first responders calling out numbers, Jessica's voice as she struggled to tell him she loved him while fighting for breath.

Now, in the quiet darkness of his bedroom, the nightmare replayed. He could hear Jessica's voice, choked with fear. He could hear the machine as she flatlined and Callahan's voice as he called her time of death.

Slade jolted awake, his heart pounding against his ribcage. He wiped the sweat from his brow, his chest heaving. The nightmares had become a nightly ritual, a cruel reminder of his failure. It was the reason he had started drinking in the first place. He'd lost Jessica, and the guilt gnawed at him, threatening to consume him whole. Then he lost hockey when he made the hard decision to leave town and everything he knew to try to heal.

He stared at the ceiling, counting the swirls in the plaster like it might undo the man he'd been pretending to be. Two years of chasing numbness, night after night, as if it could erase the fire, erase her.

He sat up slowly, nausea curling in him, a bitter reminder of what he'd become. This wasn't grief anymore. Grief had teeth; it tore at you because of love. This was something smaller, meaner. Cowardice. And he knew it.

He wasn't this bar-hopping wreck who drowned himself in cheap liquor and strangers' perfume. He was Slade Fisher, and his body still remembered the rhythm of the ice even if he'd tried to forget. Some mornings his muscles ached like they expected skates, not hangovers.

It had only been a few weeks since he admitted the truth to himself: he wanted back the life he'd been running from. Back to Silverwood. Back to the Snipers. Back to the ice. The thought rattled in him like a loose puck—equal parts dread and hunger. He hadn't told anyone yet. Not his family. Not his friends. Not even his brother. Saying it out loud would make it real.

So far, he had avoided the press picking it up.

He grabbed his phone and opened up the family chat which had been pretty quiet lately.

SLADE:

> Hey, figured I should say it here first before Samantha leaks the news to the world. I'm coming home. For good.

SCARLETT:

> WAIT. WHAT. Is this real?! You're actually coming HOME home?!

SLADE:

> Yeah, Scar. I'm coming home. For real. I'm planning a meeting with the Snipers' managers and getting back on the ice.

DAD:

That's big, son. Proud of you. You sure
you're ready?

CALLAHAN:

Looking forward to giving you a bear
hug, bro.

STRYKER:

Heck yeah, brother! Life isn't the same
without you, we need you and the team
needs you. Can I let Coach and the team
know?

BENNETT:

Glad to hear you're going home, bro! Sad I
won't be there to welcome you though.

JULIETTE:

I second what Benny said! Love you Slade.

MOM:

Oh, honey. I am so relieved to hear this. I
can't wait to wrap my arms around you!!

Chapter Nine

The crisp, early September air greeted Slade as he drove into Silverwood two weeks later. The town was just beginning to embrace the seasonal shift. Golden leaves clung to branches, though many littered the ground in vibrant piles. The streets had the familiar buzz of activity that came before hockey season.

Slade drove on Main Street, his truck headlights illuminating the businesses adorned with autumn wreaths and pumpkin displays.

He was heading to *The Cozy Cup,* a local diner where he planned to meet his sister Scarlett and hopefully avoid the press until he had a chance to shower and adjust to being back here.

Pulling into the parking lot, he cut the engine with a tired exhale, got out of his truck, and made his way toward the door.

He hesitated just outside, sliding his sunglasses into place and adjusting his baseball cap in an attempt to hide his identity.

He pushed the door open, and a bell jingled overhead, too bright, too cheerful for the mood settling inside him. Scarlett was sitting in a booth near the window, Slade slid into the seat across from her, rubbing a hand across his face.

"You look like hell," Scarlett said.

"Thanks. I've been driving all night and came straight here, brat," he snapped back.

"Sorry, just being honest." Scarlett sighed. "It's good to be able to see your face again, not just Stryker's."

They sat in silence for a moment, the hum of the diner settling around them, the neon glow from the sign outside flashing intermittently.

A waitress appeared at the edge of the table, pen poised over her notepad. "Hey Scar, y'all ready?"

Scarlett smiled. "Hey Noelle! Two of your famous hot chocolates, please. And heavy on the whipped cream, please."

Slade raised an eyebrow. "Hot chocolate? Really, Scar?"

Scarlett rolled her eyes playfully. "Yes, really. She makes the *best* hot chocolate."

"Coming right up," the waitress said before disappearing behind the counter.

They sat in silence for a beat longer.

Then, finally, she spoke. "Tell me what's going on."

A moment later, the waitress approached again with a steaming mug in each hand. Slade's gaze immediately went to her. She was petite but carried herself with confidence. Beautifully dressed in a white sweater with black leggings tucked into matching boots, her golden blonde hair was pulled back into a half ponytail cascading to the middle of her back. Her bright blue eyes sparkled behind cat-eye glasses.

She handed Scarlett one of the mugs before turning to Slade. "You must be Slade," she said, her voice warm and inviting. "I'm Noelle."

"Uh, yeah, that's me," he replied, awkwardly rubbing the back of his neck. "How did you know who I was?"

Her smile widened. "Scarlett told me all about her 'long lost brother, Slade' she was meeting today, and since you're the spitting image of Stryker, I figured you might be him."

"All good things, I hope," Slade said, his lips twitching into a small, hesitant smile.

"Mostly," Noelle teased with a glint in her eye.

"Good," he said with a teasing eye to his sister. "So you know my brother, too?" Slade didn't know why he felt jealous asking the question.

"Not very well. Just from hanging out with Scarlett. She took me in under her wing after I moved here two years ago from Vancouver." Noelle replied shyly as she handed over his drink.

Slade accepted the cup, which was filled with rich, creamy hot chocolate and topped with a generous dollop of whipped cream, a sprinkle of cocoa powder, and some candy cane sprinkles.

He took a cautious sip, his eyes widening in surprise. "Wow, this is… incredible," he admitted, the rich, velvety chocolate warming him from the inside out.

Scarlett beamed, nudging her brother. "Told you it's the best."

Noelle laughed. "I'm glad you like it. There's something magical about hot chocolate on a chilly autumn night, don't you think?"

Slade nodded slowly, the mug cradled in his hands like something fragile. For the first time in a long time, the tightness in his chest truly eased—just a little. Not gone. Not even close. But quieter. Like the walls around his heart were starting to melt.

"Yeah, there is. Thanks, Noelle."

The rink smelled the same.

Cold air, sharpened steel, faint rubber and sweat clinging to the concrete walls like a memory that refused to fade. Slade stood just inside the entrance, duffel bag at his feet, hands shoved deep into his jacket pockets.

For a second, he just watched.

The Silverwood Snipers were already on the ice, jerseys flashing blue and white as they cut sharp lines across the surface. The sound of blades biting into ice echoed through the empty stands—familiar enough to make his chest ache.

He hadn't realized how much he missed it.

"Thought that might be you."

Slade turned.

Coach Carlson stood a few feet away, arms crossed, expression unreadable in that way coaches perfected over decades. His hair was grayer than Slade remembered. His posture was just as unyielding.

"Hey, Coach."

Carlson studied him for a long moment. Then he nodded once. "You look like hell."

Slade huffed. "Yeah, that's what I hear. I earned it."

A corner of the coach's mouth twitched. "You ready to work?"

"Yes," Slade said without hesitation. "More than ready."

"Good. Because the paperwork cleared this morning from your uncle's office. You're officially back on the roster." He jerked his chin toward the ice. "Go remind them who you are."

Slade didn't need a second invitation.

He pulled on skates, the motions coming back like muscle memory never forgot him. The moment his blades hit the ice, something inside him clicked into place—quiet, steady, right.

A familiar body slammed into his side near the boards.

"You disappear for a few years and just think you can sneak back in?"

Slade grinned as he straightened, facing his twin. Stryker stood there in full gear, helmet tucked under his arm, eyes bright and sharp and entirely too amused.

"Miss me?" Slade asked.

Stryker snorted. "Like a migraine." Then his grin softened. "Good to have you back, brother."

They bumped fists, a thousand unspoken things passing between them in the contact.

After practice, they peeled off their gear side by side, the locker room buzzing with the familiar voices of Hunter and Garrett, and easy trash talk from Gunner, Jayden, Miguel and the other guys. Stryker leaned back against the bench, towel slung over his shoulders.

"So," he said casually, "I moved my stuff out of your place."

Slade blinked. "You did?"

"Yeah. Figured it was time." Stryker shrugged. "I've been crashing closer to the rink anyway. Plus"—his mouth tipped into a knowing smirk—"you're gonna need your space."

"For what?"

Stryker's eyes flicked toward the door, then back. "You'll see."

Slade shook his head, laughing under his breath. "You always talk like you know something I don't."

Stryker clapped him on the shoulder. "Twin perk. And our nosy sister."

Had Scarlett picked up on something with him and Noelle? No, impossible, there was nothing to pick up on.

As Slade placed his boots back into his bag, the weight on his chest felt lighter than it had in years.

He wasn't just back in Silverwood.

He was back where he belonged.

Slade's apartment was dark when he stepped inside. He tossed his jacket over the chair and dropped onto the couch, rubbing at his face like he could wipe her out of his head.

Noelle.

The name curled through him like smoke, sweet and bitter at once. Like Christmases past, all joy tangled with heartache.

He told himself it was nothing. Just being back in Silverwood, nerves raw, memory playing tricks. Of course the first warm smile would hit harder than it should. That's all it was.

He leaned forward, elbows on his knees. Her laugh still echoed. The way she'd looked at him as if she saw past the wreck he'd been hiding behind. He tried to fold it into the blur of every woman who'd passed through his nights since Jessica was taken from him, but the thought wouldn't dissolve.

"Just another girl," he muttered.

Hell, he'd had plenty of those. None of them followed him home when the lights went out. None of them stayed.

He dragged a hand through his hair, jaw tight. *Scarlett would lose her damn mind if she knew I was looking at her friend like that.* He could almost hear her voice, sharp and unforgiving, and for a moment he let himself cling to that excuse. It was easier than admitting the truth.

Jessica's name pressed in anyway, slicing like glass. His hand twitched against his thigh, reaching for nothing—for a stick that wasn't there.

"She's not Jessica," he said to the empty room. The words scraped his throat.

But the silence pushed back, and before he could stop himself, his fist slammed against the cushion beside him—hard enough to sting, not nearly enough to hurt.

The next morning, Slade drove north along the coast.

The sky was pale and overcast, the ocean restless but calm enough to match the knot in his chest. He hadn't told them exactly when he was coming. He hadn't called ahead. He wasn't sure what he'd say if he did.

The lighthouse came into view just as it always had—white against the gray, steady and unyielding. A constant.

He parked and sat in the truck for a long moment, hands resting on the steering wheel, breathing through the familiar weight pressing behind his ribs.

Then he got out.

The door to the small museum creaked open, warmth and the scent of old paper and polished wood spilling out to meet him. A bell chimed softly overhead.

Genevieve looked up from behind the counter.

She froze.

For half a heartbeat, Slade thought she might not recognize him.

Then her hand flew to her mouth.

"Oh," she breathed.

He managed a smile that felt fragile around the edges. "Hey, Mom."

She crossed the room in seconds, arms wrapping around him with a fierceness that stole his breath. He closed his eyes, letting himself sink into it, the years away dissolving in the familiar press of her embrace.

"I didn't know when," she said, voice trembling against his shoulder. "I just knew you'd come back."

"I'm sorry I didn't call when I got to town yesterday," he murmured.

She pulled back just enough to cup his face, eyes shining. "You're here. That's enough."

A door opened behind them.

Daniel stepped into view, his expression still and measured until his eyes landed on Slade.

They stared at each other for a long moment.

Then Daniel nodded once and crossed the room, pulling Slade into a firm, grounding embrace. No words. Just presence.

"I'm home," Slade said quietly.

Daniel's hand tightened at his back. "Thank God."

They stood like that for a moment longer, the lighthouse steady behind them, the ocean murmuring outside like it always had.

For the first time since he'd left, Slade felt the past loosen its grip.

He wasn't running anymore.

By the time the following weekend rolled around, Slade had started to feel like his feet were actually on the ground again.

He'd slept in his own bed. Had dinner with his family. Sat on the porch with Scarlett while she filled the silence with stories about town gossip he pretended not to care about. He'd even gone back to the rink twice—once to skate, once just to sit in the stands and let the cold steady him.

It helped. More than he expected.

So when Scarlett texted *Dinner at 7:00. Mom & Dad's. Don't be late.* and nothing else, he didn't think twice about it.

The house was already full when he walked in.

Not loud—just warm.

Music played low from the kitchen. The smell of something baked —chocolate, maybe—hung in the air. Stryker stood by the window with a beer in hand, Hunter and Garrett leaning nearby while Gunner and Jayden argued about something pointless. Miguel sat on the arm of the couch, scrolling his phone.

And there—half tucked into the corner of the living room—Noelle sat with Samantha, a mug cradled between her hands, listening more than she spoke. She looked up when Slade stepped inside, offering a small wave before turning back to the conversation, like she didn't want to make a moment of it.

Slade frowned. "What's going on?"

Stryker glanced over, smirking and clutching at his chest dramatically, "Don't tell me you forgot my birthday?"

Slade snorted. "Relax. I only forgot *yours*. Mine's still on the calendar."

Scarlett appeared from the kitchen, holding a cake—nothing fancy, just chocolate with blue icing and two candles in the shape of a 2 and a 4 stuck crookedly in the top. "Good, now you're both here, we can get the party started!"

Happy Birthday, Tweedle Dee & Tweedle Dumb was written across it in messy frosting.

Stryker groaned. "Wow. How sweet, sis."

Scarlett grinned. "You're welcome. Mom said to put your names on it, I was just following orders."

Slade stood there, still surprised by it all, something thick lodging in his throat. "You guys didn't have to do this."

"Yes, we did," Genevieve said easily as she and Daniel joined the group. "You don't get to skip your birthday anymore now that you're home."

They didn't sing. Thank God.

Scarlett lit the candles and shoved the cake toward them. "Make a wish. Both of you."

Noelle's face immediately came to Slade's mind. He tried to shake the thought away.

He glanced at Stryker. For a second, the years peeled back—same house, same candles, same shared breath before blowing them out.

They leaned in and blew together.

Later, after the cake had been cut and the room had settled into easy conversation, Slade found himself standing beside his brother near the window, watching everyone else talk like this was normal. Like it hadn't taken two years of loss and distance to get here.

Stryker lifted his bottle in a small salute. "Still breathing," he said. "Still skating. Still us."

Slade clinked his bottle against his. "Still us."

Across the room, Noelle caught his eye—just a soft smile, nothing more. Not claiming space. Just there.

It felt... shared.

The SILVERWOOD SCOOP

Local Sports & Community News

Slade Fisher Returns to Silverwood—and to the Snipers
Samantha Romano, Silverwood Snipers' Media Correspondent

You heard it here first, folks—Slade Fisher is making his return.

After nearly three years away, the former Silverwood Snipers star has headed back to his hometown—and back to the ice.
Fisher stepped away from hockey following the tragic fire that claimed the life of twenty-one year-old Jessica Anderson, who was reportedly set to become his fiancée that very night. The incident sent shockwaves through the community and put a sudden halt to a promising athletic career.

Since then, Slade has kept a low profile, while his twin brother, Stryker Fisher, has stepped into the spotlight, becoming the face of the Snipers in his absence.

But that's about to change.

On the first Tuesday in October, the Fisher brothers will once again take the ice together at Silverwood Hockey Arena—reuniting under the Snipers banner for the first time since the tragedy.

Will Slade find his footing after so long away?

One thing's for sure: Silverwood will be watching.

Stay with *The Scoop* for full coverage and exclusive updates.

Chapter Ten

Slade donned his Snipers jersey the first Tuesday night in October and skated onto the ice of Silverwood Hockey Arena. Every muscle in his body remembered this: the ritual of pre-game warmups, the crisp bite of the cold air, the scrape of blades cutting into the ice. He had been here before, countless times, but tonight felt different. Tonight, he was reclaiming his place.

He looked up into the stands, scanning the familiar row where his family sat—and froze. Noelle was there.

It was the first time he'd seen her since his birthday. He hadn't expected her, hadn't let himself imagine it, but now here she was—her blonde hair catching the light, her cheeks flushed as she laughed at something Scarlett said. The sound carried even through the roar of the arena, sharper and sweeter than he remembered. His chest tightened.

She wasn't like the rest of the crowd, shouting frenzied encouragement. No, she sat back with her cup of hot chocolate clasped in gloved hands, calm in the chaos, her eyes steady on the game as if she understood it. As if she understood *him*.

It hit like a cross-check to the boards. That smile, that look, carved through every wall he'd been building since he came back. She was his sister's best friend—untouchable, off-limits. He kept telling himself that. But tonight, watching her, it didn't feel true. Tonight she was the reason his heart was beating harder than it had in years.

The referee's whistle pierced the air, jolting him back. The puck dropped. The Snipers had the play. Slade weaved through his opponents, sharp, agile, the old rhythm flooding him. Jayden slid him the puck. Pass to Stryker. Down to Garrett. Over to Hunter and back to him.

The game moved fast, bodies colliding, the familiar chaos grounding him. Along the far side, the puck was chipped deep, buying a second of space. Coach Carlson made a call and Jayden peeled off toward the bench, legs burning.

Miguel vaulted the boards in one smooth motion, calling for the play as he took Jayden's spot on the blue line.

He swiftly used his stick to kick the puck loose along the boards, skittering into open ice.

Slade let instinct take over, muscle memory carrying him where thought couldn't. Midway through the first period, the puck kicked loose along the boards, skittering into open ice.

Slade saw the lane before it fully existed.

He surged forward, scooping the puck onto his stick, cutting past a defender with a sharp pivot. The crowd rose as one, anticipation buzzing through the arena. He didn't look up at the net—didn't need to.

He shot.

The puck snapped past the goalie's glove and slammed into the back of the net.

For a split second, there was silence.

Then the arena exploded.

The rest of the game flew by and before he knew it, the Snipers had their first win of the season. Out of the corner of his eye, Slade caught Noelle and Scarlett on their feet, jumping and cheering. His teammates crashed around him in celebration, but it was the sight of her—eyes bright, smile wide—that stayed with him, driving him more than the roar of the crowd ever could.

Afterward, he opened his locker and picked up his phone, seeing a message waiting for him.

STRYKER:

> Need to talk to you after everyone clears out.
> Hang back.

"Stryk, you wanted to see me?" Slade asked after the locker room had emptied.

Stryker nodded, still not looking his brother in the eyes, "Yeah. Sit."

Slade sat, curious why his twin was so serious all of a sudden.

"You know," Stryker began, fingers tapping on his knee, "when you left, the team needed someone to step up. I didn't think it would be me. I didn't even want it. You just plopped it on my shoulders."

Slade's jaw tightened. "I know, Stryk."

"No, you don't." Stryker said, finally looking at his twin brother. "I spent the last few years trying to fill a space you left behind. Not just on the ice. In the room. In the city. We may be twins, but I'm not you. You were the heartbeat of this team, Slade."

"I was a mess back then. I shouldn't have been anyone's heartbeat."

"But you were. Even after all this time, it's clear that you still are."

Stryker stood and Slade saw his jersey with the captain's C on it in his hand.

"Slade, you're back now. You're healthy. You're you again. And part of me wonders if this should go back to you."

Slade's eyes widened, "Stryk, no. You earned that. You kept this team alive. You carried what I couldn't. I didn't come back to take anything from you. I came back to play beside you."

Chapter Eleven

Between his parents, siblings, Uncle Seamus, Aunt Catherine, and cousins, Talulla, Killian, Jameson and Rowan, Thanksgiving at the Fisher house was never a quiet affair.

The cozy farmhouse smelled like roasted turkey, rosemary, and the faint bite of pine drifting in every time the door opened. Slade stood just inside the entryway, shrugging off his coat, listening to his parents argue good-naturedly about whether the gravy needed more pepper. It was familiar. Comforting. And still, it felt strange to be back for good.

"Slade," his mother called from the kitchen, "help your father with the table before Scarlett eats all the rolls."

"I heard that," Scarlett shot back, breezing past him with a grin. "And for the record, I'm saving them for Noelle and the girls."

The name landed harder than he expected. He didn't know *she* was coming and the way it both excited him and made him nervous had his head spinning. They'd seen each other a few times now since her and Scarlett were practically attached at the hip. He didn't pay any mind to the mention of the 'other girls' coming.

As if summoned, Scarlett reappeared with three guests in tow. Willow walked in first, smiling warmly, her cheeks pink from the cold. Slade's breath caught. Recognition sliced like a blade. She was the nurse.

The one who had stood in the hospital corridor two and a half years ago, her hands steady while his world shattered. They smiled politely at each other.

Behind her was her sister, Violet, who he vaguely remembered being in the waiting room that night. She was a little younger so he didn't know her as well.

"I hope Scarlett warned you we travel in pairs." Violet joked when she saw his bewildered face, shrugging off her coat. "Also—Samantha says hi to everyone. She's in Florida with her parents this week and absolutely furious she's missing your mom's cooking."

Genevieve laughed from the kitchen. "Tell her I'll save some leftovers if she brings us back a little sunshine."

"I will," Violet said, grinning. "She promised gossip as payment."

They all ceased to exist the moment Noelle walked in bundled in a pale blue sweater, blonde hair pulled loosely over one shoulder. Her cat-eye glasses caught the light when she looked up, and when her blue eyes met Slade's, something in his chest shifted and the swift pain he had just felt at the reminder of Jessica dissipated.

"Oh," she said, a little breathless, like she hadn't expected him to be there. "Hi, Slade."

"Hey," he replied, suddenly aware of his hands, his posture, the fact that he'd been gone so long he'd forgotten how to exist casually around someone new.

Scarlett watched the exchange with obvious curiosity before announcing, "Okay, everyone's here. This means we can officially eat."

"Did someone say we can finally eat? I'm famished," Stryker announced from the doorway, draping an arm over Willow's shoulder. His brothers, uncle and dad all came trampling in behind him from playing street hockey out front.

Dinner unfolded the way it always did—overfilled plates, overlapping conversations, Uncle Seamus telling inappropriate jokes and the resounding laughter echoing off walls that had heard decades of it.

At the far end of the table, Aunt Catherine leaned toward Genevieve with a nod towards Slade, her voice carrying just enough to be heard over the clatter of silverware.

"Look at him," Catherine said, smiling into her wine. "Actually here. Sitting still. I was starting to think my nephew had turned into a myth."

Genevieve laughed softly. "Don't remind me. It's such a relief to have him home. Not to mention, my brother nearly drove me mad with the pacing. Every phone call was, *'Have you heard from Slade? Has he been skating at all? Eating right?'*"

Seamus snorted from beside them. "I was worried. I'm allowed."

"You own a hockey team," Catherine said dryly. "You don't get to pretend to be subtle about your real motives."

"Might I remind you that's *our* hockey team," he shot back, grinning. "And I like my players, especially my nephews, healthy—and home."

Genevieve's gaze softened as she looked down the table at Slade. "We're just glad he's back where he belongs."

Catherine reached over and squeezed her hand. "All of us are."

Slade, seated across from Noelle, didn't hear every word—but he caught enough. Enough to feel something warm and steady settle in his chest.

Slade found he couldn't look away from Noelle who was close enough for him to notice how her button nose scrunched up when she laughed, how she listened intently when his father talked about the upcoming winter.

"It's so nice to see you again, Slade," Willow said at one point, glancing between Slade and Noelle, "Scarlett told me you're back in Maine for good."

Slade nodded. "Yeah. Took me a while, but… it felt like time."

Noelle's gaze lingered on him, thoughtful, not prying. "I'm glad you came back," she said quietly.

The sincerity in her voice caught him off guard. He didn't trust himself to respond right away, so he smiled instead—and was surprised by how natural it felt.

After dinner, Scarlett helped their aunt and mother with dessert. Stryker and Willow had taken a little stroll to walk off the food and the rest of the family sat sprawled on the couches watching football. Slade found himself alone with Noelle in the dining room as they prepped the table for dessert, the low hum of conversation drifting in from the other rooms.

"This is really nice," she said, glancing around. "Your family always makes everyone feel so welcome."

"They do," he agreed. After a pause, he added, "I'm glad you came."

She smiled at that—small, genuine, a little shy. "Me too."

For the first time in a long while, Slade realized something unexpected. The weight he'd been carrying hadn't vanished—but in moments like this, with laughter in the other room and someone like Noelle sitting beside him, it felt lighter.

And maybe, just maybe, that was enough to start with.

The meal had ended in uneasy silence, the clatter of plates replaced by the murmur of the dishwasher in the kitchen. Family voices drifted faintly from the living room, but Slade lingered near the back porch, staring out at the brittle November leaves scattered across the yard.

Behind him, footsteps hesitated. Willow.

She stood in the doorway, arms folded as if bracing against the chill. Her eyes were wary, shadowed by guilt. "I didn't mean to ruin tonight," she said softly. "I shouldn't have come. I should've known it would hurt you. Violet and I joined last year and Scarlett and Stryker insisted it would be fine..."

Slade turned, the porch light catching the tension in her face. For a moment, he saw her as she had been that night—calm in the chaos, steady when he was breaking.

He stepped closer, lowering his voice. "Willow... relax. I don't blame you."

Her brow furrowed, disbelief flickering. "But you looked at me like —like I was part of it. Like I was the reason."

Slade shook his head, the weight of memory pressing but not crushing. "You were doing your job. You were there when Jess died, yes. But you didn't cause it. You didn't fail her. Cal didn't fail her. It was a horrible accident. I know that. I was just surprised to see you, I didn't realize that you would be here and were so close with my family now, but that's on me since I've been away."

Willow's breath caught, her shoulders trembling. "I've carried that night with me. Every time I've heard your name mentioned, I wondered if I would ever see you again. I remember that night, with your shoulder and then as everything fell apart. Every time I look at you, I wonder if you hate me."

Slade's voice softened, steady now. "I don't. I couldn't. Jess's death wasn't yours to carry. It's mine. And I've been carrying it long enough."

Silence stretched between them, broken only by the faint laughter of his parents in the other room. Willow's eyes shimmered, relief mingling with sorrow.

Slade offered a small, weary smile. "You're with Stryker now. That's... complicated for me. But it doesn't mean I want you walking around afraid of me. You can breathe. You can be here."

Willow nodded slowly, the tension easing from her posture. For the first time that night, her shoulders dropped, her hands unclenched.

Chapter Twelve

Slade sat on the couch in his parents' living room, staring blankly at the muted television. The Christmas tree twinkled in the corner, feeling as though it were mocking him.

Every wreath felt like a wound. Every carol, a reminder.

She should be here. Laughing. Decorating. *Living*.

Slade rubbed a hand over his face and exhaled hard through his nose. He'd be fine with skipping the next few weeks altogether, letting the season pass like a storm he had no shelter from.

Because what was the point of Christmas when the person who made it matter was gone?

Scarlett burst into the room like a whirlwind of energy. Noelle trailed behind with an amused smile. She wore a red and white scarf around her neck and a matching hat.

Slade's breath caught before he could stop it.

It wasn't even attraction; not exactly. But it was—*something*. A flicker of life in a part of him that had gone cold.

"Alright, Slade, enough is enough," Scarlett huffed, hands on her hips. "You've been sulking around here for weeks whenever you're not at the arena. We're going to the opening night of Winter Walk," she continued, undeterred by his silence. "You're coming with us. End of discussion."

"You've got to be kidding. The Winter Walk?" Slade asked in disbelief. Scarlett knew how much he wanted to avoid that.

"Yeah, you know, the town thing. Lights, shops, hot chocolate, festive vibes?" Scarlett waved her hands in the air as if painting a picture. "It's time to live a little."

"No, thanks," Slade muttered, sinking deeper into the couch. "Not really in the mood."

"Come on," Scarlett groaned. "You can't tell me you're going to spend another night sitting around watching reruns of shows you don't even like."

Slade was about to argue when Noelle stepped forward, her soft voice cutting through his defenses. "It'll be fun, Slade. Besides, it's not just for you. We could all use a bit of fresh air, don't you think?"

He glanced at her, and the fog in his mind seemed to lift slightly for the first time in weeks. He hadn't mentioned it to anyone, but since he had met Noelle that night at *The Cozy Cup* three months ago, he had been questioning everything. His mind raced with questions and possibilities.

Can I feel something for someone again? Is it betraying Jess? What does this mean? Is it because of the season, or is this real? She's Scarlett's friend, though...

Maybe it was the way her eyes sparkled or the gentle curve of her smile, but for a moment, he considered the possibility of feeling something. Perhaps even trying to enjoy the Winter Walk again, maybe the possibility of celebrating Christmas again wasn't so far-fetched.

"Fine," he said, dragging a hand through his hair.

Downtown Silverwood bustled with activity. The Winter Walk was in full swing. Twinkling lights decorated the little shops, and the air was filled with the scent of cinnamon and roasted chestnuts. Festive music played from the speakers.

Watching Noelle weave through the crowd, he turned to Scarlett and asked, with a hint of amusement, "Is she always this... bubbly?"

His sister grinned, folding her arms, "Bubbly is just the tip of the iceberg. Noelle's like a walking Hallmark movie, except way cooler. You'd like her if you weren't so committed to being a grump."

"Scarlett, her name is Noelle. It means Christmas. We are here at the place where I was supposed to ask Jess to be my wife, and you know that night ruined Christmas for me. I haven't done anything related to Christmas for the last two years. I don't know that I ever will again. I hate everything about it now," Slade grumbled.

Scarlett's smile faded a bit as she looked at her brother with concern. "Slade, you don't have to be a Scrooge forever. Have you thought about trying to meet someone to share your life with again?" she asked gently.

Slade sighed and shook his head. "Nah, Scar, I've been too focused on my hockey comeback, and it feels weird to even think about liking someone right now. Still feels like I'd be betraying—"

Slade looked down, his eyes glistening with unshed tears. He couldn't tell Scarlett that he had been thinking about Noelle since that night he met her and was questioning everything.

Scarlett smiled sympathetically. "I know it hasn't been easy since Jessica, but Slade, you can't punish yourself forever. You are allowed to be happy again. Jessica would want that for you. You know she would."

Slade nodded, taking a deep breath. "Thanks, Scarlett."

Scarlett gave his hand another squeeze before letting go. "Anytime."

Before Slade had a chance to say anything else, a familiar voice cut into their conversation, "Well, well, if it isn't Miss Scarlett, looking as stunning as ever."

Hunter? Did he just call Scarlett stunning?

Hunter stepped up beside her, slipping his hands into his coat pockets, but the grin on his face was unmistakable.

Scarlett rolled her eyes, but a smirk tugged at her lips. "Do you always enter conversations like you're walking into a spotlight?"

Hunter chuckled, unfazed. "Only when the most beautiful woman is around and deserves my attention."

Scarlett huffed out a laugh, shaking her head, though Slade didn't miss the way her cheeks flushed.

Slade stood awkwardly to the side, hands stuffed into his coat pockets, glancing at Noelle, who had been watching the exchange with amusement since she had returned a few minutes ago. She nudged him with her elbow, a smirk playing on her lips.

"Looks like she's found her distraction," she said with a laugh, nodding toward Scarlett. "Want to keep walking?"

He hesitated, but the way Noelle tilted her head, her expression inviting and earnest, made it hard to say no. "Sure."

Slade pulled his hands from his coat pockets and gestured for Noelle to lead the way. She smiled and stepped forward, and he quickly fell into stride beside her, their footsteps syncing as they walked down the quiet street.

Fresh snow crunched beneath their boots as Slade and Noelle strolled side by side through the winding path of the Winter Walk. Twinkling lights wrapped around trees, and "Have Yourself a Merry Little Christmas" played in the distance.

The streetlights cast a warm glow over the sidewalk, illuminating the soft dusting of snow that clung to the pavement. Cold air curled around them, but Slade barely noticed. He didn't realize how close they were walking—until their hands brushed.

A spark jolted through him at the simple touch. The warmth of her skin against his sent an unexpected charge straight to his chest. Noelle paused ever so slightly, her breath catching, and Slade knew she had felt it too.

Noelle stopped in front of a small shop with a frosted window display showcasing delicate glass ornaments. She tilted her head, inspecting the twinkling decorations.

"These are beautiful, aren't they?" she said, her breath fogging in the cold air.

Slade glanced at the ornaments, but his attention quickly returned to Noelle. Something about how her face lit up and her eyes seemed to catch the light held his focus.

"Yeah," he said gruffly, shoving his hands deeper into his coat pockets, "They are beautiful."

Noelle tugged her green jacket tighter as a burst of winter air swirled around them, the scent of pine and woodsmoke wafting in the breeze. Her cheeks still ached from smiling. She hadn't felt that in... man, she couldn't remember the last time she had felt something like this. The hot chocolate warming her hands, the ornaments glittering like tiny stars, it all reminded her of childhood winters when everything felt safe.

For once, she wasn't bracing for the other shoe to drop. For once, she was just... happy.

The thought startled her almost as much as it comforted her.

And then—

A familiar chilling voice cut through the quiet, instantly shattering her peace. "Noelle."

Her breath caught as she froze, her heart lurching like ice water poured through her veins. She felt Slade stiffen beside her as well as if he picked up on her inner panic.

I know that voice. It can't be though. No, please. Not him.

She turned slowly, every muscle locked tight, until she was face-to-face with her ex-boyfriend, Beau Abbot, his dark eyes lit with the dangerous glint she knew too well.

"What are you doing here, Beau?" She managed to ask, her voice trembling.

He took a step closer to her, his presence suffocating. "You thought you could just replace me and move on?" His gaze slid to Slade in a challenging way that scared Noelle. "Find yourself a savior?"

She took a step back, her mind racing. *How did he know we were here together?*

"Beau, please just leave me—" Noelle began, but before she could finish her sentence, he grabbed her by the arm where his grip would certainly leave a bruise, and drug her away from Slade's side. Panic surged through her as she struggled to break free. "L-let me g-go."

He laughed a cold, menacing laugh. "Oh, I don't think so. You belong to me, Noelle. I'm not letting you go that easily. We're leaving."

Noelle's eyes were wide with panic, darting around the crowd like she was searching for an escape. Beau tightened his hold, making her flinch.

Slade met her eyes across the small space, and the fear in them hit harder than any check he'd ever taken. His gut clenched, heat rising in his chest. Then he noticed the hand on her arm, the way she shrank back.

He didn't think, he just moved.

"Hey," he called, voice steady as he closed the short distance. "Everything alright here?"

Noelle's eyes shifted to him, relief flashing across her face for a moment.

Beau turned, his jaw tightening. "Stay out of this, man. She's none of your business."

Slade didn't flinch. He wasn't looking for a fight, but there was no chance he was leaving her alone with someone who she was obviously scared of. He stepped closer, his presence firm but measured.

"Let go of her." His voice was low, controlled, but the heat behind it was unmistakable.

Beau turned with a sneer, his grip on Noelle unwavering. "Listen. You may think you're her new guy or something, but you're not," he spat. "I'm Beau. Noelle and I go way back. And I don't give a damn who you think you are—she's coming with me."

"She doesn't look too comfortable," Slade said, keeping his tone even and staying close. "So, how about you back off?"

Beau's grip tightened as he turned back to face Slade, pulling Noelle with him.

"Get your hands off of her," Slade growled, his eyes focused on Beau.

Beau scoffed, sizing him up. "You think you're gonna play hero? Like I said, she and I have history. Now back off." His tone was venomous, sharp enough to cut, but Slade wasn't phased.

"Yeah?" Slade raised an eyebrow. "Then maybe you should respect it enough to leave her alone when she wants you to."

Noelle gave a weak tug against Beau's hold, but he barely budged. Slade clenched his fists. The urge to rip her away from the jerk burned, but before he could move, another voice cut through the tension.

"Beau Abbot."

Stryker's tone was even, but the authority in it was obvious. He stepped up beside Slade, his stare locked on Beau. "No one wanted to see your face around here. You weren't invited."

Beau's sneer faltered, his grip twitching. "Great, that's right, there's two of you." he said sarcastically.

The moment stretched—Slade could see the calculation in his eyes, the realization that he was outnumbered. Finally, with an annoyed grunt, he let go of Noelle's wrist.

"This isn't over," Beau muttered, shoving his way into the crowd and disappearing.

"Stryk, how do you know that guy?" Slade asked, facing his twin brother.

"Beau Abbot played center for the Vancouver Vultures. We had a match-up against them the season after you left. He was an—" Stryker stopped himself from finishing the insult, glancing at Noelle.

She let out a shaky breath, her shoulders trembling as she rubbed her wrist. Slade placed a steadying hand on her back, guiding her toward the nearest bench. Stryker followed, his watchful eyes scanning the crowd, making sure Beau didn't resurface.

When they reached the bench, Noelle sank onto it, pressing her fingers against her temples. Tears clung to her lashes, but she blinked them away.

Slade crouched in front of her. "You okay?"

She let out a weak laugh—an attempt to brush it off—but he could see the weight pressing down on her. "I don't know," she admitted.

Slade exchanged a glance with Stryker. "Well, you're not alone."

The tension still clung to the air as Slade sat beside Noelle on the bench. Her hands shook slightly, one curled in a fist against her lap as she wiped at the stray tears clinging to her lashes with the other. The night's chill wrapped around them, but Slade barely felt it—his focus was solely on Noelle.

Slade shrugged off his Snipers jacket and wrapped it around Noelle's shoulders. "Take this. It's cold."

"Thanks," she said barely above a whisper as she pulled it around her shoulders. The fabric was soft and warm, and it smelled like cedarwood and clean soap.

Then out of the corner of his eye he saw movement.

She sounded cheerful at first, her usual energy breaking through the winter air. Scarlett and Hunter were rushing over, weaving past lingering groups of people. But the smile on her face faded the moment she saw Noelle. Her expression instantly shifted—tight with worry now, eyes scanning for answers.

The second she reached them, she crouched in front of Noelle, grasping her hands.

"What happened?" she demanded, scanning Noelle's face with sharp intensity, her fingers curling protectively around Noelle's.

Noelle opened her mouth, but no words came. Just a shuddering inhale, then a fresh wave of tears spilling over.

"What happened?" Scarlett asked again, her voice sharp with urgency.

Noelle didn't answer—she just curled in on herself, choking out soft, ragged sobs that she couldn't hold in any longer.

Slade glanced down at her, his chest tightening, then turned back to Scarlett.

"Her ex, Beau," he said, his voice edged with frustration. "He showed up out of nowhere and grabbed her. He tried to force her to go with him."

Scarlett stiffened. Hunter muttered something low under his breath, his jaw tight as he ran a hand through his hair.

Scarlett's gaze flicked toward Slade. "Where is he now?"

Slade shrugged, feeling tense.

Scarlett moved to the bench beside her, rubbing small circles on her back. "Do you want me to take you home?" she asked gently.

Noelle nodded. "Please."

Scarlett helped Noelle to her feet, wrapping an arm around her shoulders and guiding her toward the parking lot where Scarlett's car was parked. Noelle moved stiffly, as if exhaustion weighed down every step, but she didn't resist.

Slade lingered, hands shoved deep in his jacket pockets, watching them go. His jaw ticked slightly—frustration, worry, all of it simmering just beneath the surface. He blew out a slow breath before stepping forward, catching Scarlett's attention.

"Are you taking her to your place or hers? I'll call in a little bit," he told her, his voice steady, even. "Just to check in."

Scarlett gave him a knowing look before saying they were going to Noelle's and guiding her the rest of the way to her car.

Chapter Thirteen

Once they were in the car, Scarlett took a steadying breath, then gently turned back to Noelle. "Sweetheart, you should go to the police."

Noelle squeezed her eyes shut, her breath hitching. After a long beat, she nodded.

Scarlett softened, rubbing slow, soothing circles over Noelle's knuckles. "Glad you aren't going to fight me on that one."

Then, hesitantly, she began to say what was on her mind. "And the guys—look, I know they can be overwhelming, especially my brothers, but they were just trying to help. Slade pretends not to care since he lost someone he loved a couple of years back, but he does. That's what you saw tonight."

Noelle let out a quiet, exhausted laugh, shaking her head. "I know. I was just—" She sighed, rubbing at her face. "I don't want guys constantly thinking they have to *fix* things for me. I spent too long being told what to do by a guy who thought he was in control of every aspect of my life."

Scarlett frowned but nodded in understanding. "I get that. But you can't assume all men are like Beau."

Noelle let out another breath, her shoulders finally relaxing a fraction. She was glad she had a friend like Scarlett.

His phone pinged with a text from Scarlett that they had arrived safe. Little did she know he was already aware of that.

Slade had kept his distance, trailing Scarlett's car just far enough back that she wouldn't notice. He told himself he was only making sure Noelle got home safe—that once she was inside, he'd leave.

When Scarlett's taillights disappeared and Noelle climbed the stairs alone, his chest tightened. After the way Beau had grabbed her, after the fear in her eyes, the idea of her being left to herself didn't sit right.

He should have kept driving. Instead, he parked down the street.

Now, standing outside her building, he shifted his weight like he could shake off the unease crawling through him. He knew how this looked—showing up uninvited, hovering when she'd already had enough men trying to control her. Maybe it was too much.

But he hadn't followed because he thought she was fragile. He'd followed because, damn it—she mattered.

He should have walked away, given her space. Instead, he knocked, announcing himself.

A pause. Footsteps. The door cracked open, and Noelle stared at him with tired eyes, her lips pressed together like she wasn't sure if she wanted to let him in.

Slade stood in the frame of the door, taking in the sight of Noelle still wearing his jacket he had placed around her earlier. Something about that felt intimate and he couldn't deny how much he liked to see her in something of his.

"I just wanted to check on you," he said carefully.

"You didn't have to." Her voice was flat, more weary than sharp.

"I know." He shoved his hands into his pockets. "I just wanted to."

Her head tipped briefly against the doorframe before she sighed and opened the door wider. Not a warm welcome, but an invitation all the same. Slade stepped inside.

Her dog, Maple, lifted her head from the couch, wagged her tail once, then curled back into herself.

"I'm fine," Noelle murmured, sinking into the cushions and pulling her blanket tight around her.

Slade leaned against the armrest across from her, resisting the urge to pace. Doing nothing—just being here—was harder than taking a hit on the ice. "You should go to the police about Beau."

Her knuckles whitened around the blanket. "Slade—"

"I know you probably don't want help," he cut in, lowering his voice. "I'm sure you don't want some guy you barely know swooping in, telling you what to do."

Her brows lifted, a flicker of surprise slipping past her guard.

He rubbed the back of his neck. "But this isn't about me calling the shots. It's about making sure that Beau guy doesn't get another chance."

She dropped her gaze, pulling her knees close. "It's not that simple."

Slade nodded in understanding. The urge to push, to fix, clawed at him, but he forced himself still. She didn't need his fight—she needed his presence.

The room went quiet, save for her dog, Maple's, steady snoring. Then Noelle's voice broke the silence, softer than before: "You're stubborn."

"Maybe." The corner of his mouth tugged, though his chest stayed tight. "But I'm not going anywhere."

She looked at him then, really looked—eyes lingering like she was testing the truth of his words. Slowly, as if it cost her something, she reached out and brushed her fingers against his knee.

She pulled her hand back and leaned into the corner of the couch, exhaling slowly. "He won't come back tonight," she said, more to herself than to him. "He'll need to lick his wounds for a day or two at least."

Slade's jaw tightened. "Still doesn't mean I like the idea of you being left alone."

"I know." Her gaze flicked to the door, then back to him. After a beat, she reached for the remote on the coffee table and clicked on the TV. The screen lit the room in soft blues and golds. "It was thoughtful of you to check on me," she added, quieter. "No pressure but... you can stay for a bit. If it helps."

Something eased in his chest at that—just a notch. "Yeah," he said. "It does."

She scrolled without really looking, stopping on a familiar comfort movie. Nothing heavy. Nothing that required focus. She shifted, leaving space on the couch without saying a word.

Slade hesitated only a second before sitting at the far end, careful not to invade her space. Maple cracked one eye open, assessed him, then stretched and relocated so her back pressed against his thigh like a verdict.

Noelle noticed and huffed a tired smile. "Guess you're approved."

"I'll take it."

They didn't talk much after that. The movie played, quiet and forgettable, the kind meant to fill space rather than demand attention. The tension in Noelle's shoulders eased, just enough. Slade stayed alert without hovering, present without pushing.

When she finally relaxed against the cushions, breathing evening out, he didn't move.

For now, this was enough.

He was here.

She wasn't alone.

And that felt like a good place to end the night.

Chapter Fourteen

Noelle stared at the blinking cursor on her laptop screen, tapping her pen against her notebook in an uneven rhythm. The words were supposed to come easily—she'd researched, outlined, prepped. But no matter how hard she tried, her mind kept drifting from her novel.

Drifting to *him.*

Not Beau. Not the man she came to Silverwood to escape from—the man who somehow found his way back into her life anyway.

No. *Slade. Slade Fisher. Her best friend's brother.*

The way he'd stepped in the other night, no hesitation, no fear—just unwavering certainty that he wouldn't let Beau hurt her. It should have annoyed her. And it had. She *had* snapped at him for acting like she needed saving.

But it was also... hot.

She groaned, pressing her palms against her face. *I don't have time for this.*

A soft knock at the door pulled her from her spiraling thoughts.

"Noelle?"

It was Scarlett.

Noelle exhaled and shut her laptop, calling, "Yeah, come in."

Scarlett stepped inside, instantly greeted by Maple, who perked up from her spot on the floor and bounded toward her with eager excitement.

"Hey, cutie," Scarlett cooed, crouching to scratch Maple behind her ears. Maple's tail thumped happily against the floor as Noelle watched, arms crossed.

Scarlett straightened, giving her a once-over before sitting on the edge of the bed. "I wanted to check on you."

Noelle sighed, rubbing at her temples. "Just suffering from a little writer's block with my book. I'm fine."

Scarlett lifted a brow.

Noelle groaned. "Okay, I'm *not* fine, but I don't know what else to say."

Scarlett nudged her shoulder. "You don't always have to handle everything alone."

A few minutes later, they sat in the living room in comfortable silence. Noelle sat with her legs curled beneath her, a warm mug of her favorite hot chocolate resting between her palms. The steam curled in soft ribbons, but she barely noticed—her mind was still tangled in everything that had happened with Beau, with Slade, with the mess of emotions she couldn't seem to sort out.

Scarlett plopped down beside her, phone in hand, scrolling absentmindedly before letting out a quiet huff.

"Slade is relentless," she muttered.

Noelle glanced over, brow furrowing. "What do you mean?"

Scarlett tilted the screen toward her, and Noelle leaned in.

A series of texts. **Every day.**

SLADE:

> How's Noelle? Has that asshole showed up
> or contacted her anymore?

SLADE:

> How is she today?

SLADE:

Anything I can do? I don't have her number
and don't want to overwhelm her.

SLADE:

How is Noelle today?

Noelle blinked, straightening slightly. "Wait—he's been messaging you?"

Scarlett snorted. "Every. Day." She waved her phone slightly. "Checking on you. Making sure you're okay."

Noelle swallowed, staring at the messages, warmth curling low in her chest. Slade wasn't the guy she would've expected to hover, but there it was—proof that he had been.

She looked away, exhaling slowly. "He came by to check on me the other night after it all happened but I didn't realize he..."

Scarlett nudged her playfully. "Cared? Yeah, well, Slade's never been great at saying things out loud. He just *does* things instead."

Noelle traced the rim of her mug, the weight of realization settling in. He hadn't tried to fix things with big, dramatic gestures. He hadn't pushed, hadn't hovered too close.

But he cared.

Quietly.

Consistently.

The SILVERWOOD SCOOP

Local Sports & Community News

Slade Fisher and Beau Abbott Face Off at Winter Walk

Samantha Romano, Silverwood Snipers' Media Correspondent

Tensions flared at Silverwood's beloved Winter Walk event last weekend as hometown hockey star, Slade Fisher and former Vancouver Vultures center, Beau Abbott were seen in what witnesses described as a "heated confrontation."

Sources say the altercation occurred near the downtown ornament display, where Fisher was spotted walking with local favorite Noelle Hayes, known for her famous hot chocolate at *The Cozy Cup*. According to bystanders, Abbott approached the pair and appeared to pressure Noelle into leaving with him—until Slade stepped in.

Those close to the Snipers say Fisher has always had a strong sense of integrity, and many weren't surprised by his actions. "Slade was raised right," one local said. "He stands up for what's right—and he protects the people he cares about."

So what's really going on here? Just a tense reunion between rivals—or is there something more brewing between Slade and Noelle?

Only time will tell.

Stay with *The Scoop* for all the latest on Silverwood's favorite star—and the woman who might just be warming up his winter.

Chapter Fifteen

The cold hit his lungs sharp as he pushed off, carving across the rink. The puck skittered out ahead of him, and he snapped it into control, stick low, stride driving. He cut left, dropped his shoulder, and fired. The shot smacked off the boards, too wide.

He chased it down, circling back, the steady rhythm of blades on ice keeping his thoughts at bay. Again. He lined it up, wrist snapping clean, the puck ringing against the crossbar before

bouncing free. Better.

Slade pressed harder, skating end to end, legs burning, sweat sliding under his collar. He didn't care. The repetition steadied him—pass, carry, shoot, recover. Again. He slammed another shot past the post and let the sound echo through the empty arena.

For a moment, it was just him, the ice, and the puck. No questions. No eyes on him. Just the game.

When he finally slowed, chest heaving, he dragged his sleeve across his forehead—and that's when he saw her standing at the edge of the rink observing.

"Hey. You okay?" he asked, voice steady.

She nodded once. "Yeah." A pause, then, quieter, "I'm fine."

Her tone wasn't quite convincing, but before he could press, she sighed, shifting. "Also... I wanted to thank you for being there for me the other night."

Slade smiled. "Nah—It was nothing."

She gave him a look, a flicker of amusement behind the expression. "I'm serious. I—" She rubbed at her temples, exhaling slowly. "I felt bad you had to step in like that."

Slade studied her, sensing the vulnerability behind her words. "Well I was happy you weren't alone in that situation. "

Noelle huffed a quiet laugh and cleared her throat. "Yeah, me too, honestly. Anyway, let's put that behind us. Scarlett and I are grabbing a drink tonight. You should come."

He lifted a brow before teasingly asking, "Drinks with my sister and her best friend? Sure, what could go wrong?"

She winked at him and he caught the faint curve of her lips before she turned away.

The Fireside Pub was alive with a hum of energy—low music pulsing through the speakers, the chatter of other patrons overlapping like a comforting background melody. Warm, dim lighting bathed everything in a soft glow, casting shadows that stretched long across the wooden tables. The scent of fried food and beer lingered in the air.

Scarlett was on her way back from the restroom and had barely sat down before she glanced toward the bar, her posture shifting as recognition sparked across her face. "Oh—Hunter's here," she said casually, already half-smiling.

Slade rolled his eyes teasingly at his sister. "My boy-crazy sister, everyone."

"Stop it. Am not." Scarlett retorted with a playful shove to his shoulder.

Slade had been nursing his drink, absently listening to the chatter around him, when the door swung open. Noelle stepped inside, shaking off the lingering chill of the evening, her eyes scanning the room before landing on him and Scarlett.

Her golden-blonde hair cascaded over her shoulders in soft waves, glistening under the bar lights. A few strands framed her face, but most had been tucked neatly behind her ears, revealing her glasses' thin, delicate frames. The lenses reflected the dim lighting, making her eyes—bright and sharp—stand out even more.

Tonight, her makeup was subtle but effortlessly striking. A soft sweep of mascara darkened her lashes, making her gaze seem deeper somehow, more intense. A hint of blush kissed her cheeks, barely noticeable, and her lips—painted in a muted shade of rose—curved slightly when she spotted them.

She wore a deep burgundy sweater, oversized but stylish, the sleeves pushed up just enough to reveal the fine lines of her wrists. The color made her features pop. Dark jeans hugged her figure just right, paired with boots that clicked softly against the wooden floor as she moved toward them.

Slade watched her approach, feeling that now-familiar pull. He clenched his jaw, fighting against it. He'd sworn he was done with this—the racing pulse, the heat that spread through his chest at the sight of someone. He'd built walls for a reason. Losing the love of his life had nearly destroyed him once; he wouldn't survive it again.

Yet here was Noelle, casually dismantling his defenses without even trying. Each time he saw her, the resolve he'd built crumbled a little more. He told himself it was nothing—just basic attraction, biological, meaningless—but the lie was wearing thin.

Scarlett grinned, waving her over. "Already got you a drink," she called, nodding toward the glass sitting at the spot they had saved for Noelle.

Noelle flashed a quick smile at Scarlett as she thanked her and slid into the booth, her fingers tucking a stray strand of hair behind her ear.

She picked up the drink—a cranberry cinnamon bourbon fizz, its rich red color glowing warmly beneath the twinkle of white Christmas lights strung across the mantle. A sugared rim sparkled like frost, and a cinnamon stick nestled beside a twist of orange peel atop the ice.

As she brought it closer, the aroma drifted up—spicy, citrusy, and cozy, like winter bottled in a glass. She took a slow sip, savoring the warmth that chased away the chill, the gentle burn of bourbon softened by the tart cranberry and sweet holiday spice.

Slade swallowed, heat creeping up his neck, his pulse kicking harder than he wanted to admit. He hated how easy it was to watch her.

How the small things—the way she traced the rim of the glass with her fingertip, the way her lips parted slightly as she tasted the drink—felt... distracting.

He was painfully aware of Noelle's presence–of the fact that she was sitting directly across from him and the way the soft amber of her drink reflected in her eyes when she glanced up.

Stop. She is just here for drinks. She wasn't looking at you like that, idiot. And I sure as hell wasn't looking at her like that.

Scarlett kept glancing over Noelle's shoulder toward the bar, her attention splitting. Eventually, she stood, sliding out of the booth.

"I'm going to say hi before he leaves," she said, already shrugging into her coat. "Don't wait up."

Slade would have teased her more about Hunter but he was happy to have a moment alone with Noelle.

Across the table, Noelle stirred the last of her drink with the cinnamon stick, her expression hovering somewhere between curiosity and amusement.

"So..." she said, tilting her head, "is this the part where you pretend you weren't staring at me all night?"

Slade lifted a brow. "Was I that bad?"

"You didn't exactly try to hide it."

He laughed under his breath, rubbing the back of his neck. "Guess I wasn't trying very hard."

She smiled into her glass. "Any particular reason?"

His gaze held hers. "You have a hypnotizing way about you."

Something unreadable flickered in her eyes. "Is that so?"

"That's my best explanation," he said. "It's the way your eyes sparkle when you're about to make fun of me, like they are right now."

Their laughter softened, and the air between them shifted. Still warm, but heavier now. A quiet beat passed, full of everything unsaid.

Slade's fingers tightened slightly around his glass. His heart thudded once, hard.

Then, before he could overthink it—before the nerves won out—he leaned forward, voice low and sure. "Go out with me."

Noelle blinked, clearly surprised. He didn't give her time to recover.

"Dinner," he added. "A real date."

The space between them seemed to tighten. The bar noise faded into a dull hum, like the world had collectively decided to give them a moment.

She studied him, searching his face for something—hesitation, maybe. Or an escape route.

Instead, she smiled. Small. Measured. "Alright," she said at last. "Why not?"

Relief loosened something in his chest he hadn't realized was clenched. He exhaled a quiet laugh. "Good call."

She tipped her head, amused. "Guess I should be flattered." Then, softer, more honest: "I didn't think you'd ask."

"Why not?"

"Because you don't seem like someone who asks unless he's sure."

He considered that. Then nodded. "That's fair." His gaze held hers. "I almost didn't."

Her brows lifted. "Almost?"

"I talked myself out of it at least five times." A corner of his mouth curved. "Figured you'd think I was just another dumb jock who doesn't know when to stay in his lane."

Her laugh came easy—warm, genuine. "Well," she said, "you're definitely in your lane now."

He grinned. "Glad to hear it."

She tapped her empty glass lightly against the table. "I might need another drink to celebrate your bravery."

He glanced toward the bar. "I can make that happen."

She hesitated just a beat, then met his eyes. "Only if you walk me home after."

Something in his expression shifted—quieter, more serious. "Deal," he said.

And for the next hour, they talked like the rest of the bar had quietly slipped away.

Chapter Sixteen

A few nights later, tucked in a back room of the *Wayside Tavern* sitting fireside, Slade and Noelle gazed at one another over heaping plates of pasta. The time passed easily as they traded stories, teasing each other, slipping into the kind of rhythm that felt older than it was. She told him about her author aspirations and the book she was working on. He told her about his rookie season and the game that nearly broke him. Their knees bumped under the table. Her laughter came easier. His smile lingered longer. And in the quiet spaces between their words, something unspoken began to settle—familiar, unexpected, and real.

Their conversation took a more serious turn as they began to open up to each other in ways that they hadn't dared to with anyone else in years. Noelle's fingers twitched against her wine glass as she stared into its dark depths. "That's why I usually don't talk about... certain things. Not right away."

Slade held his breath, hoping she would go on but not wanting to force anything. "You don't have to tell me anything. But if you do—I'll be right here."

She looked up from her drink to see the sincerity in his eyes and seemed to make a decision as she let out a little sigh.

"I'm not close with either of my parents anymore," she said quietly. "My father left when I was nine. Just left. No note, no reason. And for a long time, I thought it was my fault—like I was too much or not enough or maybe both. My father... he wasn't just strict. He was cruel. I didn't understand it when I was younger, but now I know. He was abusive. Every rule, every punishment—it wasn't about discipline. It was about control. And my mother...she left the moment I turned 18. She remarried. Built a new life somewhere else. I think she wanted to forget everything. Forget him. Forget me. She always told me how much I reminded her of him."

Slade breathed out heavily. "That's not on you, Noelle."

"I know," she said quickly, then softer, "I know. But sometimes it still *feels* like it is. And like I can't outrun the abusive nature of my father. I had to leave Vancouver to escape Beau, but as you saw the other night, he's not as easy to get rid of as I'd hoped. It all makes me wary. Of letting people matter too much. Because what if they hurt me or abandon me too?"

A long silence passed.

Then Slade said, "I lost someone too. Actually, it's why I was so weird at the Winter Walk. It brings back a lot of memories. She was my high school girlfriend. I... I was planning to propose to her, but her house caught on fire, and by the time I got there, it was too late. She was brought to the hospital. My brother Callahan is a doctor, and he tried to save her, but the damage was too much. Then I... I found out she was pregnant when she died...I-I think that's why I don't let people in all the way. Because what if I care and I lose them again?"

"Slade..."

"I stopped playing for a while after that," he said. "Stopped every-thing. I basically ran away and disappeared for a couple years. I didn't want to feel anything, didn't want to want anything."

She held his gaze, steady and open, allowing him the space to share more of himself with her.

"I've dated since," he admitted. "But it was always surface. I never let anyone in. Not really."

Noelle's eyes shimmered. "And now?"

He looked at her then, like he was seeing her for the first time and the hundredth. "You make me want things again. Not just the hypothetical future. Now."

She swallowed hard, her voice barely above a whisper. "I'm not her though."

"I know," he said. "You're you. And that's why it matters."

The fire popped, sending a small ember upward. Noelle leaned into him, her head resting against his shoulder. They didn't speak again for a while. Just sat there, wrapped in silence and firelight, letting the past settle and the present begin.

"You wanna get out of here?"

Noelle looked at him for a long second. "...and go where?"

He smiled, but it wasn't cocky. Just open. Hopeful. "Somewhere quiet. Just us."

She nodded once. "Yeah. I'd like that."

They stepped out into the cold, the night crisp and still. Snow flurries drifted beneath the streetlights like falling stars, soft and slow. The world felt hushed, like it was listening.

They ended up at Slade's apartment, a small, lived-in space with hockey memorabilia on the walls and a pair of well-worn skates hanging by the door.

He pulled them down gently, the laces frayed, the leather scuffed. "These were my first pair. I was six. My parents saved up for months."

She took them in her hands, turning them over like they were something sacred. "They're beautiful."

"They're beat-up," he said with a laugh. "But they remind me of where I started. Of their belief in me, even when I didn't believe in myself."

He rehung the skates carefully, like he was putting a precious memory back in its place.

Noelle lingered by the door, taking in the apartment more fully now —the framed team photos, the stack of hockey magazines on the coffee table, the throw blanket draped haphazardly over the arm of the couch. It was unmistakably him. Comfortable. Honest.

"This place suits you," she said. "It feels... real."

He huffed a quiet laugh. "High praise."

"I mean it." She smiled. "It's not trying to impress anyone."

He glanced at her, something unreadable crossing his face. "Neither am I."

The air shifted then—not heavy, not rushed. Just aware.

Slade moved toward the kitchen, grabbing two glasses and pouring water from the tap. "You want some? Or I've got tea. Coffee. Whatever."

"Water's good, I should hydrate after those drinks at dinner," she said, accepting the glass when he handed it to her. Their fingers brushed, brief but noticeable.

She took a sip, then glanced toward the bathroom. "Would it be weird if I asked to shower off really quick? My hair still smells like smoke."

"Yeah—yeah, of course." He scratched the back of his neck. "Towels are under the sink."

She paused at the bathroom door, looking back at him. "You don't mind?"

"No," he said quickly. Then, more softly, "I like that you felt comfortable enough to ask."

Her smile warmed. "Good."

The door clicked shut behind her, and Slade exhaled, running a hand through his hair as the sound of the shower kicked on. He paced once, twice, then dropped onto the couch, elbows on his knees.

Get it together, Fisher.

He wasn't nervous—he told himself that—but the apartment felt different now. Smaller. Charged in a way he hadn't let himself feel in a long time.

When the water finally shut off, the quiet returned, thicker than before.

Noelle shivered slightly as she stepped out of the bathroom, rubbing her arms against the cool air of Slade's apartment. The warmth of the bar had faded, replaced by the quiet intimacy of his space—the low hum of the heater, the soft scent of his cologne lingering in the air.

Slade glanced up from where he sat on the couch, his gaze flicking to her and then narrowing slightly.

"You're freezing," he muttered.

"I'm fine," she said automatically, though the goosebumps on her arms betrayed her.

Slade sighed, standing and disappearing into a closet for a moment before reemerging with a worn, oversized hockey jersey draped over his arm.

"Here, put this on," he said, holding it out.

Noelle hesitated, looking at it before meeting his gaze. "That's yours."

"No kidding." He smirked. "And now it's yours for the night."

She swallowed hard, her fingers brushing the fabric as she took it, the material soft and undeniably his. It smelled like him—clean, warm, faintly like the ice—but beyond that, there was something about it that made her chest tighten.

She slipped it on, the jersey swallowing her whole, falling loosely around her legs, the sleeves dipping past her fingertips.

Slade watched her, his expression unreadable for a moment.

Then—he exhaled, shaking his head slightly, a flicker of something fond in his eyes. "You look good in it."

Noelle scoffed, pulling at the oversized sleeves. "I look ridiculous."

"Still." His grin was easy. "Looks better on you than me." He paused, then added, more casually, "You should wear it to my next home game."

That caught her off guard.

Heat crept into her face as she sat beside him on the couch. "Your next home game?" she echoed. "You want me there?"

Only then did he glance at her, like he'd suddenly realized what he was asking. "You don't have to," he said quickly. "I just—thought I'd ask."

She considered it for a second. The noise. The crowd. Him on the ice. Then she smiled, small but real. "I'd like that."

Relief flashed across his face before he masked it, stretching and running a hand through his hair. "Yeah?"

"Yeah."

A quiet beat settled between them—comfortable, warm.

She should say she was heading out. Should reach for her shoes. Instead, she stayed where she was, the jersey pooling around her legs, the night stretching ahead of them.

Slade noticed.

"You don't have to rush off," he said carefully. "If you don't want to. You can stay the night."

Her heart thudded—not from nerves, but from how gently he'd said it.

"I don't," she admitted. "Want to rush off, I mean."

He nodded once, like he'd already decided something. "Come on," he said, standing. "You should at least be comfortable."

Noelle followed him into his bedroom, nerves creeping in, though she wasn't sure why.

Slade grabbed an extra pillow, tossing it onto his bed before pulling back the covers. "You sure about this?"

Noelle hesitated, then gave him a small smile. "I wouldn't still be here if I wasn't."

Slade let out a quiet chuckle, rubbing the back of his neck before settling onto his side of the bed.

Noelle climbed in beside him, shifting slightly beneath the covers, his warmth immediately pressing against her.

For a moment, neither of them moved. The air between them was thick with nerves, desire, and something neither of them wanted to name.

Slade reached out, tracing the edge of the blanket where it rested on her hip. "You're sure?" he asked again, his voice low, rougher now.

This time, Noelle could only nod.

That was all it took. His hand slid from the blanket to her waist, tugging her gently closer. His mouth found hers, soft at first, then deeper when she opened for him. The jersey shifted as he

touched her, his palm dragging over the curve of her thigh, pushing the fabric higher.

Noelle gasped against his lips as his hand settled warm on her bare skin. He stilled at the sound,

his forehead pressing to hers. "Tell me if you want me to stop."

She shook her head quickly, her breath shaky. "Don't stop."

Slade kissed her again, slower, his tongue sweeping against hers before trailing down to her jaw, her throat. She tipped her head back, her fingers clutching at the sheets, then fisting in his shirt until he pulled it off entirely.

He hovered over her, bare chest rising and falling, the heat of him searing against her through the thin barrier of the jersey. His eyes searched hers, wide and dark, before his hand slid beneath the fabric, palm flattening against her stomach.

Her body jolted at the contact, the intimacy of it making her shiver. "Slade—"

"I've got you," he murmured, lips brushing the hollow of her collarbone as he eased the jersey higher. She lifted her arms, letting him pull it over her head.

For a moment, he just looked at her—his breath caught, eyes hungry but softened by awe. He bent, kissing down her chest, each press of his mouth unhurried.

Her hands skimmed his back, nails dragging lightly over muscle, making him groan into her skin. The sound went straight through her, heat curling low in her belly.

When his fingers slid beneath her underwear, she arched up to meet him, wordless permission in the way she clutched at him. He moved slowly, learning her pace, drawing out sounds from her she hadn't meant to give.

"Beautiful," he whispered when her body trembled against his hand.

She pulled him to her then, desperate, tugging at his waistband. He caught her wrist, kissed her palm, and then helped her, shedding the last of their clothing until there was nothing left between them but air.

The first thrust was careful, restrained, his eyes locked on hers like he was waiting for her to change her mind. She didn't. She pulled him closer, whispered his name, and he gave in.

Their movements found rhythm, bodies pressed tight, breaths mingling. Every sound, every touch felt like a discovery.

And when release finally broke over them, it was like a long exhale, the quiet shattering of walls neither of them thought they'd ever let down.

After, Noelle curled against him, her cheek on his chest, his arm wrapped tight around her as if he couldn't bear to let her go. His lips brushed her hair, lingering there.

"You okay?" he asked softly.

She smiled against his skin. "More than okay."

The sharp buzz of his alarm cut through the quiet morning. Slade groaned, fumbling for his phone on the nightstand. Practice. He should get up, lace his skates, and do what he's always done.

But then he felt her.

Noelle was curled against him, warm and soft, her breath steady against his chest. Her hand rested lightly on his stomach, the weight of it small but enough to pin him there. He froze, not wanting to shift, not wanting to risk waking her.

For years, every time he'd woken next to someone who wasn't Jessica, shame had sunk in fast and hard. He'd rolled away, sick at himself, unable to look them in the eye.

This time was different.

Noelle stirred, eyelashes brushing his skin as she blinked awake. She looked up at him, sleep still fogging her blue eyes. A slow smile curved her lips. "Your alarm's obnoxious," she murmured.

He huffed out a laugh, thumb brushing her temple. "Agreed."

"You're not getting up," she pointed out, voice muffled against him.

"I should." His gaze dropped to her hand where it rested against him. "Don't want to."

Her smile widened, drowsy but knowing. "Then don't."

Slade kissed the top of her head, breathing her in. He knew he'd drag himself to the rink

eventually, but not yet. Not when lying here felt better than anything he'd had in years.

When he finally did move, it wasn't to get up. It was to roll toward her, pulling her closer until she laughed softly and tucked herself against his side again.

Practice could wait.

Chapter Seventeen

It had been a week since Noelle spent the night in his bed. A week of coffee dates that stretched into long conversations, evenings where she ended up tucked against his side on the couch, quiet, easy company. Nothing rushed. Nothing heavy. Just enough to leave him off balance. He hadn't told the guys about her yet, but somehow Scarlett had, and now they wouldn't let it go.

The puck snapped against his stick, and Slade drove it up the ice, blades biting into the frozen surface. He cut around Garrett, shoulder low, and fired a shot that rang off the post. Too wide.

"Getting sloppy, Fisher," Garrett called, grin wide as he looped back.

Slade chased down the rebound and ripped it again. This one hit clean, burying the top corner.

Hunter's whistle cut through the cold air. "Damn. Someone's playing like he's got a girl in the stands."

The words landed like a body check. Slade's grip on the stick tightened. "Shut it."

"Don't bother," Hunter went on, circling lazily. "Scarlett already told us. *Cozy Cup* blonde. Glasses. Cute."

Scarlett. His jaw locked, irritation spiking in his chest. She was supposed to keep that quiet.

Jayden coasted past with a shrug. "Honestly, man, about time."

Miguel leaned on his stick, smirking. "So, it's true, you two are an item?"

Slade answered with another shot, the puck clanging off the glass. His voice came out low, clipped. "It's not a big deal."

Garrett laughed. "The 'not a big deal' who wears your jacket? Sure."

Slade shoved past him, skating hard until the burn in his legs dulled the twist in his chest.

Jessica's face flashed in his mind. Hearing Noelle's name tossed around the rink like a joke felt wrong. Like betrayal.

He braced one palm against the glass, sucking in a breath. "Drop it."

The chatter stopped, the rink becoming silent but for the scrape of blades. From center ice, Stryker's voice carried. "Enough." His eyes met Slade's, steady, protective. "He'll talk when

he's ready."

No one pushed further, but the sting followed him into the locker room. The teasing picked up again in bursts—Miguel pressing for details, Garrett tossing a roll of tape his way, Jayden muttering, "Good for you, man," like encouragement.

Slade ignored them all, stripping out of his gear in silence. He focused on the scrape of velcro, the snap of pads unbuckling. When he was done, he slung his bag over his shoulder and walked out without a word.

The night air outside the rink was knife-cold, biting against the sweat still clinging to his skin. He slid into his truck, exhaling into the quiet.

His phone buzzed.

NOELLE:

Want to stop by my place tonight?

His thumb hovered over the screen. A simple question, harmless on its own. But Jessica's shadow lingered, reminding him how badly it had gutted him to love someone and lose them. He should say no. Keep his distance. They were getting too close.

But he already knew he wouldn't.

SLADE:

On my way.

Noelle had Googled "best meals for hockey players" twelve times, scrapped four potential menus and had finally settled on grilled salmon, quinoa tossed with roasted vegetables and a spinach-strawberry salad with almonds.

Omega-3s. Lean protein. Antioxidants. Practically an NHL approved meal.

Her apartment smelled like garlic and lemon zest. Her nerves were somewhere between first date jitters and playoff tension. She had ironed the cloth napkins which felt both excessive and weirdly romantic.

There was a knock on the door.

"Come in," Noelle called.

Slade stepped inside and paused, his eyes scanning the room.

Noelle busied herself with plating the salmon, her heart thudding. "I read salmon was a great option for dinner for hockey players during the season. I figured since you had practice today and a few games coming up..."

Slade moved closer, his expression softening, "You made all this for me?"

She nodded, unsure why she felt so unsure of what to say, and motioned for them to sit at the table she had so carefully laid.

The silence stretched just enough to make her question everything. Slade reached for a fork and took a bite, closed his eyes like a food critic, and gave her an approving nod, "This is amazing. You might be the best thing that's happened to my diet... and my life."

Noelle laughed.

But Slade didn't just laugh with her. He set the fork down and leaned over the table to give her a kiss, still watching her. "Seriously, you didn't have to go through all this trouble. I would've been fine with takeout."

She rolled her eyes. "Yeah, but I would've known. And don't try to tell me you'd have been happy eating a soggy burger the night before a big game."

He smirked, dimples flashing. "Okay, fair. But this—" he gestured to the plates, the candles, the little details she'd fretted over "—this feels like more than dinner."

Noelle busied herself with the salad bowl to avoid his eyes. "Well, maybe I just like taking care of people."

Slade tilted his head. "And maybe I like being taken care of."

Something in his tone softened the air between them. When she finally looked up, his gaze wasn't teasing anymore, it was grateful.

She cleared her throat, breaking the moment before it grew too heavy. "You can return the favor by doing the dishes."

Slade grinned, relief in the curve of his mouth. "Deal. But I warn you, I'm way better with a hockey stick than a sponge."

"That's what dishwashers are for," Noelle shot back, and when he laughed, it wasn't just polite—it was the kind of laugh that settled deep, like he hadn't had one in a long time.

For the first time all night, Noelle's nerves ebbed. It didn't feel like she was auditioning for a role in his life. It felt like she was already part of it.

Later, after the last bite was gone, Slade gathered the plates and carried them to the sink. Noelle leaned against the counter, arms folded. "Huh. Look at you. So domestic."

"Don't spread it around the locker room," he said, rolling up his sleeves. "The guys would never let me live it down."

She handed him the sponge anyway. Their hands brushed, and both froze for a split second before he cleared his throat and turned on the faucet.

"You're actually not terrible at this," Noelle teased as he scrubbed a pan with exaggerated concentration.

He shot her a grin over his shoulder. "Careful. If you compliment me too much, I might start showing up uninvited just to cook and clean."

Her laugh slipped out before she could stop it. "Somehow I don't think I'd mind."

The words surprised them both. He stilled, suds dripping from his hands, then looked at her with something softer than teasing in his eyes. For a moment, the only sound was the low buzz of the overhead light.

Then Slade smiled, boyish and a little uncertain. "Guess that means I'll have to bring dessert next time."

Noelle's heart gave a ridiculous little leap. "Next time?"

He dried his hands, leaning close enough that she caught the faint scent of soap and citrus on his skin. "Yeah," he said simply. "Next time."

When he finally left, the apartment felt too quiet, the quiet murmur of the TV like an echo of their laughter. Noelle leaned against the closed door, palms pressed flat to the wood. On the counter, two wine glasses sat half-full, catching the glow of the candles she hadn't blown out yet. She smiled, picked up her phone, and opened her messages.

No new texts. No distractions. Just her, the soft scent of lemon and garlic still in the air, and the knowledge that tonight had been different. She typed out a quick message to Scarlett—*Don't say 'I told you so'*— then deleted it before sending.

Instead, she slid her phone aside and curled into the couch, letting herself replay the way Slade had looked at her when he said "next time."

Her chest tightened, but not with nerves this time. With hope.

Chapter Eighteen

Slade could feel Scarlett watching him—waiting—but he kept his focus on the fridge, scanning shelves like the answer to her inevitable interrogation might be buried somewhere behind a leftover takeout container.

He wasn't ready to turn around, wasn't ready to deal with the knowing glint in his sister's eyes, or the way she had a freakish ability to see straight through him. He grabbed a bottle of water, shut the fridge with more force than necessary, and finally faced her.

"So," she drawled, crossing her arms. "You gonna tell me about you and Noelle, or am I supposed to just keep pretending like nothing is going on between you two?"

"Nothing's going on."

Scarlett lifted a brow. "Uh-huh. Sure. Because *nothing* explains why you keep looking at her like she's the most complicated puzzle you've ever tried to solve for the last few weeks. And *nothing* explains why she's walking around like a lovesick teenager lately. You realize she's my best friend and tells me everything, right?"

Slade exhaled, rubbing the back of his neck. "I—" He shook his head, taking a sip of water before leaning against the counter opposite her. "I don't know what to say."

Scarlett softened slightly, tilting her head. "You *do* know. You just don't want to say it."

Slade let out a sharp laugh, shaking his head. "She's different, okay? It's—complicated."

Scarlett's expression eased into something more knowing, more amused. "You *like* her."

He sighed, pinching the bridge of his nose. "Scarlett—"

"You *like* her," she repeated, grinning now.

Slade muttered something under his breath but didn't deny it.

She stepped closer, leaning against the counter across from him. "Don't act like you're confused, Slade. You're just scared."

He scoffed quietly. "I'm not scared."

She gave him a look. "You disappeared for years. You're terrified."

That landed.

Slade stared down at the bottle in his hand. "She matters," he said finally. "More than I expected. And I don't want to be the reason things get complicated for her."

Scarlett nodded slowly. "She already knows things can be complicated. That's not what scares her."

He glanced up. "Then what does?"

Scarlett smiled faintly. "Feeling like something good might actually stick."

Slade exhaled, the truth of it settling into his chest.

"She didn't seem unsure when I saw her yesterday," he admitted. "If anything, she looked... hopeful."

"Because she is," Scarlett said gently. "She just doesn't rush. And neither do you, we both know that."

He shook his head with a quiet laugh. "You're saying we're the same kind of mess."

"Exactly," she said, grinning. "Which is why it might actually work."

He leaned back against the counter, staring at the ceiling. "You always do this. Make it sound simple."

"Oh, it's not simple," Scarlett said. "But it's real. And I think she feels that with you."

She pushed off the counter, heading toward the hallway. "Just... don't overthink yourself out of something good."

Then she paused, turning back. "Oh—and maybe start with her birthday."

Slade blinked. "Her what?"

"Birthday," Scarlett repeated, raising an eyebrow. "It's Christmas Eve."

He stared at her. "You're joking."

"She doesn't talk about it much," Scarlett said, walking over to the pantry. "Says it gets lost in the holiday noise. But it matters to her."

Slade frowned. "She never mentioned it. Not once."

He leaned against the counter, the weight of that settling in. "Christmas Eve," he murmured. "That's... soon." Just a little over a week away, in fact. He hadn't realized Christmas was so near since he still tried to forget the season existed at all. He wasn't sure how he felt about that.

Chapter Nineteen

The fudge shop sat tucked between a vintage bookstore and a florist. Its sign was hand painted, slightly faded with the words *Sweet Haven* curling in soft script above the door.

The bell above the door jingled as Slade held the door for Noelle and she stepped inside; her red scarf still looped loosely around her neck. Inside the air was warm and thick with the scent of melted sugar, toasted nuts, and cocoa. A chalkboard listed the day's specials in looping handwriting: Amaretto Swirl, Maple Walnut, Espresso Crunch.

He tugged off his beanie, his hair still wet from practice and glanced at her. "You weren't kidding. This place really does smell like heaven."

She smiled; cheeks pink from the cold. "Wait until you try the amaretto. It's the pink and brown swirl one- kind of almondy, kind of cherry, kind of nostalgic. It's my favorite."

He leaned over the glass scanning the trays until he spotted it. Soft marbled ribbons of blush and cocoa, cut into perfect squares. "You've got a whole memory wrapped up in that square, huh?"

She laughed. "Maybe."

He nodded then turned to the woman behind the counter. "Two pieces of the amaretto swirl, please."

They took their fudge to the bench outside, the street quiet except for the occasional car passing by. Slade watched her take a bite, her shoulders relaxing as if the cold couldn't touch her. She closed her eyes for a second, smiling, and the sight tugged at something in him.

"It tastes like Christmas when I was little," she said. "Back when it all felt... safe."

"Speaking of Christmas, a little birdy told me that your birthday is Christmas Eve; I can't believe you didn't tell me it was so close!"

"Oh, yeah, I'm assuming that nosy 'little birdy' was Scarlett. I was trying to avoid it, honestly. I usually do. Christmas is more important than my birthday anyway," she said with a shrug.

Slade wasn't sure how to respond to that last part; he didn't expect the gut punch that it landed to his core. Rather than let himself focus on that, he pulled a package from inside his jacket pocket onto the table and slid it her way. "Happy early birthday, Noelle. I didn't want it to be overshadowed by Christmas."

She looked genuinely surprised and hesitantly opened the gift. Her eyes lit up when she saw it. "Oh Slade, this is gorgeous and thoughtful of you. Thank you so much," she gushed as she pulled out the long, ruby red scarf that had her initials, NH, and little stars embroidered in silver along one bottom edge.

He just smiled, pleased he had made her happy, and bit into his square as he watched her wrap it around her slender neck. Almond and cherry bloomed across his tongue. The taste of the treat and the look on Noelle's face shifted his perspective in an instant that almost made him dizzy. The season didn't taste like smoke, or hospitals, or loss. Just sweetness. Just now. He looked at her, laughing at the way the fudge stuck to her teeth, and the ache in his chest loosened—quietly, unexpectedly.

Maybe this Christmas could be different.

Noelle tilted her head, catching his gaze. "Worth the hype?"

"Yeah," he said, softer than he meant to. "Better than I expected." And he wasn't talking about the fudge.

Noelle's phone suddenly lit up in her lap and her expression went cold.

BEAU:

Miss me yet?

BEAU:

Thought you could hide? Cute scarf.

BEAU:

I always know where you are, Noelle.

Noelle turned the screen down, fingers trembling. The sweetness of her smile turned sour.

Slade watched the way her jaw tensed as she handed him her phone for him to see. The soft part of him—the part that smiled at fudge and small moments—snapped shut.

"Beau?" he asked, voice close to a growl.

She nodded, small, furious and ashamed all at once. "Beau."

The phone buzzed again. Another message.

BEAU:

I'm not afraid of your dumb jock boyfriend
either.

Slade's hand clenched around the phone. His expression went granite. "That's it. We're getting out of here and you're not staying at your place. Not tonight."

Noelle blinked. "Slade—"

He was already on his feet, tugging her up with him. "You're coming back to my place. He wants to play games, fine. But he doesn't get to play them while you're alone."

Her pulse thudded unevenly. "I don't want to drag you into this—"

"You think I'm not already in it? He texted *you* while you're sitting next to *me*. He's openly stalking you. That makes it my problem." His voice was sharp, absolute. He grabbed his coat, scanning the quiet street with a predator's attention. "He wants to try something? Let him come. He'll have to go through me."

The words were too fierce, too certain, and yet she felt herself breathing easier with them pressed between them.

Slade didn't wait for her agreement. He wrapped an arm around her shoulders, steering her toward his truck. The night air bit down, but his presence was heat and shield all at once. On the drive, he kept one hand on the wheel, the other tight around her phone. Every time it buzzed, he didn't even glance down—he just tossed the vibration a glare like it was daring him to stop.

When they pulled into his driveway, he killed the engine and turned to her. His voice dropped, low and final. "He doesn't touch you. He doesn't even get close. Not while you're with me."

Noelle's throat worked, the fight to argue still there—but softer, dimmer now. She just nodded. Slade got out first, scanning the street before opening her door. His hand brushed hers, steady and grounding as he led her inside.

Inside his house, the locks clicked shut behind them. Slade checked them twice before dropping his keys on the counter with a sharp clatter.

"You're safe here." Not reassurance—command.

Noelle unwound her scarf slowly, as if shaking off the words that had followed her inside. Beau had always promised she'd never be free. The echo of that threat clung beneath her skin. Slade's place was quiet, ordinary, but her pulse still raced like she'd dragged the danger in with her.

He gestured toward the couch. "Go ahead and have a seat. I'll put something on. Better than staring at your phone all night."

Her laugh came thin. "That's your plan for terrifying texts? A movie?"

"Got a better one?" He flipped on the TV. "Besides, I've got decent taste."

She sank into the cushions, a blanket pulled over her knees. The first flicker of film filled the silence. For a while she sat rigid, waiting for the phone to buzz again, but it stayed still. Gradually, her shoulder brushed his. His arm stretched along the back of the couch, then settled warm and solid around her. She leaned into it, just enough to breathe.

Onscreen, a couple kissed beneath falling snow. Noelle turned her head and found Slade watching her instead. His gaze was sharp, unyielding.

"We should be paying attention," she whispered.

"I am."

The kiss landed before she had time to think. Hard, hungry, years of restraint splintering at once. She clutched at his shirt as he dragged her closer, his mouth claiming hers like he'd been starving. The blanket slid to the floor.

"Tell me to stop," he rasped against her throat.

Her breath stuttered, but her voice didn't falter. "Don't stop."

He rose, pulling her with him, hand steady at the small of her back as he led her down the hall. The bedroom was plain—bed, dresser, shadows—but it shifted the instant he closed the door.

"I don't want you half under a blanket on my couch," he murmured, forehead pressed to hers. "I want you here. With me."

Her answer was steady. "I want you, too."

Clothes fell in a careless trail. She sank into the mattress, the dip of his weight above her. For a moment he stilled, just looking, like he wasn't sure she was real. She touched his jaw, felt the scrape of stubble. "You don't have to hold back."

His laugh cracked, hoarse. "I've been holding back since the second I met you."

The kiss that followed was slower, reverent, but when he entered her it was steady, grounding, a vow in motion. She gasped, clutching tighter, and he bent low, voice breaking against her skin. "He doesn't own a single part of you. Not anymore. Not ever again."

The words hit deeper than the thrust of his body. She rose to meet him, every movement, every kiss burning through the fear Beau had planted. For the first time in years she realized she wasn't being claimed —she was choosing.

They moved together in a rhythm that blurred urgency with something dangerously close to devotion. The storm rattled the windows, but inside there was only heat, breath, and the startling relief of giving in.

After, she curled against him, his arm heavy across her, heart still pounding beneath her cheek. He pressed a kiss into her hair, voice raw and unguarded. "You're mine to protect. Always."

She closed her eyes, holding the warmth of him, the truth of it. And in the quiet where doubt usually crept in, it didn't. For once, she let herself believe him but in the back of her mind, she wondered how long it would last.

Chapter Twenty

The bus ride would normally have pulled him into game mode—headphones on, playlist loud, eyes shut against the dark. Usually it worked, cutting him off from everything but the ice. Tonight, every track blurred into noise. His thumb kept flicking over his phone, checking for a message that wasn't there.

Why hadn't she responded to his earlier texts? What had he done? Did she not want him to feel so protective over her? Had he overstepped like that jerk, Beau, always did with her? He couldn't help wanting to keep her safe. Always. Crap! His mind raced faster than his skates could carry him across the ice and it was showing in his performance.

Jayden leaned across the aisle. "What's wrong, Fisher? Forget your teddy bear at home?"

Slade shoved the phone into his pocket. "Shut up."

Hunter twisted in his seat, grinning. "It's the girl, isn't it? Haven't seen you this twitchy since rookie year."

"Focus on yourself," Slade muttered, sharper than he meant.

The rink should've fixed him, but the noise in his head followed him out onto the ice. The roar of the crowd, the bite of cold air, the snap of tape under his gloves—none of it burned through. He missed an easy shot. Took a hit along the boards he should've braced for. Came up gasping, angrier at himself than the guy who leveled him.

"Fisher, lock in!" Coach's voice cut like a whip.

"Nice shot," Garrett called as he skated past. "You aiming for her number in the rafters?"

Laughter spilled down the bench. Slade ripped off his helmet, glare sharp enough to cut. The noise died, but it didn't stop the static inside his skull. His vision filled with all the little things that had added up in his heart over the last few months–her scarf draped over his chair. Her toothbrush by his sink. The dent her body had left on what had become "her" side of the bed. His place had felt gutted without her.

After the game, the locker room was all victory noise—towels snapping, tape ripping, voices riding high. Slade sat at his stall, untying his skates slow, deliberate, like he could drag his head back into order. His phone burned in his pocket. He pulled it out, thumb hovering over her name.

Wish you were here. He typed it. Stared. Deleted. Tried again. *Good night.* Deleted that too.

Garrett glanced over, smirk tugging at his mouth. "You played like a guy homesick for his girl."

Slade snapped his phone shut, shoved it deep in his bag, and raked a hand through his damp hair. "Get it together," he muttered. But the ache in his chest pressed harder, sharp and unyielding, like something he couldn't skate off.

The lunch rush had thinned, but Noelle still moved fast behind the counter, stacking mugs and wiping down tables. The bell over the door jingled, and her stomach jumped before her brain caught up. Just a pair of college kids, laughing their way to a booth. Not Beau.

She pasted on the smile she'd practiced until it felt natural. "Be right with you."

The air smelled of espresso and burnt sugar, steady as a heartbeat.

She sank into the rhythm—pour, ring up, deliver. Normal. Ordinary. Except her phone weighed heavy in her apron pocket, and every time it buzzed with an order ticket, her pulse leapt.

Slade had reached out a few times since the Beau incident two nights ago, checking in on her and trying to plan their next date. She had felt so safe and content with Slade in that moment of him comforting her but the familiar fear Beau had instilled in her had begun creeping its way through her veins, turning her icy once more and she couldn't help but retreat into her protective shell–even if that meant hiding from a man she instinctively knew would never treat her like Beau. *Why do I always have to self sabotage myself like this?!*

Mr. Keene, one of her regulars, lifted his empty mug with a crooked grin, breaking her out of the doom and gloom of her mind. "Afternoon, sunshine. You're looking tired today. You working too hard?"

"Just keeping busy," she said, forcibly pushing all thoughts of Slade to the side in a feeble attempt to focus on her job.

He squinted at her, not buying it. "Well, don't let this place run you ragged. World's tough enough without burning yourself out."

Noelle's fingers tightened on the pot. Beau used to say things like that too—little comments that sounded caring until he twisted them into control. She slid the mug back onto the counter, careful not to spill. "Thanks, Mr. Keene."

"You okay, kid?"

"I'm fine." She backed away before the lie could crack.

Scarlett appeared as Noelle was counting the till, sliding onto a stool with the energy of someone who never asked permission. "You look like you're waiting for a grenade to roll across the floor."

"I'm fine," Noelle repeated, shutting the register drawer with more force than necessary.

Scarlett arched a brow. "*Fine* fine, or fine because you've been tangled up with a certain someone?"

Noelle's face heated. "Scarlett."

"What? Half the town saw you go to his house the other day," she teased, "but it sounds like maybe there's a bit of a lull in your little Hall-mark romance?"

Noelle set her rag down a little too hard. "He saw Beau's texts. He wouldn't let me go back home alone."

Scarlett's smirk died instantly. "Beau texted you again?"

Noelle nodded. "Said he knew where I was."

Scarlett's jaw tightened. She slapped her palm against the counter, making the napkin holder rattle. "That son of a—" She cut herself off, voice sharp. "I swear, if he so much as breathes near you, I'll run him over myself."

The fierceness in her friend's voice rattled something loose in Noelle. Relief. Shame. Gratitude. "Slade was...just there. It felt like I could breathe again, but now I can't stop overthinking things–that I shouldn't drag Slade into my mess, that I'm afraid he will get fed up with the drama of it all and leave me eventually anyway."

Scarlett leaned across the counter, eyes burning. "Then let him be there, let him make you feel safe. Stop pushing him away and trying to do this alone."

Noelle's throat closed. "Safe isn't the same as happy. What if it's only temporary?"

Scarlett softened, tilting her head. "Or what if it's real? Sometimes safe and happy show up together. Sometimes you get both."

The silence stretched. Scarlett tilted her head, studying Noelle with narrowed eyes and a knowing little smile.

"So," she said lightly, "are you in trouble yet?"

Noelle blinked. "What kind of trouble?"

Scarlett's grin widened. "The *love* kind. The kind where you pretend you're totally fine and definitely not thinking about my brother every five seconds."

Noelle laughed, shaking her head. "You're ridiculous."

"Am I?" Scarlett leaned closer, lowering her voice conspiratorially. "Because your cheeks just turned the exact color they do when you lie."

Noelle sighed, giving up. "I don't know. It's... different. He feels different."

Scarlett softened immediately. "Different good?"

"Yeah," Noelle admitted. "Different good."

Scarlett nudged her elbow with an excited squeal. "That's how it starts. Next thing you know, you're in love and my brother's walking you down the aisle."

Noelle's smile lingered, thoughtful now. "I don't know about love."

"You don't have to," Scarlett said gently. Then, with a wicked grin returning, "But you *do* have to text him back before he spirals."

Noelle laughed, pulling out her phone. "You're the worst."

"I know," Scarlett said cheerfully. "It's my brand."

Noelle peeked at her through her fingers, half-exasperated, half smiling. Scarlett sat back, grin widening, knowing she had convinced her friend not to give up. "Tomorrow is Friday night. Girls' night. Pizza, wine that costs less than your apron, and a bad movie marathon."

Noelle shook her head. "I don't know. I just want to stay home."

"Uh-uh." Scarlett wagged a finger. "No sulking alone. You've earned a night where the scariest thing is whether Chris Evans looks better in a cable-knit sweater or a leather jacket."

Despite herself, Noelle laughed again. Scarlett always had that effect. "You're relentless."

"And you love me for it. So, girls' night tomorrow?"

Noelle hesitated, then sighed. "Okay. Yeah, let's do it."

Scarlett beamed like she'd just won a championship. "Good girl. Now go clock out before I drag you out of here myself."

For the first time all day, Noelle felt the tightness in her chest ease.

Slade shut the hotel door behind him and dropped his gear bag by the bed. The room was the same as every other road stop—beige walls, scratchy carpet, a heater rattling in the corner like it might give out. It smelled faintly of bleach and nothing else. Empty in a way that gnawed at him.

His heart leapt as his phone buzzed and Noelle's name lit up the screen. FaceTime.

He swiped before he could think.

She was curled on her couch, hair in a messy knot, sweatshirt slipping off one shoulder. The sight hit harder than a cross-check.

"You win?" she asked, smiling like it mattered more than the scoreboard.

"Yeah," he said, leaning back against the headboard. "Not my best game."

"You look tired."

He smirked. "You don't look too wide awake yourself."

She smiled back nervously and took a deep breath. "Well I wanted to call and apologize for going MIA on you the last couple days. I was just overthinking things but Scarlett helped me realize how stupid I was being. I'm sorry, I hope we're okay."

"Oh yeah, yeah, of course," he stammered, "I'm sorry if I was too much, I didn't mean to upset you. I never thought I'd be happy for my sister meddling but glad we're good."

"No, not at all," she replied quickly. Scarlett's voice called from somewhere off screen—something about popcorn. Noelle rolled her eyes. "She's dragging me into a girls' night. Pizza, cheap wine, bad movies."

"Sounds like hell." He meant it as a joke, but the thought of her laughing on that couch without him dug under his skin.

They slipped into easy chatter like nothing had ever happened. What she'd served at the shop. Scarlett's movie pick. Garrett chirping him on the bench. Nothing important, but he couldn't stop staring—at her smile, at the way her laugh softened the edges of his day.

Scarlett popped into view with a heaping bowl of popcorn and he took that as his cue to let them get back to their girls' night. They said their goodbyes and the screen went dark. The silence hit hard. The hum of the heater, the buzz of a light bulb, the stale air of a room that wasn't his. He reached for his phone again, thumb hovering over her name.

Wish you were here. Hate this bed without you.

He stared at the words until they blurred, throat tight. Then he deleted them, one letter at a time, until nothing remained but the blank glow of the screen.

He tossed the phone onto the nightstand like it had burned him and pressed a hand over his face. He'd told himself he just wanted to make sure she was safe, that was all. But the ache in his chest said otherwise.

It wasn't about safety at all. It was about the way she made him feel alive.

And that scared him more than Beau ever could.

"Damn it, Fisher," he muttered into the quiet. "You're gone on her."

Chapter Twenty-One

The first snow of winter came hard and fast a few days later, covering Silverwood in a blanket of white that felt more like a warning than a comfort.

Lights blinked from windows, and wreaths hung on doors and the streets filled with the kind of joy that made Slade's skin crawl.

He still hated this time of year. Even after three years had passed which felt like a lifetime and yesterday at once.

The music, the forced cheer, the memories clawing from places he had tried to bury deep.

December. The fire.

He was wandering aimlessly around his apartment with these thoughts whirring in his brain when something caught his eye on the top shelf of the closet.

A small box. Undisturbed. Untouched for months.

He hesitated–then pulled it down.

It's been a while since I have opened this box.

A silver necklace, its clasp melted halfway shut. A Polaroid of her in his team hoodie, half-laughing, hair windblown, light in her eyes. The ultrasound picture.

His chest tightened.

He sank onto the edge of the bed, the box cradled like the baby they never had.

I should have left this box alone. I shouldn't have opened it.

He closed his eyes and suddenly images that hadn't haunted him in a while flashed through his mind; flames licking up walls, smoke-blurred memories, a rescue that came too late. And Jessica. *Gone.*

The room was too quiet.

The air smelled faintly like vanilla. Like her. *Noelle.*

Noelle had been here last night. Her laugh still echoed in the walls. Her toothbrush in the bathroom. Her touch hadn't felt dangerous.

Not until now.

He stared at the necklace, at the way the metal warped, delicate and ruined.

Damn it Jess. I didn't forget about you. I swear I didn't. I haven't looked at this stuff in a long time. It hurts.

What if letting Noelle get closer meant risking this pain all over again?

He pictured her in this apartment—hair messy from sleep, cooking barefoot, curling up on his couch like it had always been hers. It hit so suddenly, it stole his breath.

Her laugh echoing from the kitchen.

Her jacket on the hook beside his.

Her key next to his on the counter.

And for a split second, he wanted it. Wanted all of it.

Then the weight of it crashed in—fast, sharp, familiar.

Too much. Too soon. Too good.

He rubbed the back of his neck, heart thudding with something that wasn't adrenaline.

He was good at power plays. Angles. Muscle memory.

He was terrible at peace. Terrified of softness.

The team had lost—hard-fought, brutal, the kind of game that left every muscle aching and every mistake replaying on a loop. Slade should've been angry, replaying shifts, dissecting what he could've done better. Instead, all he felt was hollow.

The moment he stepped into his hotel room, it closed in on him: too quiet. Too dim. And way too empty.

He tossed his duffel onto the floor and flopped onto the bed, phone in hand before his head hit the pillow. Her name stared back at him, already typed in the message bar.

SLADE:

Can you talk?

The video rang once. Twice.

Then Noelle appeared, wrapped in a blanket, glasses sliding down her nose, hair a sleepy tumble. "Hey."

Slade exhaled like he'd been holding his breath since warmups.

"You look wiped," she said, her voice soft and warm through the pixel haze. "Rough game?"

He nodded, throat tightening. "Yeah. We lost."

"I'm sorry." Her brows drew together, sympathy immediate and unguarded. "Was it close?"

"Too close," he admitted. "One of those games where you keep thinking if you'd just done one thing differently..."

She studied him for a moment, seeing past the words. "That's not what's bothering you, though."

Slade huffed a quiet breath, gaze drifting to the far wall. "No. Guess not."

The silence stretched, comfortable but heavy. Finally, he asked, "Are you free around lunch tomorrow when I get back to town? Maybe we could meet at the diner—talk for a bit?"

"Yeah," she said without hesitation. "I'd like that."

"Okay." His shoulders eased, just a fraction. "Thanks."

"Get back safe," she added gently.

After the call ended, Noelle sat there a moment longer, phone still in her hands. Normally she'd be replaying his smile, the sound of his voice. Instead, a nervous pit settled in her stomach.

Whatever was weighing on him hadn't stayed on the ice.

Chapter Twenty-Two

It hadn't been an impulsive decision. He'd sat with it—rolling it over in the back of his mind until the answer hardened in him when he saw Jessica's box. Noelle's laugh still haunted the quiet, her small touches etched themselves into his space, but every time he caught himself wanting more, the same fear clawed back in.

Now, facing her in the diner, the words pressed heavy on his tongue. He felt terrible doing this two days before her birthday but he just couldn't cope with the wave of emotions tossing him around in the endless sea of loss he had been sailing for so long.

Slade took a deep breath, his heart pounding in his chest. "Noelle, I... I can't do this. I can't get close to you," he said, his voice strained. Slade exhaled sharply, rubbing a hand over his face. "I'm—look, I'm just not built for this."

Her chest tightened. "Built for *what*?"

Slade let out a humorless laugh, shaking his head. "For all of it. Love. Family. Whatever future you think we might have. I *can't*."

Slade shifted, crossing his arms, his body stiff. "I don't know how to do this, Noelle. I'm trying to do the right thing."

"And crushing me like this is the *right* thing? I thought you were different," she said. "Not because you don't have scars. But because you didn't run from mine."

"I'm not running from you," he said, urgent now. "I'm running from the part of me that ruins things."

She studied him for a long moment, like she was memorizing his face.

Noelle's throat tightened. "Ruining it anyway by pushing me away?"

His jaw clenched. "By not leading you on."

"Leading me on?" She scoffed, taking a step forward. "We've been inseparable for weeks. You hold me like you need me. You kiss me like you mean it. You look at me like—" Her voice cracked, but she didn't stop, "like you *love* me, Slade."

"I don't love you," he said, the words cutting through the air like a knife.

Noelle froze, her breath catching in her throat. "What?" she whispered, her voice trembling.

"I can't love you. Your name means Christmas, the thing I've hated most in the world for three years now and has caused me unbearable pain. It's better for both of us if you move on and find someone who can make you happy." Slade swallowed hard, running a hand through his hair, looking away.

Tears welled up in Noelle's eyes, her heart shattering at his words. She shook her head, her chest aching, "If you really mean that, then look me in the eye and say it again."

Slade turned to face her, his expression cold and distant. "I don't love you," he repeated, his eyes hardening.

Noelle's stomach dropped.

She nodded slowly, blinking away the sting in her eyes. "Then I guess that's it." She turned, heading toward the door, her steps steady despite the storm raging inside her, threatening to rip her to shreds.

The sad truth was, he *did* love Noelle. He could picture a future with her, which scared him more than anything.

Noelle gripped her phone tightly, pressing it against her ear as she sat in her car, parked on the side of the road, breath uneven. The lump in her throat was impossible to swallow, and she hated the way her fingers shook against the steering wheel.

Scarlett picked up after the second ring.

"Noelle?"

The sound of her voice nearly undid her.

Noelle inhaled sharply, blinking rapidly, willing herself not to cry. "I—I don't know why I'm calling."

Scarlett exhaled slowly, like she already knew. "What happened?"

Noelle let out a breath that sounded too much like a laugh, but there was nothing funny about it. "I- I lost him, Scar. He- He broke up with me," she whispered.

Scarlett stilled. "Slade?"

Noelle nodded, even though Scarlett couldn't see her. "He said he can't love me."

Silence stretched across the line, heavy and suffocating.

Scarlett let out a sharp breath, frustration bleeding into her tone, "I was afraid of this. My brother is a *moron*."

"I knew this would happen," Noelle murmured. "I knew he'd pull back eventually, I just—" She squeezed her eyes shut, pressing her forehead against the steering wheel. "I let myself hope."

Scarlett's voice softened, though the edge of her anger still lingered. "He's scared. I'm sure he'll come to his senses."

Noelle swallowed, fingers tightening around the phone. "I know. I told him that. But he told me he never loved me. He said he couldn't. "

"Where are you now?" Scarlett asked.

"I think I am just going to go home. I have to stop at the store and pick up dinner, maybe ice cream and something to drown my sorrows," Noelle said.

"Call me when you get home. There is a snowstorm that is heading this way within the hour. I'll swing by later to check in on you when I'm done with my shift at the bookstore."

Scarlett went over to Noelle's after work to comfort her.

By the time she arrived, the snow had started to drift in thin, uncertain flurries, the kind that hinted at something heavier coming. Noelle answered the door in socked feet, hair pulled into a loose knot that had clearly been retied too many times.

Scarlett didn't ask questions. She stepped inside and pulled Noelle into a hug so tight it stole what little breath she had left.

Noelle crumpled against her.

Scarlett's eyes drifted to the calendar taped to the fridge, its corners curling.

She paused.

"Hey," she said carefully.

Noelle followed her gaze and felt the familiar sting bloom in her chest.

December 24th.

Two days away.

"I know," Noelle murmured before Scarlett could say anything. "I didn't forget."

Scarlett's mouth tightened. "I wasn't worried about that. I just—" She shook her head. "I hate that this is happening now. I really didn't see this coming."

Noelle let out a breath that sounded tired more than sad. "You and me both, but bad things always seem to happen to me around the holidays. I guess this year just decided to be on theme."

"No," Scarlett said firmly. "This year is going to be different."

Noelle glanced at her, unconvinced.

"You don't get to spend your birthday pretending it doesn't matter," Scarlett went on. "Even if it's small. Even if it's just us and cake from the grocery store."

A faint smile tugged at Noelle's mouth. "You don't have to—"

"I want to," Scarlett said. "We can make it a slumber party; by the looks of the snow coming down, we won't have a choice in the matter. Good thing I came loaded with snacks and wine."

Noelle leaned back against the couch, staring at the ceiling as the snow outside began to fall a little thicker.

They ended up being snowed in for the next two days into Noelle's birthday. And the quiet one-on-one time with her best friend, talking for long hours, watching movies, and playing cards did things to heal her heart in a way she didn't think was possible. It was the best gift she could have asked for, all things considered.

The snow had come and gone, burying Silverwood in silence, but the storm inside Slade hadn't broken. Days blurred into practices and nights into restless hours where Noelle's absence pressed in heavier than the cold. He told himself he'd done the right thing, pushing her away, but the lie wore thinner every time he laced up his skates.

The puck slammed off the boards, ricocheting into the far corner. Slade chased it down with more speed than precision, body low, muscles coiled too tight. Practice drills had dissolved into something feral—he wasn't skating so much as attacking the ice.

"Nice pass, Fisher," Garrett barked sarcastically from behind him. "If we were aiming for the ghost of your attitude."

Slade didn't turn. Just gritted his teeth and swung his stick harder just missing the puck.

Coach's whistle cut through the rink.

"Fisher. Bench. Now."

Slade skated off, chest heaving. He yanked off his helmet and dropped it onto the bench with a hollow clatter.

"You good?" Hunter asked cautiously. "You've been... sharp lately."

"Just play better," Slade snapped.

Hunter straightened, "What the hell is your problem, man?"

Stryker leaned against the boards, watching. "This about Noelle?"

Slade froze. He didn't answer.

Stryker stepped forward, voice low. "You're miserable, man. And now the whole team's feeling it. Maybe call her. But don't tear us up because you lost someone you still want."

Slade's jaw clenched. *I didn't lose her,* he told himself. *I let her go. I pushed her away. I told her I couldn't love her and I do. Damn it, I miss her. What did I do?*

The cemetery was empty, blanketed in a thin layer of snow that softened everything it touched. Headstones stood like sentinels beneath the gray winter sky, the world hushed in a way that felt almost reverent.

Slade stood with his hands shoved deep into the pockets of his coat, breath fogging in front of him as he stared down at the familiar stone.

Jessica Anderson.

The letters were clean. Too clean. Like time hadn't earned the right to wear them down yet.

"I told myself I wasn't coming back," he muttered, voice low, almost embarrassed. "Guess I lied."

The wind stirred the bare branches overhead. No answer. There never was.

He shifted his weight, boots crunching softly in the snow. For a long moment, he said nothing at all—just stared, chest tight, jaw locked, like if he stayed quiet long enough the ache might ease.

"It's been three years," he said finally. "Everyone says that's enough time."

He let out a breath that trembled despite his best effort. "I still can't breathe around Christmas."

His throat tightened.

"I met someone," he went on, eyes burning now. "She's... good. Steady. She sees me. And I let myself believe—just for a second—that maybe I could have that again. That I could build something and not ruin it."

His laugh came out hollow. "Stupid, right?"

Slade rubbed a hand over his face, anger flashing hot and sharp before collapsing into something quieter.

"She deserves better than someone who flinches at the word *future*. Better than someone who hears her name and thinks of funerals instead of promises."

He swallowed hard, "So I did what I did when I lost you. I ran."

The admission sat heavy in the cold air.

"I told her I didn't love her," he whispered. "Looked her right in the eyes and said it like it was nothing."

His voice cracked then, just barely, "And I hated myself the second the words left my mouth."

Silence stretched. Snow drifted down in slow, lazy flakes.

"I don't know how to love without losing someone," he said. "I don't know how to survive it if it happens again."

His gaze dropped to the ground between his boots.

"But I think... I think I've already lost her."

Slade exhaled shakily and straightened, forcing himself to stand tall like he always had—like grief hadn't hollowed him out years ago and left echoes behind.

"I know it's probably dumb but I needed to talk to you about it all. I hope you'd understand," he said quietly. "I hope you'd forgive me."

He reached out, brushing snow from the top of the headstone with a bare hand, the cold biting into his skin.

"Somehow, I think this helped even though I can't hear you talking back. Thank you for that. Goodbye, Jess."

He turned and walked away without looking back, the snow swallowing his footprints almost immediately—like proof he'd been there was never meant to last.

The SILVERWOOD SCOOP

Local Sports & Community News

Love on Thin Ice: Are Slade Fisher and Noelle Hayes Still a Team?
Samantha Romano, Silverwood Snipers' Media Correspondent

Is there trouble in paradise? Has hometown heartthrob and Snipers star Slade Fisher already hit the penalty box in love? For weeks, fans couldn't get enough of Slade's whirlwind romance with local sweetheart Noelle Hayes, but sharp-eyed readers have noticed something strange: it's been *days* since the pair were spotted together.

No coffee runs. No cozy dinners. No sideline smiles. Nada.

So what gives? Our sources say Noelle has been keeping a low profile at work while Slade has been looking more than a little tense on the ice. Could this picture-perfect couple be skating toward a breakup? Or are they simply dodging the cameras and enjoying some private time out of the spotlight?

Either way, the silence has tongues wagging. Is Slade Fisher—Silverwood's most eligible bachelor and resident bad boy on blades—about to be back on the market?

Stay tuned, *Scoop* readers. You know we'll be the first to spill the tea when this love story takes its next turn.

Chapter Twenty-Three

Noelle barely registered that Christmas and New Years came and went. She had picked up extra shifts at the diner and buried herself in her writing, ignoring calls from Scarlett, Violet, and Samantha, all in a weak attempt to avoid her current reality.

The newest snowstorm had started swirling just before dusk, blanketing Silverwood in the quiet beauty of a Maine winter. The streetlights flickered, casting golden halos on the empty roads as the snow fell harder. Noelle hadn't intended on being out in this but the snow came quicker than expected. Her coat was warm but not warm enough. The early January wind whipped her blonde hair into her face, her cheeks stung from the cold. As snowflakes fell on her glasses, it made it almost impossible to see as she walked along.

Her boots sank into the drifts, each step a fight. They were still damp from the slush outside the arena. Slade had a home game tonight. She was normally supposed to be there. She had wanted to be there to support him. So she had gone in and watched some of it from the back, but she left without saying anything to anyone before the game ended. She hadn't even told Scartlett she was going to show up. She couldn't bear to see Slade with his teammates laughing and pretending like nothing had happened. Her breath came in sharp bursts, fogging the air, her tears freezing before they could fall. The streets were empty, the world swallowed by white.

She didn't know where she was going. She had to get as far away as possible from Slade and from the words that had gutted her and would echo around her heart long after the snow melted.

Why am I torturing myself over him? I'm done.

She repeated it like a prayer she didn't believe in. A mantra that cracked a little more each time she thought it.

Her fingers were numb inside her gloves, the cold biting through the seams. Her legs ached with every step, thighs burning, calves tight, but she welcomed the pain. It gave her something solid to focus on. Something that wasn't *him*.

Snow swirled around her, thickening as the night pressed in. The world felt muffled, distant—like she was walking inside a snow globe someone had shaken too hard.

She passed the park without really seeing it. The swings hung frozen and half-buried, chains creaking softly in the wind. The benches were iced over, their familiar shapes blurred beneath white. This was a place she'd walked a hundred times before. Tonight, it felt unfamiliar. Hostile.

Her vision wavered. She blinked hard, but it didn't help. Her breath came out in sharp, uneven bursts, fogging the air in front of her face. The tears she refused to let fall burned hot behind her eyes.

I should've eaten something, she thought.

I should've slept.

She clutched the scarf around her neck, the one Slade had given to her as an early birthday gift so Christmas wouldn't overshadow her day. Ironic after everything that had happened, but still she couldn't help but wear it to have some piece of him near.

Now it was soaked through, stiff with ice, the fabric clinging to her coat like it didn't want to let go. She pressed it closer anyway, breathing in faint, fading traces of his cologne beneath the cold.

Her phone was dead. She'd noticed it too late—black screen, no response. No Scarlett. No way to call anyone. She told herself it was fine. She was fine.

She wasn't fine.

I should have told someone I was going to the arena.

Should have charged my phone.

Her stomach twisted, empty and hollow. Her head throbbed with a dull, pulsing ache.

The wind picked up, pushing her sideways. Snow swirled in frantic spirals, making it hard to see more than a few feet ahead. Her steps grew unsteady, her legs heavy.

Her heart thudded too fast.

Her breath came too shallow.

Her thoughts felt slow, foggy.

She wrapped her arms around herself, trying to steady her shaking.

Just get home, she told herself. *Just a little farther.*

She didn't see the patch of ice.

Her foot slid.

It happened too fast and in slow motion all at once. The world tilted. Her stomach dropped as she tried to catch herself, arms flailing uselessly. Her boots scraped for traction that wasn't there.

"Oh—"

Her body twisted, panic bloomed sharp and bright as she went down, and all of the air rushed out of her as she made contact, surely cracking a rib or two. Her head struck the pavement with a sickening crack that echoed louder than it should have, even under the snow.

The cold rushed in everywhere at once. Her vision exploded into white and black, stars bursting behind her eyes. She lay there, stunned, the snow immediately beginning to gather in her hair, on her lashes, down the front of her coat.

The sky above her was nothing but swirling gray.

I shouldn't have come...

Her thoughts started to feel slippery, slow, like they were drifting away from her before she could hold onto them.

I shouldn't have been alone...

Her fingers twitched, trying to move. One hand scraped weakly against the ice. Her head throbbed, a deep, nauseating pain that made the world pulse.

Fear crept in then—quiet, insidious.

What if I can't get up? What if no one comes?

Her chest tightened. She sucked in a shaky breath that burned her lungs.

"Help," she tried to whisper, but the word barely escaped her lips.

The snow kept falling, soft and relentless, covering her footprints, erasing her path like she had never been there at all.

Her vision blurred again, this time darker at the edges.

Slade...

His name, his handsome face, was the last thing that filled her mind.

And then the world tilted once more—slowly, gently—until everything went dark.

The trauma bay doors burst open, letting in a gust of frigid air and a stretcher dusted in snow. The paramedics were layered in frost, their boots soaked, their voices urgent.

"Female, mid-twenties," one shouted. "Found unconscious off Camden Street near the harbor trail leading away from the arena. Head trauma, hypothermia. We think she's been down for hours."

Dr. Callahan Fisher was already moving, pulling on gloves, his breath fogging in the cold air that hadn't yet settled from the storm. The ER was understaffed tonight—half the roads were still impassable—and he'd been on shift for eighteen hours.

"Let's get her core temp up," he ordered. "Warm saline, heated blankets, oxygen. I want a CT on her head as soon as she's stable."

He moved to the side of the stretcher, eyes scanning vitals, assessing damage. Then he looked at her face.

And froze.

"Noelle?"

The name slipped out before he could stop it. His hands hovered mid-air, his breath caught.

Willow, who was on shift and hurrying to the commotion, jolted when she heard the name. "Noelle?"

Callahan swallowed hard. "Yeah, I think you know her too. She's— she's my sister's best friend...and my brother's girlfriend."

Willow's eyes widened in recognition. "Yeah. She's my friend, too."

Callahan looked at her knowingly and said, voice determined now. "Okay, we've got her together—as a team. As long as you feel alright, or should I get someone else?"

Willow just jumped into action as affirmation.

Chapter Twenty-Four

Back at the arena, the air hummed with anticipation as Slade stepped onto the ice. The crowd roared, the sound echoing against the rafters, a wall of noise he usually let wash over him until it sharpened his focus. Hockey was supposed to be his sanctuary—ninety feet of ice where the rest of the world didn't matter. Just the puck, the net, the rush of adrenaline in his veins.

But tonight, the ice felt foreign. Harder, colder. The crowd blurred into static.

Noelle should've been here.

He tightened his grip on his stick, pushing harder, trying to drown her out with motion. But the memory clawed back anyway—her tear-streaked face, her voice breaking when he told her he didn't love her. The lie burned on his tongue even now. He hadn't said it to hurt her; he'd said it to keep her out. To keep himself safe.

Safe from what? Losing again? Breaking all over?

The puck dropped. Stryker won possession for the Snipers. Slade watched as Stryker hit the puck to Hunter, who then passed it to Jayden, back to Stryker who sent the puck to him. He surged forward, muscle memory taking over, but his head wasn't in it. His first pass went wide. He chased it down too late. By the time he caught up, an opponent stripped the puck clean and sent it flying the other way.

"Lock in, Fisher!" Coach Carlson barked from the bench.

He ground his teeth and skated harder, lungs burning, but nothing clicked. Every shift, every stride, her face bled through the noise.

He knew Noelle had been right. He had pushed her away. Pride, fear, the ghosts of everything he'd already lost—he'd thought those things would protect him. Instead, they'd left him hollow.

He slammed an opponent into the boards harder than necessary, the jolt rattling up his shoulder. The crowd roared with approval, but it felt empty. He wasn't proving anything. He wasn't fixing anything.

By the final whistle, his chest heaved with more than exertion. He skated to the bench, helmet heavy on his head, mind spiraling.

Slade stayed planted at the bench, breath ragged, sweat dripping, the noise of the arena fading into something distant and muffled.

What if he had just made the biggest mistake of his life? The thought knifed through him sharper than any hit he'd taken.

And for the first time in years, hockey didn't feel like a refuge. It felt like a reminder—of everything he couldn't outrun.

His phone started to vibrate relentlessly.

Once.

Twice.

Again.

He barely had time to untape his wrists before it buzzed again.

His emotions already stretched thin, he grabbed it off the bench, pressing it to his ear without checking the screen.

"This better be worth the fine I'm gonna get for taking this during a game," he barked.

The voice on the other end was tight, strained.

"Slade."

Callahan.

Slade's stomach dropped, his pulse spiking instantly, the tremor in his brother's tone putting him on edge.

Something was wrong. "What is it?" Slade asked, standing up, tension coiling through his muscles.

Callahan exhaled sharply. "It's Noelle."

Everything stopped. He couldn't see the game in front of him anymore.

Slade's grip on his phone tightened, his heartbeat hammering in his ears, drowning out the post-game chatter around him.

"What do you mean *it's Noelle*?" His voice came out too sharp, too desperate, but he didn't care.

"There was an accident," Callahan finally said, voice low, like he was trying to steady himself. "She was found unconscious in the snow. She was hypothermic when she was brought in and she still hasn't regained consciousness. We know she has a couple broken ribs and hit her head, making it probable that she has a concussion as well. It's looking critical but we're doing everything we can to stabilize her now. Slade, you're all she has besides our family. You need to get here."

Slade's knees nearly buckled.

No.

No, no, no.

His entire body locked up, panic clawing at his throat, at his chest,

Unconscious.

In the snow.

Snow.

It was December.

Hypothermic.

Concussion.

She hit her head.

Hospital.

The words were a jumble that hit like a freight train, suffocating, unbearable.

And the last thing he had said to her—*"I can't love you."* Slade inhaled sharply, ripping off his jersey. He shoved his skates into his bag, moving on instinct. "Cal- Cal, stay with her. Don't leave her alone until I get there." His voice was rough, broken.

"Slade— there's something else," Callahan said. "She was found by the arena."

But Slade was already moving, already running, his body acting before his mind could catch up because if she didn't make it—if she didn't wake up—he would never forgive himself.

Stryker appeared next to him. "Slade, where are you going? What's going on?" he asked, his voice singed with concern.

Slade opened his mouth to answer, but the words stuck in his throat. Memories of losing Jessica in the fire flooded his mind—her lifeless body, Callahan's voice telling him she was gone. The pain of that loss surged through him, paralyzing his ability to speak.

His knees nearly buckled.

Stryker's grip tightened on Slade's shoulder, his eyes searching his brother's face. "Slade, talk to me. What's wrong?"

Slade's breath came in ragged gasps, his heart pounding as the memories and reality collided. He tried to find the words, it felt like that terrible night with Jess in the fire all over again, all he could see was Jessica's face, hearing that dreadful night's echoes enter his present day nightmare.

Slade clutched his chest, fear constricting his lungs. The pain and panic bore down on him. Finally, he forced the words out, his voice splintering. "Noelle... accident... She's in the hospital. Critical condition. I... I can't..."

Stryker's eyes widened in shock, then hardened with determination. He understood the depth of Slade's fear, the trauma that was surfacing. "She's alive though. She's hurt, but she's alive."

"I messed up, Stryk. I pushed her away. I ended things with her. Told her I couldn't love her—didn't love her. She was supposed to be at the game—She was here... she was here... and I didn't know. Now—" he couldn't finish the thought and he turned to go.

Slade's breath came in ragged bursts, the adrenaline pushing him forward. The double doors swung open, and the frigid night air slapped his face. He stumbled down the steps, his hockey bag slung over one shoulder.

He headed towards his truck, his thoughts a chaotic whirl of fear and regret.

Just as he reached the driver's side door, Stryker grabbed him by the shoulder, his grip firm and grounding. "Slade, give me your keys. You're not in a condition to drive right now."

Slade hesitated, the weight of the moment pressing down on him.

He handed over the keys, his hands trembling. Stryker took them with a nod of understanding, his eyes filled with concern.

Rapid fire texts started to flood in via a group thread that Willow started:

WILLOW:

Hey guys. CODE RED. Need you all at
Silverwood General ASAP.

SCARLETT:

What's wrong??

WILLOW:

Noelle was brought into the ER about twenty
minutes ago. She slipped on ice and hit her
head. She was found by a passerby,
thankfully they found her before hypothermia
could become severe.

VIOLET:

What?! Is she okay??

WILLOW:

She's stable, but it's been confirmed she has
a concussion and we're still running scans.
Callahan is with her. He asked me to let you
all know the updates.

SAMANTHA:

Oh no! I'm so glad someone found her. Is
she conscious at all?

SCARLETT:

This can't be happening. Does Slade know?
I'm on my way right now!

WILLOW:

Yeah. At least I think so, Callahan told me he
called him. I added him to this thread to be
sure. She's on the second floor—Trauma
Wing, room 214. Please come to the nurses'
station first.

STRYKER:

Yeah, he called Slade. We just finished the
game and I'm bringing him to the hospital
now. Hunter is with us too.

SLADE:

Help her.

VIOLET:

I'm grabbing my coat right now and on my
way too. Praying so hard.

STRYKER:

Five minutes out.

WILLOW:

Doing everything we can. See you guys
soon.

Chapter Twenty-Five

The sterile scent of antiseptic hung heavy in the air, and the fluorescent lights cast harsh shadows. The automatic doors slid open, and the warmth of the lobby, still decorated for Christmas, greeted them. The sight triggered a rush of memories for Slade, taking him back to that fateful night years ago when he had lost Jessica.

The waiting area was adorned with twinkling fairy lights and garlands of evergreen. A decorated Christmas tree stood in the corner, its ornaments reflecting the soft glow of the lights. The air smelled faintly of pine and cinnamon, a scent meant to comfort, but that only heightened Slade's anxiety.

Slade's breath came in shallow gasps as he stepped into the waiting area, his hand instinctively going to his heart. He rushed past the memories in the direction of the nurse's station, Stryker, and Hunter following close behind him.

Willow was pacing behind the nurses' station but she came around it to greet them as soon as she saw them.

"Noelle," Slade said, voice rough, too sharp, like he barely had control over it. "Noelle. P-please. You've gotta t-take me to her!"

"Yes, I can't quite let all of you back yet to see her but let me double check with Callahan that you can go see her, Slade."

"Slade?"

He turned. Callahan was striding toward him in dark scrubs, ID badge flashing against his chest. The look on his face—sharp, tired, instantly alert—told Slade everything he didn't want to hear.

"Cal- on the phone you said there was an accident. What happened? Where is she?"

"Noelle was found unconscious in the snow. We don't have all the details but we had to do a CT scan to check for head trauma; she hit her head pretty good. She has a concussion and a slight case of hypothermia as well as a couple fractured ribs from the apparent fall."

Slade felt his knees weaken and leaned against the wall for support. "Cal- I can't do this again. This hospital. I can't lose her. Not like Jess."

Critical. The word echoed in Slade's mind, a relentless drumbeat.

He stumbled back a half-step, the fear sending ice down his spine.

Callahan put a hand on Slade's shoulder to steady him. "We're taking good care of her, I have faith she's going to pull through this."

Slade's fingers curled into fists, his heartbeat slamming against his ribs, his entire body screaming to do something, to fix this, to make sure she was safe—

"Slade."

The voice pulled him out of the spiral. He turned fast, eyes landing on Scarlett.

"You *absolute* idiot."

Slade barely had time to brace himself before her hands shoved at his chest—sharp, frustrated, raging with fury. "If she dies, Slade—" Her voice cracked, and she shut her mouth, inhaling sharply through her nose.

Hunter wrapped his arms around her in a bear hug from behind, pulling her off Slade as she continued to try to beat at his chest, strong but trying to soothe the rage storming within her. "C'mon babe, this wasn't Slade's fault. It was nobody's fault."

Slade flinched, her words had hit him like a knife to the gut. "She's not going to die," he muttered, voice low, tight, like saying it would make it true.

Scarlett laughed—a humorless, bitter sound. "You don't know that! You *pushed* her away," she snapped. "You hurt her so deeply and for no reason. Now—now she was alone and hurt and she's fighting for her life, Slade, and I—" She exhaled harshly, her fingers shaking as she shoved them through her hair.

Slade looked away, his jaw clenching. He knew.

And that was the worst part.

Scarlett stepped closer, voice lower now—deadly quiet.

"She loved you, and you broke her."

"Sis, you need to try to calm down, it's not helping anything right now. Noelle is in the best of hands. Slade, bud, you can see her soon. We just need a little longer to finish some tests," Callahan said with his composed doctor's authority.

She looked at him as if she'd turn on him next but ended up stomping over to Violet who had just walked in, the two of them collapsing on a bench, hugging each other.

Slade stood in the dimly lit hospital corridor, his eyes raw from tears. His fists clenched at his sides, knuckles white against the sterile walls.

His footsteps faltered on the worn linoleum, echoing in the otherwise silent hallway. The slightly open chapel door was a sliver of light beckoning, a symbol of hope in this sea of sterile corridors.

He hesitated, the weight of memories pressing down on him again. The air smelled of aged wood and candle wax, the flicker of candles dancing on the walls, casting shadows that seemed to sway with their prayers.

Slade's fingers grazed the doorframe as he stepped inside. The silence enveloped him like a shroud, each step echoing through the stillness. The polished mahogany pew creaked under his weight as he settled into one. The wooden kneeler invited him to bow his head, to surrender to something greater than himself.

He bowed his head, the chapel's tranquility cocooning him.

"God," he began, his voice barely audible, filled with desperation. "If you're there... if you're listening..." His voice cracked. "Let her live. Please. I've made mistakes—so many of them. I pushed her away, thinking it was safer. But now, Noelle is fighting for her life. And I—"

He buried his face in his hands, his body shaking with sobs. "Please, God, don't take her from me," he pleaded, his voice breaking. "I can't lose her too."

His throat tightened. The memories flooded back—the arguments, the missed chances, the walls he'd built around his heart. He'd convinced himself that love was a risk he couldn't afford. When he heard Noelle was hurt, he realized how much he'd been lying to himself. He couldn't live without her, but he had been so scared of being hurt or losing her that now, in the end, he might lose her just like he lost Jessica.

"I'm sorry," Slade continued. "I'm sorry for every time I held back, for every 'maybe later' and 'not now', I was rotten with women after Jess but Noelle has opened my eyes again. If you're listening, Lord, please don't take her. Don't take my girl. Let me make things right. Love is worth the risk—I understand that now."

The candle flickered as if acknowledging his plea.

A quiet knock at the door pulled him from the spiral.

He looked up, breath caught in his throat.

Callahan stepped inside. "She's still asleep but we're done testing and have her comfortable now. You can see her," he said, offering a reassuring smile.

Relief washed over Slade, but it was tempered by the lingering fear and guilt. He followed the doctor down the sterile corridors, his footsteps echoing in the silence. Each step brought him closer to Noelle, to the moment of truth.

As they reached her room, Callahan paused, allowing Slade to enter first. He hesitated at the doorway, his breath catching in his throat. There she was, lying so still in the hospital bed covered in warm heavy blankets and a heating pad, her face pale and bruised. The machines beeped softly, a constant reminder of her fragility. Tubes and wires connected her to various monitors, each one a lifeline.

Slade approached her bedside slowly, his eyes never leaving her face. He sank into the chair beside her, his legs shaky from the prolonged vigil. He reached out, taking her hand gently in his, feeling the coolness of her skin. Tears blurred his vision as he whispered, "I'm so sorry,

Noelle. I never should have left. I was a fool, scared of what I felt for you."

He stayed by her side, holding her hand, whispering apologies and promises, his heart breaking with each passing minute. The weight of exhaustion finally pulled him into a restless sleep, his head resting on the edge of her bed, his hand still holding hers.

Noelle's eyes fluttered open, disoriented and in pain. She winced, the memories of the last few days flooding back. She turned her head slightly, her gaze falling on Slade, sleeping beside her. His face was lined with worry even in slumber, and a tear escaped her eye, trailing down her cheek. She raised her free hand, hesitating before gently touching his hair.

What was he doing here? He said he didn't love me. He ended things.

"S-slade?" Noelle asked groggily.

Slade stirred, his eyes slowly opening, and he met her gaze. "Noelle!" he exclaimed, sitting up quickly, his voice a mix of relief and worry. "Thank God! You're awake."

"What h-ha-happened?" she choked out.

"You took a bad fall on some ice outside the arena, love. Do you remember anything? You've had us all so worried. I can't tell you how relieved I am to see you awake and to hear your voice. I was terrified you left me."

"Y-yes. S-sorry they called you. I shouldn't have gone to the game... did you just call me l-love?"

He looked at her, his eyes filled with regret and pain. "I messed up in the worst way. I'm so sorry for everything. I was afraid... of losing you, of loving you. But I can't imagine my life without you. Please, please, forgive me."

Noelle didn't speak—didn't trust the way emotion burned behind her throat.

"I told myself pushing you away made me strong and protected us both," Slade said. "But I was wrong. I haven't slept, haven't played right, haven't laughed once since that night. You make me better, Noelle. Not weaker. And I love you. I'm late saying it, and I might not deserve a second chance, but I am asking you for one. I was so scared."

Noelle closed her eyes, her pulse thudding dully against the side of her skull. She thought of the nights she'd lain awake replaying those words, trying to convince herself she'd imagined them.

"I was scared too," she whispered finally. Her breath fogged the glass, soft and unsteady. "Not of you. Of how much I wanted to stay. Of what it would do to me if you meant it when you left me. Because I love you too, Slade."

His eyes shone with emotion. When he spoke again, his voice came out hoarse. "I'll spend the rest of my life proving I didn't mean it. If you let me."

She studied him for a long moment—the dark circles under his eyes, the tension in his shoulders, the way he kept swallowing like he was trying to force down panic.

"You look like you're about to fall over," she whispered.

He huffed a breath that wasn't quite a laugh. "I'm fine."

"You don't look like you are. Come here," she murmured, shifting just enough to make space. "Please."

He hesitated—not because he didn't want to, but because he was afraid of hurting her, afraid of doing the wrong thing, afraid of how much he needed the closeness she was offering.

"I don't want to jostle you," he said quietly. "You're hurt."

"You won't," she whispered. "I just... I don't want you over there. Not right now."

Something in him broke at that.

He exhaled shakily, stood from the chair, and moved carefully to the side of the bed. He hesitated one last time, searching her face for any sign she wasn't sure.

She nodded.

That was all he needed.

He slipped onto the bed slowly, cautiously, lying on top of the blankets so he wouldn't disturb any wires or hurt her ribs. He curled his body around hers, close but gentle, his arm sliding beneath her shoulders, his other hand finding hers again instantly.

The moment he settled beside her, his entire body sagged—like he'd been holding himself upright by sheer force of will and finally let go.

She rested her head against his chest, listening to the uneven, too-fast rhythm of his heartbeat.

He pressed his forehead to the top of her head, breath trembling. "I thought I lost you," he whispered, voice breaking. "I can't—God, I can't go through that again."

She squeezed his hand, her thumb brushing his skin. "You didn't lose me."

He exhaled slowly, eyes searching for something—anything—to let him know she meant that.

It had been a month since their first night at the bar—the bourbon fizz, the laughter, the way she made him feel like maybe things could be okay again. Since then, they'd spent stolen hours in coffee shops, long walks under string lights, and quiet conversations that stretched into the early morning. Every day, she'd let him in just a little more. And he had just let it all go.

"I know this has been a scary night," he started softly. "But I need you to hear me. I need you to know that I see you and I'll never pull a stupid stunt like that ever again. I'm not just saying that because I thought you might die."

She stayed silent, but nodded with a small smile.

He hugged her a little closer. "I know your favorite color is red, and not just any red but the red that is the color of rubies and holly berries."

Her head tilted slightly to look up towards his face, curious.

"I know your favorite treat is amaretto swirl fudge, the pink and brown swirl one- kind of almondy, kind of cherry, kind of nostalgic as you always say, which can only come from *Sweet Haven*."

A flicker of amusement ghosted across her face.

"I know that your favorite flowers are those little blue ones—Forget-Me-Nots. Although, you do love holly as a decoration which goes perfect with your name for Christmas and if you ever have a daughter you want her name to be Holly."

She blinked, clearly surprised.

"I know you love the scent of fresh lavender, but you never buy it for yourself—you just linger a little longer in stores when they have lavender candles out."

Her fingers tightened around her grip on his hand.

"I know that your favorite dish from Veranda Thai is the orange chicken, and you have to get it with fried rice and those incredible spring rolls."

Her gaze had become more focused, studying him.

"I know you prefer your incredible hot chocolate over coffee, except on Sunday mornings when you take exactly two sips of my coffee just to pretend you like it."

Her lips pressed together, a sparkle lighting up her eyes.

"I know that when you're upset, you count things in your head—how many books are on the shelf, how many steps it takes to get from the bedroom to the kitchen. I know that you hum under your breath when you're nervous, even though you don't realize you're doing it."

Has he really noticed all these things about me?

Still, Slade went on.

"I know you also pretend to love stormy nights because they seem poetic, but deep down they make you uneasy, and you sleep better when the weather is still. And I also know you say you like horror movies, but you only watch them so you don't seem like a coward."

Her lips parted, but no words came out. She was dumbfounded.

"I know that you twirl your hair when you're deep in thought. I know that even when you think I'm not paying attention, I always am."

She finally found her voice, and the weight in her eyes nearly undid him. "You really noticed all of that?" she asked barely above a whisper.

He nodded, offering a small, sad smile. "How could I not? You're my favorite thing."

And just like that, the storm that had swelled between them cracked, making way for something warmer—something truly worth holding onto.

Then slowly, she lifted her uninjured hand toward his face. Fingers trembling. Asking nothing, offering everything.

He held it gently against his cheek, cradling it as if it were sacred.

The discharge papers crinkled as Noelle shoved them into her purse, unread. Scarlett and Violet had offered to bring her home. But Slade hadn't left her room in the last four days, and now he stepped forward with his keys in his hand and his voice soft.

"Noelle, I can take you. If you want."

She nodded, too tired to speak. They had a lot to figure out, but she was exhausted, and right now she just wanted some moments alone with him.

Her body ached. Her head throbbed. The thought of sitting in silence without him felt heavier than it should. The drive was quiet at first. Snow dusted the streets, the tires hissing softly over slush. Noelle leaned her head against the window, watching the world blur. Her scarf —the one Slade had given her—was wrapped around her shoulders, carrying the faint, warm scent of him.

As they pulled up to her place, his voice broke the quiet. Low, rough. "I'm so thankful you're finally out of the hospital and home where you belong. With me."

Her eyes fluttered open, "You and me both. It felt like forever."

He got out and went around to her side to open the door for her and ease her out. He still couldn't help but feel like she was about to break.

The door clicked shut behind them. Noelle leaned against the frame, breath hitching from the pain shooting through her ribcage. Maple was over at Scarlett's where she'd been staying since Noelle's accident.

"Easy. I got you."

His hands steadied her—one at her elbow, one hovering just beneath her ribs where the bruises bloomed. "Bed or couch?"

"Bed," she whispered.

He poured her a glass of water wanting to make sure she stayed hydrated and placed her pain meds on the nightstand. Then he added a soft hoodie of his—worn and warm—just in case.

Finally, as she settled in, he stood in the doorway, hesitating.

"Slade," she said.

He turned.

"Stay. Not because I'm hurt. Just because."

He crossed the room, climbed in beside her with care. The mattress dipped under his weight. His arm curled behind her like instinct, protective but tentative. She leaned in, head on his shoulder, hand resting over his heart. And for the first time in days, the ache in her body dulled beneath the steady rhythm of him beside her.

Chapter Twenty-Six

The first few mornings blurred together.

Pain, pills, sleep.

The soft sound of Slade moving through the apartment like he was afraid to wake her. He'd mostly learned where she kept everything—mugs, the extra blankets in the linen closet, her tea in the wrong canister. She never corrected him if he didn't get it right.

One afternoon, she had been taking a nap on the couch when a dream of the night she slipped on the black ice jolted her awake. She tried to stand too fast, trying to escape that moment, and Slade was there in a split second before she could fall.

"Slow down," he murmured, steadying her with one arm around her waist. "You've got nothing to prove."

She wanted to argue, but her body disagreed.

As another evening settled in around them, he helped her to the couch, wrapped her in a throw blanket that smelled faintly of his cologne. He handed her a steaming mug of something that was mostly honey and sympathy.

"I can make my own tea," she said, her voice rough.

"I know," he said. "You don't have to."

The TV flickered in the corner. Some mindless movie they both pretended to watch. When she shifted, pain flashed across her face. He noticed every time.

Later that night, she woke to find the lamp still on and Slade asleep in the chair beside her bed. His head tilted back, arms crossed, exhaustion softening the edges of him. A paperback sat open on his lap.

For a long moment, she just looked at him—the way his lashes rested against his cheek, the faint shadow of stubble along his jaw. He'd been through hell once before. She'd read about it in headlines and heard tidbits from Scarlett. Now he was living through a smaller version for her.

"Slade," she whispered.

He startled awake, eyes instantly alert. "You okay? Pain bad again? What can I get you?"

"No," she said quietly. "Just... didn't want you to wake up with a sore neck."

His mouth curved faintly. "You worry too much."

"You hover too much."

He grinned, and for a heartbeat it felt like old times. When he moved to adjust the blanket around her, his fingers brushed her wrist— an accident, maybe. The smallest touch, but something inside her steadied.

"You don't have to stay every night," she said, eyes on the ceiling.

"I know," he said again. "But I want to for as long as you'll let me."

The clock ticked on. She drifted back to sleep to the sound of him breathing beside her.

The world outside was half-thawed snow and salt lines on pavement. The kind of morning where the cold sank slow, steady, right into bone. Slade insisted on driving. He didn't ask—just showed up at her door with two coffees for the ride and that look that meant arguing would cost her more energy than it was worth.

She watched him over the rim of the cup as he scraped frost from the windshield. The movement tugged at something inside her—how easily he fit here again, like he'd never walked away.

The drive was quiet. The radio hummed something low and forgettable. His hand rested on the gearshift between them, and once, when he hit a red light, she caught his thumb tapping against the console in rhythm with her heartbeat.

At the clinic, a nurse called her name. Slade rose as she did, like her shadow.

"I can go in alone," she murmured.

"I know," he said, not moving but she didn't make him wait in the hall.

Dr. Patel, who was on duty in place of Callahan, smiled when he saw her. "You're healing beautifully, Noelle. No concussion symptoms, bruising's fading nicely. You'll be sore for a few more weeks, but you're out of the woods."

She nodded, half listening. Slade stood in the corner, arms crossed, pretending not to hang on every word. When the doctor left, she reached for her coat. Her wrist twinged. Before she could grab it, Slade was there, easing the sleeve up her arm, careful with the movement.

"I'm fine," she said.

"I know," he said softly. "Let me anyway."

Something in her chest fluttered—quiet, traitorous hope.

They walked back through the sterile hallway, the sound of their footsteps in sync. Outside, the air smelled faintly of melting snow and coffee. In the truck, she leaned her head against the window, exhaustion settling deep. He started the engine, heat sighing through the vents.

"Doc says you're healing fast," he said after a while. "Guess that means I'm out of a job."

She smiled, eyes still closed. "You were never good at sitting still."

"Maybe I finally found something worth slowing down for."

Her breath caught. She turned toward him, and for once, he didn't look away.

By the time the first weekend of February came, she could walk without wincing. "That was progress," Slade had said. He'd been saying that a lot lately—progress, not pressure.

He showed up at her door with a paper bag and a grin that didn't quite reach his eyes. "No hospital food. No takeout. Just me trying to cook for you."

She blinked at him. "Should I be worried?"

"Probably," he said with a chuckle, "I'll keep it simple."

The smell hit first—something buttery and warm. Grilled cheese and tomato soup, the kind of comfort that tasted like childhood and second chances. They ate on the couch, legs tucked close, the hockey game on. The buzz of the crowd filled the silences they hadn't learned how to fill yet.

When she laughed at one of his sarcastic mutters about the commentators, he froze for half a beat. Like the sound startled him. Then he smiled—real this time. After dinner, he reached for the remote. "Movie?"

"Dealer's choice."

He chose something old and predictable. Safe.

Halfway through, she noticed his arm stretched along the back of the couch, not quite touching her. Close enough that the air between them felt charged. Her fingers found the hem of his sleeve, just a brush.

He didn't move away.

She leaned into him, slow, testing. His arm came around her like it had always belonged there.

"I missed this," he said quietly.

She tilted her head back to look at him. "Which part?"

"All of it."

Outside, the streetlight flickered through the window. Inside, everything felt still.

When the credits rolled, neither of them moved. His thumb traced circles at her shoulder, and her pulse settled into something steady against him.

He shifted slightly, his voice almost lost in the sound of the heater. "You know, I was going to take you out tonight. A real date. But—"

"This is better," she said.

He smiled. "Yeah. It is."

Her head rested on his chest, the rise and fall of it a quiet kind of rhythm she hadn't realized she'd been missing.

The night had settled into a quiet comfort that was quickly feeling like second nature at this point. The warmth of the blankets wrapped around them like a cocoon on the couch while the light of the TV flickered between scenes. Noelle snuggled beside Slade, her body relaxed, her fingers absentmindedly tracing the ink sprawled across his skin.

Slade let out a slow breath, his muscles shifting slightly beneath her touch, but he didn't pull away.

Instead, he let her explore.

Her fingertips ran over the intricate lines of a faded script along his forearm, then trailed up to the bold edges of the tattoo on his bicep.

"You like doing that, huh?" Slade murmured, his voice husky with exhaustion.

Noelle huffed a small laugh, her fingers gliding along the curve of his shoulder. "It's weird, I guess. But it's... grounding."

Slade tilted his head, watching her, his chest rising and falling steadily beneath her cheek.

"It's not weird," he murmured. "Feels good."

Her movements slowed, running along the edge of ink near his collarbone, feeling the warmth of his skin beneath her touch.

Slade sighed, leaning back into the cushions, his arm draped loosely around her waist.

Noelle shifted slightly, settling her head against his chest, her fingers resting flat over the ink she had just traced.

"Can you tell me?" Slade asked.

Her breath caught at his request, the quiet plea buried in his gravel-rough voice.

"What do you want me to say?" she whispered, tilting her chin to look at him.

"That you're here with me—really here," he said. "That you forgive me and we're going to be okay again."

Something in his tone undid her. He wasn't demanding; he was confessing. Asking for something as fragile as her trust again. Her hand slid higher, tracing the strong line of his jaw. "I'm here, I don't want to be anywhere else." Then she added quietly, "And I do forgive you."

The way relief flickered through his eyes felt like a match struck in the dark. He kissed her then—slow at first, testing—but the dam had already cracked, and the hunger came rushing through.

She surprised herself by moving first, sliding onto his lap, knees bracketing his hips. The closeness stole her breath. His hands gripped her waist, steadying, anchoring, as he drank in the sight of her straddling him.

When his thumb brushed the edge of the bandage still hidden under her sleeve, he stopped. "Tell me if it hurts."

"It doesn't," she whispered. "Not when you touch me like that."

He exhaled shakily, forehead resting against hers. "I don't deserve you."

"Maybe not," she said. "But here we are."

"You are so beautiful, I never want to let you go," he rasped against her mouth, the words frayed at the edges, his restraint hanging by a thread.

"Then don't," she murmured, tugging at his shirt like she'd been waiting her whole life to say it.

He groaned softly, then shifted, guiding her down against the cushions as though she were something breakable he refused to drop. His mouth traced from her lips to her throat, each kiss leaving a trail of warmth that lit her nerves like tiny sparklers.

When he helped her pull her shirt over her head, she expected to feel exposed. Instead, she felt...seen. His gaze roamed her like he was memorizing her.

Heat rushed through her, but she didn't let him linger in his awe. She tugged him closer, skin to skin, her laughter breaking out when he nearly fumbled in his urgency. That laugh earned her a grin, boyish and unguarded, before he kissed her again—deep, claiming, desperate and tender all at once.

Every shift, every touch built like a song gathering momentum—her nails skimming his shoulders, his mouth brushing places she never thought could feel like promises. When he finally slid into her, she gasped, the world narrowing to the press of him, the rhythm they found together.

He pressed his forehead to hers, breath ragged. "Look at me," he whispered.

She did—and the intensity in his gaze stripped her bare. It wasn't just lust. It was grief and hope and love jumbled together, both of them daring to believe in something new.

Her release came sharp and unexpected, like the rush of cold air when a storm finally breaks. She clung to him, whispering his name, and a heartbeat later he followed, his body shuddering against hers.

For a long time they stayed tangled, catching their breath, hearts still racing in sync. His weight pressed her into the couch, grounding her in the best way. Sweat dampened her hairline, her thighs ached, and she wouldn't have moved for the world.

Slade's hand found hers, their fingers interlacing. He turned his head just enough to press a kiss to her temple. "You're not just grounding me, Noelle," he murmured, voice hoarse. "You're saving me."

Her chest tightened at the rawness of it. She kissed his jaw, smiling faintly against his skin. "Then I guess we're saving each other."

Neither of them spoke after that. They didn't need to. The hum of the city outside the window, the blanket sliding half off the couch, the rise and fall of his chest beneath her cheek—these were the words that mattered now.

The snow started again later that night—light and slow, each flake catching the glow from the lamppost outside her window.

They stood there for a while, quiet, watching the world blur white.

"It's peaceful," she said softly. "Like the world finally exhaled."

Slade's reflection hovered beside hers in the glass—broad shoulders, tired eyes, a man who looked like he'd been waiting a long time for the storm to pass.

"Feels like we're inside a snow globe," she added.

He smiled faintly. "And I'm looking forward to shaking it."

When she turned, he was already looking at her. The air between them felt fragile, like if either of them spoke too loudly, it might break. Her hand lifted, fingers brushing the line of his jaw. He caught her wrist before she could pull away, holding it just long enough for her to feel the warmth of his skin.

"Ready for round two already?" Noelle asked enticingly, lightly tracing her fingers along the waistband of his sweats.

He gripped her behind in response. "I can't help it. The need to be close to you and to make up for lost time is all I can think about.

"Slade." Her voice trembled, but it wasn't fear.

He searched her face, a playful grin on his face. "You're sure? You're not in pain?"

She nodded. "I've never been more sure of anything."

He hesitated, then leaned in. The first kiss was soft—barely pressure, a breath against her lips. The second found its rhythm, slow and aching. He kissed her like she was something he'd lost and somehow been given back.

His hands moved up her back, tracing the shape of her shoulder blade through the fabric of her shirt. She could feel the careful strength in him—the restraint, the reverence.

The kiss deepened, and she rose onto her toes, her hand sliding beneath the collar of his shirt. His skin was warm, solid. The heat of him grounded her, steady and real.

When he lifted her, she gasped—a sound caught somewhere between surprise and want—but he moved slowly, careful of her ribs, lowering her onto the bed like something breakable.

"Slade," she whispered again, as if saying his name could anchor her to this moment.

He brushed his thumb across her lower lip, eyes searching hers. "I've missed you."

"Then find me," she said.

He did—slowly, reverently, like a man relearning a language he thought he'd forgotten. Every touch was gentle, every breath measured. There was no rush, no firestorm—just heat that simmered like sunrise, patient and quiet.

When he finally sank down beside her, her hand found his, their fingers lacing. The world outside was nothing but snow and silence. He pressed his lips to her temple. "You okay?"

She smiled against his throat. "I think for the first time in a long time, I really am."

The room was dim, the air warm, their breathing the only thing that moved. Her head rested on his chest, his arm around her waist, thumb tracing slow circles against her hip.

"Feels like our snowglobe finally stopped shaking," she murmured, echoing their earlier conversation.

He laughed softly—one of those rare, unguarded sounds that felt like home. His reply came low and certain, a promise wrapped in quiet, "No other snowglobe I'd rather be in."

The SILVERWOOD SCOOP

Local Sports & Community News

Slade Fisher Steps Up After Scare

Samantha Romano, Silverwood Snipers' Media Correspondent

It seems trouble found *someone else* this time—but Silverwood's favorite left-wing was there to catch her.

Sources confirm Noelle Hayes was treated at Silverwood General earlier this week after a minor accident on icy roads. Witnesses say Slade Fisher hasn't left her side since, helping with appointments and keeping close watch during her recovery.

Friends say the pair have been "inseparable" lately, and after everything they've weathered, it looks like their story might be finding its stride again.

Looks like love's back on the scoreboard in Silverwood.

Chapter Twenty-Seven

The hotel room was beige, bland, and buzzing with a heater that coughed more than it warmed. Slade sat on the edge of the bed, gear bag tossed in the corner, his shoulders still aching from the game. Usually, he hated road trips for the sameness of them—the identical rooms, the recycled air, the way the walls closed in once the adrenaline drained out. Tonight, he hated them because Noelle wasn't here.

He picked up his phone before he could stop himself. The screen lit, and his thumb hovered over her name. He didn't even have to type first. Her message blinked across the screen, like she'd been waiting too.

NOELLE:

> Your team still alive, or did Garrett chirp you
> into an early grave?

He snorted under his breath.

SLADE:

> I'll chirp him into the boards tomorrow. Don't
> worry.

The dots appeared, paused, reappeared.

NOELLE:

Don't get suspended. I like you better on
the ice.

SLADE:

You like me better in your bed.

NOELLE:

Cocky.

SLADE:

True.

Her typing bubble disappeared, then came back. He leaned against the headboard, waiting, pulse tapping a little faster than it should.

NOELLE:

I like you better in both.

Slade swore softly, a grin tugging at his mouth before he could stop it. He wasn't a grinner. He didn't sit around smiling at his phone like some rookie with his first girlfriend. And yet here he was, staring at her words until the screen dimmed.

A knock sounded at the door. Garrett stuck his head in, smirk already in place. "Who's got you all soft, Fisher? I thought you were married to the game."

"Go to hell," Slade muttered, tossing a pillow at him.

Garrett ducked out, still laughing. "She's got you wrapped up, man. Don't fight it too hard."

Slade ignored him, jaw tight, but when he looked back at the screen, his chest eased.

SLADE:

> Get some sleep, Trouble. I'll text after the
> morning skate.

NOELLE:

> Only if you promise not to pout when I beat
> you at Wordle again.

SLADE:

> Never gonna happen.

NOELLE:

> Sweet dreams, Hockey Star.

The room went quiet again, but it didn't feel so empty this time. He fell asleep with the phone still in his hand.

Chapter Twenty-Eight

Winter had melted into springtime and warmed into summer. The weather was too gorgeous not to take advantage of so Slade and Noelle decided a date in the sunshine was in order.

Silverwood Lake lay smooth and reflective around them, tall pines and wildflowers framing the water like something out of a postcard. The town had recommended the canoe rental as a *romantic must-do*, and so far it had delivered—sunlight dancing across the surface, the distant sound of loons. The canoe rental guy had smiled at them in a way that suggested he already knew how this was going to end.

Slade didn't notice. He was too busy tightening the straps on his life vest like he was preparing for a minor expedition. Noelle watched him from the dock, arms folded, sunlight catching in her hair.

"You know," she said, "most people just... put those on."

Slade glanced up. "I *am* putting it on."

"You've adjusted it three times."

"Fourth time's the charm."

She laughed and stepped into the canoe once he held it steady, the wood warm beneath her hands. The water was glassy and calm with surrounding evergreens that leaned toward the water like quiet onlookers. It was the kind of place that felt untouched, as if it had been waiting for afternoons exactly like this.

They pushed off, and for a moment, everything really was perfect.

The canoe cut gently through the water. Slade paddled with enthusiasm if not precision, and Noelle matched his rhythm, watching the ripples fan out behind them.

"This is nice," she said.

"Told you," Slade replied, pleased. "Romantic. Scenic. Zero chance of disaster."

She tilted her head. "Hey now, be careful with what you say or you'll jinx us."

He grinned. "Have a little faith."

They drifted farther from shore, passing a pair of ducks that eyed them curiously. Noelle dipped her paddle into the water and felt the cool resistance travel up her arms.

By the time they were in the middle of the lake, Noelle knew two things for certain: First, the lake was much colder than it looked. Second, trusting Slade's steering skills had been a mistake.

"Just relax," Slade said, dipping the paddle into the water with confidence that absolutely did not match his experience. "It's all about balance."

Noelle raised an eyebrow. "You say that like we're not wobbling."

They were, in fact, wobbling, but Slade sitting across from her with that familiar half-smile that always made her feel settled and bright all at once was distracting.

Then the canoe tipped.

It wasn't dramatic. No crashing waves, no shouting. Just a slow, inevitable lean, followed by a shared moment of realization.

"Oh no," Noelle said.

"Oh no," Slade echoed.

They hit the water with a splash and a burst of laughter, the cold shocking enough to steal Noelle's breath before she started laughing so hard she had to grab the side of the canoe to steady herself.

"I *told* you," she gasped.

Slade had surfaced beside her, hair plastered to his forehead, grinning unapologetically. "Okay, maybe I underestimated the balance part."

They dragged themselves back to the dock, soaked and shivering, laughing the entire time. Slade offered his towel, and Noelle accepted, bumping her shoulder into his as they attempted to dry off.

Moments like this had become easy with them again.

That was the surprising part—not the spark; that had been there from the start, but the comfort that followed. The way being together felt natural, like Silverwood itself had quietly made room for them.

They sat side by side on the dock, shoes off, legs dangling over the edge as the sun worked to warm them again. The lake had already returned to stillness, as if nothing unusual had happened at all.

They talked about other dates as they watched the lake: the afternoon they spent wandering Main Street with coffee in hand, sharing a blueberry scone from the bakery; the night at the old drive-in just outside town where they'd watched a grainy black-and-white movie and laughed more than they paid attention; the Saturday mornings at the farmers market where Slade insisted on buying honey "from the *best* beekeeper," as if Noelle hadn't already noticed he did that every time; watching the Fourth of July firework show then heading home to create fireworks of their own behind closed doors.

And then there were the quiet nights.

Takeout spread across the coffee table. Shoes kicked off by the door. Noelle curled around Slade on the couch with a rerun of some show that they were too busy with each other to watch. Sometimes they talked until midnight. Sometimes they didn't talk at all. Both felt equally right.

As the sun dipped lower over the lake, Slade glanced at her. "I still say this counts as romantic."

"It does," Noelle agreed. "But next time, I'm steering."

He nodded solemnly. "I accept my demotion."

Silverwood stayed calm around them and for the first time in a long while, both of them felt certain—not just about this moment, but about all the ordinary, wonderful ones still waiting ahead.

Chapter Twenty-Nine

The months folded in on themselves—slow mornings, shared meals, soft laughter. Hockey season roared back to life around them, but inside the small, careful world they'd built, everything else fell quiet. It felt like they'd barely blinked before winter found them once more.

Noelle woke to Slade's arm warm and heavy around her waist, the room still dark, the snow outside turning the morning blue. For a moment, she forgot what day it was. Forgot the ache that had lingered from last year—how her birthday had come only days after he'd walked away, how she'd told herself she didn't care while something inside her cracked anyway.

"Hey," he murmured, voice rough with sleep. "Happy birthday."

Her breath caught. Not because of the words—but because he said them like they mattered.

"You remembered," she said softly.

"Impossible to forget," he replied, tightening his arm just slightly, like a promise.

He shifted, reaching for the nightstand. "I've got something for you."

She pushed herself up on one elbow, watching as he handed her a small box—plain, unwrapped, like it hadn't needed dressing up to mean something. Inside was a delicate silver necklace, a thin chain with a tiny charm at its center: a simple snowflake, understated and bright.

"I know it's not much," he said quietly. "But you love winter. And you love finding beauty in the quiet parts."

Her throat tightened as she lifted it from the box. "Slade..."

"I wanted you to have something that stayed close," he added. "Something that didn't disappear when the season changed."

Maple gave a little bark that seemed to be a nod of approval to the gift. Noelle didn't trust herself to speak though. She just leaned forward and kissed him—slow, unhurried, the kind of kiss that said *thank you* and *I'm still here* all at once.

He fastened the clasp for her, fingers brushing the nape of her neck. She rested her forehead against his shoulder, breathing him in.

No candles. No wishes spoken out loud. Just the quiet certainty of being chosen.

It wasn't a celebration anyone else would notice.

But it was the first birthday in a long time that didn't hurt.

That night back at Slade's, the tree in the living room leaned a little to the left. He had been fighting it for ten minutes.

"Maybe it's the floor," he muttered.

"It's the tree," Noelle said from the couch, wrapped in a blanket, the faintest smile tugging at her mouth.

He gave it one more shove. The stand creaked. The tree tilted the other way. He sighed. "I think it's mocking me."

"That makes two of us."

He glanced over. Her hair was damp from her shower, her sweatshirt one of his. The sight softened him in ways he couldn't name.

They worked in near silence, the air filled with the whisper of pine and the faint crackle of the radio. Mismatched ornaments—her old ones mixed with a few he'd grabbed at the corner store—clinked against one another. Near the bottom of the box, he found one he didn't recognize. Blue glass. Hand-painted. The kind Jessica used to love.

His breath caught.

The ornament slipped before he realized his hand was shaking. The sound when it hit the floor was small but sharp. It echoed longer than it should have.

He crouched, gathering the shards, the edges cold and biting against his fingertips. "I didn't—" his voice cracked, the words collapsing halfway out.

"Hey," Noelle said softly, kneeling beside him. "It's okay."

He shook his head. "It was... hers."

She studied the fragments in his hand. Her voice stayed quiet. "Then maybe it's time to let a little light through the cracks."

He let out a breath that sounded like surrender and dropped the pieces into her palm. She carried them to the trash, came back with a new strand of lights, and plugged them in.

The room filled with gold.

They stood together, watching the glow shift across the ornaments. The broken spot on the floor glittered faintly in the light.

"Better?" she asked.

"Yeah," he said. His voice was rough, but steady.

Not fixed. Not healed. But quieter.

When she brushed past him to straighten a ribbon, his hand closed around hers—unthinking, instinctive. He didn't say anything. Neither did she. She just stayed.

Later, they sat on the floor, backs against the couch, mugs of cocoa cooling between them. The tree glowed softly behind their shoulders, steady and warm.

Slade didn't talk about the holiday. He didn't have to.

He just let her rest against him. Let the lights stay on. Let the moment exist without bracing for what came next.

Outside, snow started again—slow, deliberate, blanketing the world in something clean for the night.

The world outside was white and still—the kind of silence that only came after snow.

Noelle woke first. The room smelled faintly of pine and cinnamon from the candle they'd forgotten to blow out. The lights on the tree still glowed, soft and steady in the dim morning. Slade lay beside her, one arm slung across the blankets, hair falling into his eyes. For a long moment she just watched him. Without the tension in his jaw, he looked younger. Lighter.

When she shifted, the mattress dipped and his eyes opened.

For a moment, he just looked at her—like he was orienting himself to the world again.

"Merry Christmas," she whispered.

He didn't flinch.

Didn't joke. Didn't deflect.

He exhaled slowly, then said, almost to himself, "I don't hate this one."

Her chest tightened.

She smiled, reached out, and brushed her thumb along his wrist. "Good. Then stay right here."

He nodded, already doing exactly that.

She slipped out of bed and tugged on one of his sweatshirts, the fabric hanging long and familiar. "Coffee first, I'll be right back," she said.

He watched her go, the tree lights from the living room reflecting in his eyes.

For the first time in years, he let them.

Noelle entered the cold kitchen, the tiles biting against her bare feet. She turned on the stove and reached for the pancake mix. He appeared in the doorway as she poured batter onto the griddle, watching like he wasn't sure whether to help or let her.

"That smoke alarm's gonna file for overtime," he said.

She glanced back. "Merry Christmas to you too."

He grinned, came up behind her, and took the spatula from her hand. "Here. Before you burn the next one."

His arm brushed hers as he flipped the pancake. The smell of butter and coffee filled the space between them. In that moment, everything felt startlingly ordinary.

They ate standing at the counter, shoulder to shoulder, their chewing the only sound. The quiet felt different this morning—lighter somehow. He caught her looking at him once, and she didn't look away.

Afterward, he stepped out to take a call. Through the window, she saw him standing in the snow, phone pressed to his ear, head bowed. His voice was low, threaded with something between sorrow and relief. When he came back in, snow clung to his hair and the cuffs of his sleeves.

"Everything okay?" she asked.

He nodded slowly. "Stryker. Just wanted to check in. He asked how I was doing this year."

"And?"

He looked toward the tree, where the lights blinked lazily across the room. "Told him it still hurts. Just not the same way anymore."

She reached out, curling her fingers around his. "That's still healing," she said. "It just hurts differently after a while."

He studied her hand in his, as if the idea needed time to settle. "You make it sound easy."

"No, I know it's not," she said. "Just saying it's worth it."

They sat together by the tree as the light shifted across the floor, gold creeping into gray. His thumb traced small, absent circles against her wrist. When she leaned into him, his breath hitched, barely audible.

He tilted his head toward her, and she met him halfway. The kiss was soft at first, cautious, but deepened slowly until it felt like something loosening inside her.

Her hand found the hem of his shirt. His palm slid against her jaw, thumb brushing the edge of her mouth. Everything between them felt slow and deliberate, as if they were relearning each other through touch and silence.

He hesitated when her breath caught, pulling back just enough to search her face.

"You okay?"

She nodded. "You don't have to stop."

When he kissed her again, it wasn't apology or desperation—it was warmth. Real warmth. The kind that steadied her pulse until the world felt still again.

Later, they lay tangled in the sheets, the glow of the tree spilling across the room. Her cheek rested against his chest, his heartbeat slow beneath her ear. Snow drifted outside the window, soft and endless. Inside, the lights flickered warm against the dark.

By the last week of December, the snow had turned to slush and back again. Silverwood was gray and half-frozen, same as always, but this time the gray didn't get under her skin.

The arena, though, was alive.

December home games always were. The stands were packed despite the cold, scarves and knit hats everywhere, the air buzzing with the promise of tradition. Slade had never stopped skating. Even after the accident, even when everything between them had splintered, he'd kept to the rink—early mornings, long drills, endless laps. But lately it felt different. Less like running from something. More like coming home.

The puck dropped.

Slade took the pass at the blue line and drove hard toward the net, muscle memory taking over once more. The shot came clean off his stick —sharp, precise—and buried itself behind the goalie before the crowd could even inhale.

The red light flashed.

Cheers roared, horns blared—and suddenly, the air filled with color.

Teddy bears rained down from the stands. Hundreds of them. Plush and lopsided and joyful, tumbling onto the ice in a blur of fur and stuffing. The annual Teddy Bear Toss, unleashed after the first goal, a tradition meant for kids who needed something soft to hold onto.

Slade stood frozen near the crease, breath coming hard as bears bounced at his skates. He laughed, lifting his helmet as one clipped his shoulder.

And then he looked up again.

Noelle was on her feet, clutching a teddy bear to her chest—one she must have brought with her—hesitating only a second before throwing it onto the ice. It landed closer to him than any of the others.

Their eyes met.

The noise faded to a dull roar. The world narrowed to that small moment—her smile tremulous but real, his heart pounding so hard it hurt. He pressed a fist briefly to his chest, a silent acknowledgment, before his teammates crashed into him in celebration.

As the ice crew began collecting the bears, Slade skated toward the bench, adrenaline humming through him—but something else burned beneath it now.

Hope.

Impossible to ignore.

Later, Noelle sat in the bleachers with a thermos of coffee, wrapped in his scarf, watching him move. He was precise as ever, his stride clean, each pass cutting smooth lines into the ice. When he looked up and spotted her, the edge in his focus softened.

He skated over during a stoppage, tugging off his gloves. "How'd I do?"

"Graceful as ever," she said, smiling into her cup.

"That bad?"

"Only a little."

He dropped onto the bench beside her, stealing the thermos from her hands. "You realize this is cheating—me skating, you sitting there with hot chocolate."

"I'm in recovery," she said.

"So am I."

Their eyes met; the silence between them didn't need translating.

When they left the rink, sunlight spilled pale and thin over the snow. They stopped at the grocery store, his hat pulled low, her hand looped through his arm. A few people recognized him—quick nods, quiet smiles—but he didn't flinch. When someone called his name, he only reached for her hand and kept walking.

Back at her place, they unpacked the bags side by side. She lined up the soup cans; he stole a grape and earned a swat for it. The rhythm between them felt easy again—half work, half something gentler.

He checked his phone, thumb hesitating on the screen. She caught the look. "Everything okay?"

He turned the phone so she could see—a photo of him and Jessica, medals around their necks, snow falling behind them.

"Sorry, this Facebook memory notification just popped up. Christmas tournament," he said quietly. "Feels like another lifetime."

"You don't have to hide that from me."

"I'm not. I just forget sometimes that it's allowed to hurt and still be okay."

She stepped closer, hand resting over his chest. "You're allowed both."

He looked at her then, eyes tired but open. "Yeah," he said. "Guess I am. Thanks."

He kissed her, slow and certain, the taste of hot chocolate between them. When he pulled back, she smiled. "Hey, you should teach me to skate."

"Pretty sure that's a terrible idea."

"Maybe. But I still want to try."

They bundled up and walked to the frozen pond behind her building, their breath coming out in white clouds. The ice glimmered under the weak sun, smooth and unbroken.

"I've never skated in my life," she admitted as he laced up.

"Lucky for you," he said, offering his hands, "I've got experience keeping people upright."

"Cocky."

"Confident."

Her laugh echoed across the quiet pond. He guided her carefully, slow steps, hands steady at her waist. She wobbled, cursed, and he laughed so hard he nearly lost his balance too. When she stumbled again, he caught her before she fell, arms around her, breath warm against her hair.

"See?" he said. "You catch me, I catch you."

"That's the deal?"

"Always will be."

They stayed out until the cold bit through their gloves and the stars began to shine, faint against the pale sky. When they finally made it home, they collapsed onto the couch, still laughing. Her hands were freezing; he caught them in his and rubbed warmth back into her skin.

"You smell like snow," she murmured.

He smiled against her hair. "Guess that's better than sweat."

He leaned back, eyes half-lidded, the grin fading to something softer. "This feels like —."

"What?"

"Normal. Good. I don't know."

She brushed her thumb over the scar on his hand. "Then maybe that's what this year's been for."

He turned his hand, catching hers. "Or starting fresh."

She shifted closer, knees touching. His gaze found hers, steady now. When he kissed her, it was just connection, clean and quiet. Outside, the last days of the year were fading into dark, and for once, neither of them minded.

Snow drifted beyond the window, soft as ash under the streetlights. The apartment glowed in candlelight, cinnamon curling through the air, the quiet thrum of the heater the only sound between them.

Noelle watched from the window while Slade opened the champagne. He didn't rush it. He never did anything halfway. The cork gave a low pop, the sound swallowed by snow.

"You sure you don't want to go out?" she asked, her reflection faint in the glass.

He set the bottle down and crossed the room to her, sleeves pushed up, a crooked smile on his mouth. "I'd rather stay in. Fewer people to steal my date."

"You just hate crowds."

"I hate bad music." He paused, voice softening. "And I like you better when it's quiet."

His reflection moved behind hers—broad shoulders, warm breath brushing her neck. The heat of him was a counterpoint to the cold seeping through the windowpane.

"New year, new us?" she said, half-teasing.

"Same us," he murmured. "Just... not broken anymore."

When she turned, his hand found her jaw, thumb tracing the corner of her mouth. The first kiss landed like a promise—slow, deliberate, the kind that made everything else in the room go still. Her hands slid up his chest, catching in the fabric of his shirt, pulling until he followed her back a step, then another.

He tasted like champagne and winter. When she rose onto her toes, he scooped her up, one arm beneath her thighs, the other steady at her spine. She gasped, startled, then laughed against his mouth.

"Easy?" he asked, his voice rough.

"Easy is no fun," she whispered, breathing against his ear.

That unstrung him. His laugh broke apart against her skin, and then his mouth was at her throat, tracing heat down to her collarbone, leaving small, careful marks that still felt like claiming.

He set her down on the couch, the cushions dipping under their weight. The world outside blurred to silence. His hands moved with slow certainty, finding skin, learning her all over again. She caught his face in her palms, fingers trembling not from pain now but from wanting.

Every touch deepened. His breath hitched once when she tugged him closer; she answered with a sound that belonged to neither of them alone. It was all rhythm and trust, a slow-burn tempo that climbed higher with each heartbeat.

There was nothing tentative anymore. Only warmth, breath, the slide of skin against skin, and the quiet hum in her chest that said *this is what it feels like to be alive again.*

When the world finally broke open around them, it wasn't fireworks or music—just the raw pulse of shared breath, a single exhale that carried them both.

Later, she lay draped across him, skin flushed, heartbeat still tripping against his ribs. Outside, the first bursts of the new year shimmered faintly through the snow-soft glass.

"Happy New Year," he murmured into her hair.

She smiled, eyes closing. "It really is."

Chapter Thirty

The puck flew across the ice, a blur of black against the surface of the ice. Slade's focus was razor-sharp as he chased it down. He barely had time to register the player from the other team closing in on him before it was too late.

A shoulder slammed into his ribs with bone-jarring force, knocking the air from his lungs. The collision sent him sprawling, his body twisting mid-air before crashing down hard onto the ice. His helmet flew off, skidding across the rink as his momentum carried him straight into the unforgiving metal of the goalpost.

The sound was sickening—a hollow, echoing thud that silenced the roaring crowd.

Pain exploded through his shoulder, sharp and searing, radiating down his arm and into his chest. His head snapped back, the world tilting violently as stars burst behind his eyes.

For a moment, everything was a blur. The lights above seemed too bright, the noise of the arena muffled and distant. Slade tried to move, but his body felt heavy and unresponsive.

"Slade!" Stryker's voice cut through the haze, sharp and panicked.

Slade blinked, his vision swimming as his brother's face came into focus.

"Slade, can you hear me?" Stryker asked, gripping Slade's arm tightly.

Slade's lips moved, but the words came out slurred, barely audible. "N-Noelle..."

Stryker's jaw clenched, his eyes darting to the medical team rushing toward them. "Stay with me, man. Don't you dare check out on me."

"Stryk..." He tried again, but his voice cracked, the weight of exhaustion pressing down on him. "She... She has to know..."

Stryker tightened his grip on Slade's hand, his jaw clenched with barely restrained fear. "I'll call her, okay? I promise."

Slade's head lolled to the side, his vision darkening at the edges. The pain was overwhelming, a relentless wave that threatened to pull him under.

Stryker swore under his breath, his heart pounding as the medics worked on his twin.

He dashed over to the bench and pulled out his phone with shaking hands. He hit Noelle's contact, raising the phone to his ear. He knew no one would dare fine him for breaking the no phones rule at a time like this.

Noelle sat frozen on the couch, her eyes glued to the TV screen as the replay of the collision played again. The sound of the impact made her stomach churn, her heart pounding so hard it felt like it might burst.

"No, no, no," she whispered, her hand flying to her mouth, her breath hitching as she watched Slade crumple against the goalpost.

She shook Scarlett awake who had come over to watch the game but dozed off on the couch after a long shift at work. Noelle's voice was trembling, "Scarlett, wake up! Something's happened to Slade."

Scarlett blinked groggily, sitting up as alarm spread across her face. "What? What happened?"

Noelle pointed at the screen, her voice breaking in a sob, "He got hit... he's not moving."

"I'm calling Stryker," Scarlett said, becoming more alert and grabbing her phone off the coffee table as they watched the game coverage.

Before she could hit Stryker's contact, Noelle's phone rang. She grabbed it and saw Stryker's name flash on the screen.

Her fingers trembled as she answered and put it on speaker phone. "Stryker? What's happening? Is Slade okay?"

Stryker's voice was steady, but the worry behind it was unmistakable. "Hey. He got hit hard. He's probably got a concussion at the very least, but it looks like he's going to be okay. The medical team is with him in the locker room now."

Noelle's knees buckled, and she sank onto the couch, her chest tight with relief and fear. "Thank God. I—I was so scared. I saw it happen live."

"I know," Stryker said, his voice softening. "It looked bad. But they're getting ready to take him to the hospital to check him over just to be safe. Your name was the first thing he said right after the hit."

Was I really the only thing he was thinking about during such a scary and painful moment? Noelle wondered. She felt like she finally understood that they had become the most important people to each other—and through the fear, that thought kept her floating.

Scarlett sat beside her, her face pale, her hands gripping the blanket tightly. She launched into questioning Stryker. "Stryk, what are they saying? Is he going to be okay? I wish I was there. Who was that player? Did he get penalized?"

"Scarlett, hang on," Stryker said, his voice sharp. "I'll answer all of your questions, but right now, I am going to go with Slade to the hospital and make sure he is okay. I am driving his truck, I will keep you guys updated, or we will just come there after. Just relax."

Scarlett and Noelle decided to use the spare key to wait at Slade's apartment until Stryker could get him home after the doctors looked him over. What felt like a lifetime later but was really only a few hours, the front door creaked open, and Noelle's heart skipped a beat as she saw Slade and Stryker walk in. Looking exhausted with a bandage wrapped around his head and arm in a sling, Slade managed a weak smile as he inhaled the familiar, comforting aroma.

Stryker was holding Slade's hockey bag. "Willow was on shift. She glued our little man back together and only threatened to charge us extra for emotional damages," he said teasingly.

Scarlett crossed the room immediately, her eyes scanning Slade from head to toe. "You're not allowed to scare us like that," she said, voice tight but steady. "Next time, maybe just score a goal instead of sacrificing your skull."

Slade huffed out a breath that might've been a laugh. "I'll keep that in mind."

Noelle rushed forward before anything else could be said, unshed tears glistening in her eyes. Her lips trembled, caught between a smile and a sob; as she approached him, Slade opened his arms and pulled her in. Before he could say anything, she wrapped her arms around him, holding him tightly, her face buried against his chest as she breathed him in. The familiar scent of ice and sweat clinging to his jersey filled her senses. The cold, sharp smell of the rink, mixed with the warmth of his body, grounded her in the reality that he was home and safe—feeling the rhythm of his heart beating.

Slade exhaled, the weight of the past few hours sinking into him, but the warmth of her—the way she clung to him—made it all a little easier to carry.

"You scared me," she whispered, voice shaking. "I saw it happen, and then you weren't moving."

Slade rested his chin against the top of her head, his good arm tightening around her. "I'm okay."

"Easy, brother. That was quite a hit." Stryker said as he set down Slade's hockey bag.

Scarlett lingered a moment longer, watching them—Noelle wrapped around Slade, Slade holding her like he needed her just as much. Then she cleared her throat. "I'm going to make some tea," she said. "And then Stryker and I will disappear before you two start pretending we're not here."

Stryker nodded. "Doctor's orders. Rest. Hydrate. No heroic nonsense."

Slade gave a tired smile. "Thanks for getting me home."

"Always," Stryker said.

Noelle cupped his face in her hands, her eyes searching his. "I'm so sorry I wasn't there. I should have been there," she whispered, tears spilling over.

Slade pulled her close, resting his forehead against hers. "It's okay, Noelle. You're here now, and that's all that matters," he said, his voice filled with love and reassurance.

Noelle sniffled, trying to hold back more tears. "I was so scared, Slade. Seeing you like that... I felt so helpless.

Slade kissed her forehead gently. "I know, babe. But I'm okay. Just a little banged up. You being here means everything to me."

Local Sports & Community News

Slade Fisher Injured During Snipers Game
Samantha Romano, Silverwood Snipers' Media Correspondent

Silverwood fans were left stunned Friday night when forward Slade Fisher went down hard after a mid-ice collision in the third period of the Snipers' matchup against the Portland Breakers.

Fisher struck the goalpost before collapsing on the ice, motionless for several tense moments as the arena fell silent. Medical staff rushed to assist, and he was eventually helped to his feet and escorted to the locker room amid a standing ovation from the crowd.

Team representatives confirmed shortly after the game that Fisher was evaluated for a possible concussion and other minor injuries. "He's alert and in good hands," a spokesperson said, declining further comment.

The Snipers have not yet announced whether Fisher will miss any upcoming games, though insiders suggest he'll undergo standard league concussion protocol before returning to play.

No penalty was issued for the hit, a call that's already sparking heated debate among fans online.

For now, Silverwood waits—and hopes—to see its favorite left wing back on the ice soon.

Stay with *The Scoop* for updates on Fisher's condition and the Snipers' next game.

Chapter Thirty-One

The next day, the apartment was filled with voices—concerned, familiar, loving.

Slade barely had the energy to respond.

Stryker was in and out of the room, making sure he had everything he needed but hovering like he was afraid to leave for too long.

"Dude, you scared the hell out of us," Hunter said, arms crossed, trying for casual but falling short.

"You hit the post like it owed you money," Miguel added, smirking, but there was tension behind it.

Slade gave a tired huff, shifting against the pillows. "I'll send it a bill later."

Scarlett sat at the foot of the bed, arms wrapped around her knees. "Are you actually okay?" she asked, quieter than the others.

Slade sighed. "Yeah. Just tired."

And then, it was Noelle.

Just her.

Finally.

She moved closer, sitting gently beside him, and the tension in his body eased instantly.

"You've had a lot of visitors," she murmured.

"Yeah." Slade blinked heavily, his voice softer now. "But I was waiting for you."

Noelle swallowed, her fingers brushing over the blanket absently. "I'm here." His hand found hers, slow, clumsy, but warm.

"Stay, please... stay," he mumbled, his voice thick with drowsiness. "I want you close."

Noelle swallowed, her heart giving a strange little lurch at the words.

"You should rest," she murmured, though she made no move to leave.

"I know," he said, barely audible, his grip tightening slightly. "But if you're here, it's easier to do that." So she stayed, just relieved to be at his side.

He slept for most of the afternoon. When he opened his eyes again, Noelle was still there, curled up in the chair beside the bed. A book lay face-down on her knee, her hair coming loose in soft waves around her face.

"You're still here," he said, voice rough.

"You asked me to be."

He smiled a little, tired. "Guess I did."

She leaned forward, checked his pupils the way Willow had shown her. "Still hurting?"

"Feels like someone's playing drums in my skull," he muttered.

"Then no lights. No screens. Just quiet."

"You always this bossy?"

"Only when it keeps you alive," she said, setting the book aside.

He shut his eyes again, half-smiling. The room smelled faintly like her shampoo and the lemon soup she'd reheated earlier. It was the first thing that had felt normal since the hit.

The next few days blurred. She kept him fed and mostly horizontal, reading to him when he got restless, checking in with the team's doctor, keeping his phone out of reach.

He tried to argue once about coffee. That ended with her handing him tea and a look that didn't need words.

"You're cruel," he said.

"You'll live."

"Barely."

"Good. Then my job's done."

He drank the tea. Complained about it. Drank it anyway.

By the end of the week, the headache had eased to a dull throb. The world didn't tilt when he stood. The bruises were starting to fade. But the boredom hit harder than the concussion ever did.

He decided to clean. Or at least, that was the lie he told himself when he went for the broom.

It wasn't heavy, but the reach was bad. His shoulder pulled, sharp and fast, heat flaring under the old scar. He swore, froze, waited for it to fade.

By the time Noelle came back from a grocery run, he was pretending everything was fine and doing a terrible job of it.

"What did you do?" she asked immediately.

"Nothing."

"Slade."

"It's fine," he said, but his arm was hanging too stiffly at his side.

She crossed the room, took one look at the tension in his jaw, and sighed. "Sit."

"I'm—"

"Sit."

He did.

She checked the shoulder he'd bruised, the old injury damaged again with the impact, fingers careful and cool. "You definitely irritated it. You need ice. Have you set up that PT appointment with Talulla yet?"

"Nah, it's getting better everyday. I don't need to bug my cousin about this." Slade responded as nonchalantly as he could.

"That's not going to fly, mister. You needed to set that up with her like yesterday, there's a reason she's the Snipers' physical therapist. Now stop acting like you're indestructible."

He winced. "You sure? Because I was going for heroic."

"You're not allowed to be heroic. You're benched." She left for the freezer, came back with an ice pack. "Next time you wait for me."

"Bossy," he said again, quieter this time.

"Accurate," she said, wrapping the sling back around his arm. "And keeping you alive. Which is the goal."

He looked at her—at the crease between her brows, the focus in her face—and felt something in his chest loosen. "Okay fine, I'll call Talulla in the morning. You ever stop worrying?"

"Nope." She pressed the ice against his shoulder, softer now. "You make it too easy."

A storm came that weekend, the kind that buried cars and turned the city into quiet white. The team texted to check in; Scarlett threatened to come over with board games. They took the excuse of the storm to stay in alone.

They watched bad TV with the sound low and the captions on. He dozed off with her hand on his chest. She read while the wind knocked the windows, glancing over every so often like she couldn't quite believe he was real.

By the second week, his shoulder still protested if he pushed it, but the pain had dulled to a grumble.

Noelle started bringing over more of her things—an extra hoodie, her favorite mug, that stupid cherry lip balm she thought he didn't notice her using. She was just... there. A quiet constant.

He didn't say it out loud, but he liked the way her voice sounded in his apartment. Like the place had finally remembered what warmth was supposed to feel like.

By the time Valentine's week rolled around, he was done being patient. The doctor had cleared him for light training and warned him about doing anything "stupid." Which, of course, was the first thing on his list.

He wanted to do something for her. Something normal. So he made dinner.

It wasn't much—pasta, garlic bread, salad. He set the table, found a runner Scarlett had bullied him into buying, and even dug a crumpled pack of candles out of a drawer. The flowers on the counter were a haphazard jumble, but he'd tried.

When Noelle knocked, he opened the door with a huge smile, "Happy Valentine's Day, my love!"

She stepped inside, cheeks pink from the cold, eyes going wide at the sight of the table. "You did all this?"

"Don't sound so surprised," he said, grinning. "I can read directions."

She laughed softly. "You shouldn't have."

"I wanted to, you've done so much for me these last couple weeks."

Her smile faded just a little at that, replaced by something quieter. She brushed her fingers over his arm, careful near the shoulder. "You look better."

"Getting there."

They ate, trading stories between bites. She told him about work, about her and Scarlett's plans for a girl's night that weekend, about how weird it felt to go home to an empty apartment now that she and Maple spent most nights here. He listened, and every so often, she caught him watching her like he was memorizing the shape of the moment.

After dinner, he leaned back, rubbing his thumb over the rim of his glass. "You know, other than my hiatus in North Carolina, this is the longest I've gone without skating since I was twelve."

"Should I be worried you're about to use me as a stand-in?"

He smiled. "You'd be better at it than half the guys I've played with."

She rolled her eyes, but the color in her cheeks gave her away. "Smooth."

"Effective?"

"Maybe."

He reached for her hand, slow enough to give her room to pull back. She didn't.

The space between them got smaller without either of them deciding it should. One heartbeat, and her hand was on his jaw, thumb brushing the corner of his mouth.

"Your head okay?" she asked quietly.

"Clear."

"Shoulder?"

"Manageable."

She studied him a second longer. Then, "Okay."

The kiss started soft—testing, cautious—but deepened quickly and wasn't careful for long. It felt like something they'd both been circling for weeks without realizing how close they already were.

When they finally broke apart, both of them were breathing unevenly.

"You should probably sit down before you fall over," she said.

He grinned. "I'm fine."

"You're full of bad ideas."

"Always," he said, and kissed her again.

Later, the room was quiet except for the radiator clicking on again. Noelle lay half-asleep against him, her head tucked under his chin, one arm draped across his chest, Maple snoring at their feet.

He ran his thumb over her wrist, tracing the pulse there. "You're still here," he said, a little dazed.

She smiled without opening her eyes. "You keep asking like I might leave."

"Habit."

"Break it," she murmured, settling closer.

He watched the snow slide off the ledge outside, the streetlight catching the melt. For the first time since the hit, his head didn't ache. His shoulder hurt in the background, sure, but the rest of him felt lighter—like the noise in his life had finally gone quiet enough to hear himself think.

"Hey," she said, half asleep.

"Yeah?"

"Next time you try to reach the top shelf, I'm tackling you."

He laughed, pressing a kiss to her hair. "Deal."

Chapter Thirty-Two

The next few weeks slid by in a calm daze as Slade returned to normal while the hockey season came to an end. Easter came and went, the streets of Silverwood still jeweled with frost. Noelle had insisted on getting out of the house—"fresh air cures everything," she'd said—so Scarlett let her drag her downtown for some girl time.

They wandered through the small boutiques, their reflections fractured in the frosted glass displays. Scarlett talked nonstop—wedding rumors, team gossip that Samantha got from Miguel, Hunter, the bakery adding peppermint mochas year-round—while Noelle smiled and pretended to keep up. But her smile didn't quite reach her eyes.

Inside the bookstore, she paused too long under the soft lights, pressing her fingers to her temple.

"You okay?" Scarlett asked, frowning.

"Yeah, just—" Noelle's voice wavered. "Just a headache. Probably the lights."

Scarlett handed her a bottle of water from her bag, mothering as usual. "You sure? You look kind of pale."

"I'm fine," Noelle said, though she wasn't. The edges of her vision shimmered and her stomach turned. She blinked, hoping it would pass.

But when she straightened, the shelves seemed to tilt, and Scarlett's voice came from far away.

The next thing she knew, the cold air outside hit her face. Scarlett was holding her upright, panic written all over her.

"Whoa, hey. Don't scare me like that. Sit—sit down. You nearly passed out."

"I told you," Noelle murmured weakly. "Just a migraine."

"Just a migraine," Scarlett repeated, unimpressed. "You're calling Slade. He's going to be worried if you don't."

Noelle groaned, shielding her eyes from the pale afternoon sun. "Please don't tell him. It's not a big deal."

Scarlett gave her a look that said *oh, it's a big deal.*

Slade tapped his foot against the floor, scrolling through his texts. Noelle hadn't replied since early afternoon, and they were supposed to meet at her place around six. Movie night. Nothing fancy. But still—the silence nagged.

Scarlett hesitated. "I saw her earlier. She looked awful, she said it was just a headache but once in a while she will get these awful migraines and they take her out for hours sometimes for a whole day. She hasn't had one in a while, at least not that she has mentioned to me but maybe since the accident..."

Slade sat up straighter. "Wait, seriously? She hasn't said anything about a headache or anything like that. I need to talk to her."

The apartment was dim, the overhead lights too sharp for Noelle's aching eyes. She'd pulled the curtains, lit the stovetop carefully, and moved slower than usual, her limbs heavy with exhaustion. The air smelled faintly of lemon and garlic—comforting, though even that was turning her stomach.

Slade opened the apartment door balancing grocery bags, snowflakes clinging to his hoodie. "Soup delivery!" he called out, grinning—until he saw her.

He stepped inside and stopped cold.

"Noelle," he said, voice low, careful. "Scarlett told me you weren't feeling well so I figured I'd bring you soup."

Snow dusted his sleeves, but his gaze locked instantly on her pale face and glassy eyes. She stood at the stove, stirring a pot of rice, her motions too slow, too deliberate.

A familiar plate of lemon garlic chicken sat on the counter, perfectly portioned. She smiled weakly and murmured, "No worries. Dinner's ready."

His expression shifted instantly. "Noelle... wait, what? You shouldn't have gone to all this trouble. Not when you aren't feeling well."

She gave another tired smile, pressing a hand to her midsection.

"I figured you'd be hungry. You just got back from two away games and then had practice today, right? Chicken's good protein to keep you strong since your injury."

Slade didn't move. Then, slowly, he set the bags on the counter and pulled out a container of soup. "You look like you're burning up," he said gently.

"It's just the flu. I'm fine," she insisted, though her voice came out hoarse. "I didn't want to let you down."

Slade crossed to her, slower than usual. "You could've texted. Canceled. I'd have shown up with soup and snacks and zero complaints."

She looked down, fingers twitching at the edge of her sweatshirt. "I didn't want to be a burden."

He exhaled, then took her hand—warm, trembling. "You're never a burden."

Her eyes met his, unsure. "People say that until it's inconvenient."

"Well, then I guess this is me proving I'm not 'people'," he said softly. "You need rest. You don't owe me dinner."

Noelle blinked back a sudden rush of gratitude. "You didn't have to..."

"No," he interrupted, "you didn't have to. Noelle, you can barely stand upright."

"You're being dramatic."

"And you're ridiculous," he murmured, handing her the soup. "And kind. And—kind of a badass."

She chuckled weakly. "You really think soup and chicken qualify me for that?"

"No." He softened. "Getting up and making dinner when you clearly need rest does."

Then, without asking, he pulled her into him, arms wrapping around her like warmth itself. Her forehead pressed against his chest, her body limp from fever and fatigue.

She let out a breath that sounded too much like surrender.

"You don't have to earn my care," he murmured into her hair. "Not with dinner. Not with pretending you're okay. Just let me hold you and take care of you."

She didn't respond—just stayed still, wrapped tight against his heartbeat.

"We're reheating this later," he said softly. "Right now, I'm putting you to bed with cold packs and silence. My kind of romantic."

She chuckled faintly, gripping his sweatshirt as he scooped her into his arms.

Chapter Thirty-Three

Outside, the early May wind rattled the tree branches that were just starting to show the first signs of spring on their bones. The sky was a pale, unforgiving gray—neither stormy nor clear, just suspended, the kind of day that held its breath.

Inside Noelle's apartment, Scarlett was visiting, curled up on the couch beneath a knitted blanket, halfway through a movie neither of them were really watching.

Noelle's phone buzzed again. She didn't look at it right away.

Scarlett glanced up. "Popular girl. Your phone hasn't stopped going off for like ten minutes. Is everything okay?"

"It's nothing," Noelle said, though her voice was thinner than she meant it to be.

Scarlett frowned. "You've said that twice already."

Noelle hesitated, then flipped the phone face down on the coffee table. "It's just Beau. He—uh—found my number again, I guess."

Scarlett straightened, her easy warmth gone in an instant. "Wait—*Beau,* Beau?"

"Yeah."

"What on earth does he want now?"

Noelle exhaled. "I don't know. He keeps saying he wants to talk.

Says he's changed. Stuff like that." She tried to sound casual, but her fingers were tight around the mug in her hands.

Scarlett leaned forward. "Let me see."

"No." Noelle's voice came out sharper than she intended. "It's fine, just texts. They're harmless and I'm ignoring them."

"Harmless guys don't send a dozen messages to someone who's not answering."

Noelle's phone buzzed again, as if on cue. She tried to ignore it, but Scarlett snatched it up before she could stop her.

The newest message glowed on the screen:

BEAU:

> You don't get to ignore me, Noelle. Not
> again.

Scarlett's face drained of color to match the sky outside. "I thought this jerk was long gone by now. This isn't harmless."

Noelle took the phone back, pressing the lock button hard. "He's just trying to get a reaction. If I don't answer, he'll stop."

Scarlett shook her head. "You need to tell Slade."

"No." The word was immediate. "He's got enough going on. The last thing he needs is me dragging up old drama."

"This isn't drama," Scarlett snapped. "This is a man who doesn't know when to quit."

Noelle tried to laugh, but it came out hollow. "You're overreacting. It's fine."

But outside, the wind howled harder, scraping against the windowpanes like fingernails. The sound made both women glance toward the dark glass.

Scarlett didn't say anything else. She just reached over and switched on the lamp, flooding the room with light.

For a long time, neither of them spoke. The phone stayed facedown between them, silent—for now.

Hockey season was over but Slade never took that as a reason not to be practicing. He wiped the sweat from his brow, rolling his shoulders as he stepped off the ice at the end of his practice session. His breath came in clouds under the rink lights, the faint echo of pucks clattering still hanging in the air.

Scarlett stood by the benches, arms crossed, her expression tight. She waited until the last few players had trickled toward the locker room before speaking.

"We need to talk," she said.

Slade frowned, slinging his stick over his shoulder. "That sounds promising."

"It's about Noelle."

He froze halfway through untying his skates. "What about her? Is she alright?"

Scarlett hesitated, chewing her bottom lip like she was trying to find the least explosive version of the truth. "She's been getting texts. From Beau."

Slade's eyes darkened. "What?"

"She didn't want me to tell you," Scarlett rushed on. "Said it was nothing—just messages and she's 'ignoring them'. But they're not nothing, Slade. They're... off."

He dropped the skate laces from his hands. "Define off."

Scarlett sighed, lowering her voice. "Threatening. Possessive. The kind of tone that gives you that crawl-up-your-spine feeling. There were a dozen of them at least, all in a short span of time. I only saw one, and it was enough."

Slade's jaw flexed. "She should've come to me."

"I told her that but she *knew* you'd react like this," Scarlett said, exasperated. "She doesn't want to make things worse. But I think he's dangerous, Slade. You didn't see her face. She tried to play it off, but she was shaken."

Slade ran a hand through his damp hair, pacing. The boards creaked beneath his boots. "Do you know if he's still in town?"

Scarlett shook her head. "No idea. But the way he's sending those texts—he knows how to get under her skin. And I don't like it."

Slade exhaled slowly, the sound more like a growl than a breath. "I've got to talk to her."

"She'll be mad I told you," Scarlett warned, softer now.

"Yeah," he said, eyes hard. "But I'd rather she be mad than scared or in danger."

Scarlett nodded once, her gaze steady. "That's how I feel too so I felt like you needed to know. Just... be careful, Slade. After hearing all the awful things he did to her in their relationship, he really gives me the creeps. You have no idea what kind of man he is."

Slade slung his gear bag over his shoulder. "Then it's time I find out."

The smell of roasted garlic and basil filled Slade's kitchen. The tall white pine outside tapped lightly against the window as if asking to join the aromatic meal.

Noelle sat at the counter, legs crossed, a faint smile on her lips as she watched him cook. "You always make it look so easy," she said.

"That's because I'm pretending I know what I'm doing."

"Confidence counts," she teased.

He grinned, pouring the sauce over the pasta. For a little while, it felt like the world had narrowed to this — two plates, the sound of rain ticking against the glass, the candles flickering shadows on the walls.

Then her phone lit up on the counter. Once. Then again.

Slade glanced down. The name flashing across the screen made his stomach tighten.

Beau.

He picked up the phone, eyes scanning the message before thinking twice:

BEAU:

> You think you can ignore me forever? We're
> going to be together again, Noelle.

Slade's jaw clenched. He set the phone back down carefully, not wanting to alarm her, but the tension in his chest wouldn't let him stay quiet.

"Noelle..." His voice was low, controlled, but sharp with concern. "Beau's still contacting you?"

She looked up from her seat, expression calm but attentive. "Yeah. I told Scarlett, and she's keeping an eye on it."

"Okay, I'm not sure my sister can do anything about this. I thought we agreed you were going to have the police get involved," he said, running a hand through his hair. "I just... I hate that he's still in your life, even if it's just in text messages."

She reached across and placed her hand over his. "I can handle it. I'm just going to block his number. I've got this. But thank you for worrying."

Slade exhaled slowly, tension easing slightly, though the protectiveness lingered in his eyes. "I don't want to overstep. I just... I care about you. And I'll do whatever it takes to keep you safe. I love you."

Her smile was small but reassuring. "I know, I trust you, but I also trust myself. That's the important part. And I love you too."

He nodded, swallowing the tight lump in his throat. "Still... if he shows up? If he tries anything? I won't let him near you."

"I wouldn't want you to," she said softly, her fingers curling around his. "But I'm stronger than you think, Slade. You don't have to be my shield all the time."

He squeezed her hand, a silent promise passing between them. "I'll try to remember that. But I'll never stop caring."

The two of them returned to their meal, the snow outside continuing its quiet dance, the kitchen warm with the smell of basil, garlic, and something more—a sense of safety, however tenuous, held in the space between them.

Chapter Thirty-Four

Back at her own apartment later that night, it felt too quiet—the kind of quiet that thrummed beneath the skin.

Noelle sat curled on her couch, Maple's head heavy in her lap, the TV muttering through a rerun she wasn't really watching. The only light came from the lamp by the window, throwing her reflection across the glass—pale, tired, hollow-eyed, the ghost of an argument still clinging to her.

Maple's ears flicked. Her gaze locked on the window. A low growl vibrated through her chest.

"Hey," she murmured, smoothing his fur. "It's just the wind."

Outside, a spring storm hissed sideways, tapping against the panes like impatient fingers.

Her phone buzzed on the coffee table. She reached for it automatically, expecting Scarlett, maybe Slade—apologies, explanations. Anything human.

Unknown number.

UNKNOWN:

Nice view tonight.

A photo followed.

For half a second her brain refused to understand what she was seeing. Then the image sharpened—her own reflection, captured from outside, framed by the same lamp still glowing behind her.

Her breath hitched. Maple barked once, sharp and warning.

She rose slowly, pulse pounding in her throat. "Who's there?"

Nothing. Only the sound of the radiator hissing and the wind pressing harder at the glass.

The phone buzzed again—another message she never had time to read.

The window exploded inward.

Glass burst across the room, the shockwave stealing her breath. Maple lunged, teeth bared, as a figure hauled itself through the shattered frame.

Beau.

He hit the floor hard and fast, one gloved hand clamping over her mouth. The smell of whiskey, metal, and his familiar cologne filled her lungs.

"Miss me?" he hissed.

She drove her elbow back, connecting with his ribs—a dull thud and a grunt—but he only tightened his grip, dragging her toward the broken window. Maple snarled, snapping at his leg.

"Stop it, Noelle," Beau growled, shoving her through the jagged opening, glass slicing through her skin. Her scream fractured into the night as he forced her out onto the fire escape. "You made me do this. You left me with nothing but silence. Do you know what silence does to me? It eats me alive. And now—now you'll find out what that feels like."

Rain tangled in her hair. Streetlight silvered Beau's face—eyes wild, mouth twisted between fury and triumph. He leaned close, words slicing through the storm.

"You thought you could erase me. But I'm carved into you, Noelle. Every fight, every kiss, every promise—I'm still here. And tonight, you'll remember who you belong to. And it's not that other hockey player, Fisher."

Inside, Maple paced the broken glass, whining at the wind that still whispered her name.

Rain slicked the street as Slade pulled up to Noelle's building. The porch light flickered weakly, haloed in mist. He sat in the truck for a long minute, forehead pressed to the steering wheel, rehearsing the apology he'd been carrying all day.

I shouldn't have tried to get in the middle of the Beau situation. You were right. I'm sorry.

The words still felt too small. But he needed to say them.

He climbed the stairs, heart thudding, and hesitated at her door. His knuckles hovered just above the wood before he forced himself to knock.

Once. Twice.

"Noelle? It's me."

Silence.

He waited, listening—hoping for footsteps, a laugh, the click of Maple's nails on the floor.

Nothing.

He knocked again, softer. "C'mon, open up. I just want to talk."

Still nothing.

Something just didn't feel right. He fished the spare key from his pocket —the one she'd handed him with a grin. *In case I lock myself out again.*

The lock turned with a soft click.

The apartment was dark and cold.

"Noelle?" He stepped inside. "Maple?"

The dog appeared from the hallway, tail tucked low, eyes wide and frantic. She let out a thin whine and stopped short, trembling like she didn't know whether to run to him or hide.

Slade crouched instinctively. "Hey, girl. Where is she?"

Maple didn't move.

He straightened and took another step—and his stomach dropped.

Glass glittered across the rug, catching the streetlight in sharp, ugly fragments. The window stood open, curtain torn, rain spilling over the sill and creeping onto the floor. Cold air rushed in, sharp and wrong.

"No," he breathed.

He moved slowly, every instinct on edge. And the air—

Slade inhaled and stiffened.

It wasn't her.

The familiar warmth of vanilla and ink was buried beneath something sour and heavy. Sweat. Oil. Male. Recent and fresh, cloying at his nostrils.

His pulse roared in his ears.

"Oh no," he groaned. All his worst fears began galloping around his mind, Beau at the center of them in particular.

Maple whimpered behind him.

His phone buzzed in his hand. Scarlett.

He answered automatically, eyes locked on the shattered window. "Hey—have you heard from Noelle? I'm at her apartment but she's not here and something is very wrong."

Scarlett hesitated. "Maybe she just needed space. You know how she gets after a fight—she shuts down."

"If she needed space," he said sharply, the words tumbling out, "she wouldn't have left the window like this."

A beat. "Like what?" Scarlett asked, her voice tightening.

"It's broken from the outside," he said. "Glass is strewn all over the floor."

Silence stretched on the line. Then her breath hitched.

"Oh no, do you think—"

"Yeah," Slade said hoarsely. "There's someone else's scent in here too. Scarlett, it's clear she didn't leave by her own choice."

Another pause—shorter this time. Focused.

"It must have been Beau," she said.

Slade swallowed hard, his gaze never leaving the open window. "I don't know for sure," he said. "But I can't imagine it was anyone else. I'm going to tear him apart when I find him."

Ten minutes later, headlights cut through the mist. A truck pulled up, then another. Doors slammed. Voices carried up the stairwell—low, urgent, too many at once.

Scarlett burst in first, hair plastered to her cheeks, eyes wide. "Slade —have you found her?"

He didn't answer right away. He just pointed at the shattered window.

Scarlett pressed a hand to her mouth, shaking her head. "No. No, this isn't okay—"

Behind her, Stryker shouldered through, followed by Willow, Hunter, Gunner, and Garrett —still in jackets, smelling of sweat and damp ice from the earlier scrimmage. Their laughter from practice had vanished; now their faces were tight, wary.

"Jayden, Miguel, Violet and Sam are checking around outside," Garrett informed them, staring at the glass glittering across the rug.

Stryker crouched, running a hand over the shards. "You're right, brother, this wasn't an accident. Someone obviously forced their way in." He looked up, eyes hard.

"Beau." Slade hissed, the certainty of it growing in his gut as he followed Stryker out onto the fire escape. Rain slicked the metal, dripping through the jagged frame. Stryker's beam swept across the railing— then froze.

Blood. A smear, fresh, glistening in the light.

Slade's stomach dropped. "She fought him."

Stryker's jaw tightened. "And he dragged her down. We have to call the police."

Below, where Miguel and Samantha were searching the alley, there came a sudden shout from Miguel, "Tracks! Fresh ones—boots, heavy tread. Heading east!"

Everything moved at once after that.

Slade was already pulling his phone from his pocket, hands shaking as he stepped back inside and dialed. He paced the length of the apartment while it rang, eyes never leaving the broken window, the rain still whispering through it like the place itself was holding its breath.

"Yes," he said the moment the call connected, his voice sharp, unsteady. "I need the police at my location immediately. There's been a break-in. My girlfriend is missing. Her window was shattered, there's blood, and we believe she was taken. This isn't an accident—she's in danger. We need help immediately."

When Slade ended the call, the apartment felt too small for all of them. Too loud. Too helpless. "The police are on their way," he said. "They told us not to touch anything else."

Scarlett stepped closer to him, her voice low but fierce. "We're not leaving you alone."

"I know but we can't all stay here," he said, swallowing hard. "We cover more ground if we split up."

No one argued. They all understood what that meant.

They made quick decisions—who would stay to speak with the police, who would keep searching nearby streets, who would go home but stay awake, phones charged and volume up. Keys were exchanged. Locations shared. Promises made that sounded fragile even as they were spoken.

Scarlett squeezed Slade's arm before stepping back. "The second we hear anything—anything—we call. No matter the hour."

"Keep your phones on you," Stryker added, eyes sweeping the group. "No silent mode. Not tonight."

Not tonight.

As they filtered out, one by one, the apartment emptied until only Slade remained, standing in the middle of the wreckage—glass, rainwater, the echo of her absence pressing in on him from every direction.

He stared at the shattered window, at the smear of blood on the railing beyond it, and clenched his fists.

Wherever Noelle was, he knew one thing with terrifying certainty:

She wasn't alone.

And neither was he—not anymore.

The night had fractured them, scattered them across the city, but every phone was lit, every breath held, all of them waiting for the same sound.

A call.

Chapter Thirty-Five

When Noelle came to, her first thought was that the air was wrong. Too cold. Too still.

Then she felt the rope.

Her wrists were tied in front of her—tight enough to bite into her skin. Her ankles too. A dull ache pulsed at the back of her skull.

She blinked until the room steadied: wood walls, a cracked window, a lamp burning low beside the door. A cabin.

Her stomach turned.

"Hey," a voice said from the corner. "You're awake."

Her pulse jumped. She knew that voice.

Beau stepped into the light, hair messy, eyes bloodshot. He looked strung out with a combination of lack of sleep and rage.

"Beau." Her throat burned. "What are you doing? Where are we?"

He smiled like he'd been waiting for her to ask.

"Bringing you home," he said.

Her pulse kicked harder. "You took me. You can't—"

"I can't?" His voice cracked, sharp. "I can't come get what's mine? You think you can just walk away from me? Let that hockey star replace me?"

Noelle pressed back against the wall she was propped against. "You need to untie me."

He laughed—a sound with no humor in it. "You're not going anywhere."

He started pacing. The floor creaked under his boots, each step uneven.

"I tried to give you time," he said. "You ignored me. Blocked my number. Pretended I didn't exist."

"Because you scare me." The words slipped out before she could stop them.

That made him still. He looked at her for a long moment, expression twisting. "No. You only think I scare you because *he* got in your head. Slade. You think he's some good guy? You think he's better than me?"

Her wrists throbbed as she worked at the rope, little by little. "You don't have to do this," she said carefully. "We can talk. But you have to untie me."

He crouched in front of her, close enough that she could smell the mix of whiskey and stale coffee on his breath.

"You'll say anything when you're cornered," he said, quieter now. "That's what you do."

He stood again, pacing faster, muttering. "You think I don't remember what we had? You used to look at me like I was the only one who saw you. Now you look at me like I'm the problem."

Her gaze flicked toward the counter. Her phone sat there, next to a water bottle.

If she could just reach it—

Beau caught her staring, "You don't need that." He grabbed the phone and tossed it across the room, where it hit the wall with a dull thud. "You don't need anyone else but me."

Noelle's heartbeat pounded so hard it hurt. "You can't keep me here."

He turned back, eyes glassy and mean. "I can do whatever I need to do."

Her hands burned against the rope. She swallowed, voice barely steady. "You hurt me, try to control me. That's what you do, that's all you ever do to me. That's not love, Beau."

He froze—just long enough for her to see the flash of guilt behind the rage.

Then he shoved it down and tried to flip things back on her, "You made me do that. You made me crazy. You think you're better than me now, but you'll remember. You always do."

He ran a hand through his hair, pacing again. "You just need to calm down. It'll feel like before once you stop fighting it."

She didn't answer. She was already thinking two steps ahead—eyes darting back to the counter when he turned and reached for the kettle. Her phone felt like her only lifeline.

She heard it vibrate, the screen glowing faintly, she almost couldn't breathe. "Beau," she said, forcing her voice to be small. "Can I have some water? Please?"

He stopped, glancing back at her. "See? That's better. You can ask nicely for things."

He grabbed the half-empty bottle, twisted the cap, and held it to her lips. She drank, staying still while his fingers brushed her chin. Her stomach rolled.

"Good girl," he muttered.

Her throat burned as she swallowed.

He turned away again, muttering about how everyone had turned on him, how no one ever stayed.

She worked the rope harder. The knot scraped, loosened. Her fingers were slick with sweat and blood by the time it started to give.

"Beau," she said softly, "please. Let's just talk like we used to, okay?"

He stopped pacing, half-smiling. "You really think you can play me like that?" He stepped closer. She didn't move. "You think I can't tell when you're lying?"

She shook her head fast. "I'm not."

He stared at her a moment longer, then turned back toward the counter. "You don't get it. You're mine. You were always mine."

Her hands slipped free.

She kept them low, breathing shallow as she covertly untied her ankles as well, then waited for the sound of his steps to cover hers. When he turned and refilled his mug, she moved—quiet, quick—reaching for her phone beside the sink.

The screen was unlocked.

Her hands shook so hard she could barely type.

> HELP. CABIN. NORTH OF SILVERWOOD.
> BEAU.

She hit send. The bar flickered—no signal—then lit again.

Beau began to swivel back around to her.

She slid the phone under a stack of napkins and stepped back just as he turned.

"What are you doing?"

Her heart stuttered. "My wrists. They're bleeding. I was looking for a towel–"

He studied her through his whiskey haze, eyes narrowing. Then he exhaled, the shift sudden and terrifying. "You'll be fine," he said softly. "We just need time. That's all."

He walked toward the back door. "I'm getting firewood. Don't try to leave. You're in the middle of nowhere anyway." The door slammed, the sound echoing in the empty space.

Noelle stayed still, listening—waiting for his footsteps to return. Nothing. Just the wind pressing against the windows and her pulse hammering in her ears. She counted her lucky stars that he was too inebriated to register that she was no longer bound up.

She went closer to the counter again, wrists raw, eyes fixed on the faint glow under the napkins.

Delivered.

Her breath hitched. Relief surged—thin and fragile—but it was something. And then—

Life360.

The thought came out of nowhere, sharp and sudden. Slade had set it up months ago, half-joking, half-serious. *Just in case,* he'd said. She'd almost forgotten it existed.

Her fingers flew again, heart pounding so hard it hurt. She tapped the app. The screen loaded slowly, painfully—then the small blue dot appeared.

There you are.

She didn't know if Slade would remember. Didn't know if he'd even think to look. But the dot was there. Real. Trackable. It gave her hope.

She eased the rope back over her wrists, keeping it loose so it would look untouched. Every muscle trembled with the effort of staying still. The wind rattled the cabin again. Then silence.

Please find me soon.

The message came through just after nine, interrupting Slade's pacing.

A single text. Noelle's name.

NOELLE:

> HELP. CABIN. NORTH OF SILVERWOOD.
> BEAU.

For half a second, Slade's brain refused to make sense of the words. Then it hit like a slap across his face. He was moving before he even realized it—grabbing his keys, scrambling to get his jacket on.

His hands were shaking. His chest felt too tight.

Cabin. North of Silverwood. That could be anywhere. Too much ground. Too many miles of trees and back roads and *nothing*.

Think.

He called Scarlett on speaker while yanking on his beanie.

She answered mid-sentence. "Hey, I was just—"

"Just got word." His voice came out low, sharp. "Noelle. She got a message through."

"What? What do you mean?"

"We were right, she's with Beau." He slammed the door behind him, leaves swirling into the stairwell. "Somewhere north of Silverwood. I'm heading out."

"Slade—wait." She was already moving, her voice going brisk and professional. "I'm calling the cops to update them that we heard from her and know the area to search. You can't go in alone."

"There's not a snowflake's chance in hell that I'm waiting around for the cops." He dropped into the driver's seat, breath fogging the windshield. "I have to get to her. You have my location now, send them after me."

"Slade—"

He hung up before she could finish.

The tires spun on slick road before catching, throwing up a spray of rocks as he hit the road. His phone vibrated—Scarlett again—but he ignored it. The world had narrowed to the beam of his headlights and the cold pulse of the steering wheel under his hands.

He drove fast, too fast, the needle climbing. The wipers smeared raindrops across the glass. Every turn in the road looked the same— blacktop vanishing into the white haze of the droplets. He could almost hear her voice, that tight, scared edge she got when she tried to sound calm.

Help.

Cabin.

North of Silverwood.

"Damn it," he muttered, slamming his palm against the steering wheel. "Think!"

And then it hit him.

Life360.

The memory came rushing back—him setting it up on her phone months ago, joking about it, brushing it off like it was nothing important. *Just in case,* he'd said. And then he'd forgotten about it. Because things had been good. Because he'd let himself believe nothing bad would touch her again.

His chest lurched.

He fumbled for the app, nearly dropping his phone as he opened it. The screen loaded too slowly, the spinning icon a cruel taunt.

Come on. Come on.

Then the map appeared.

A blue dot blinked into place.

There.

North of Silverwood. Off the main road. Deep into the trees.

Relief and terror slammed into him at the same time, sharp enough to make him gasp.

"I see you," he breathed, eyes locked on the screen. "I've got you." He texted the location to Scarlett.

He gritted his teeth and pushed harder on the gas. The farther north he went, the thinner the traffic. By the time he hit the tree line, it was just him and the wind. Branches bowed under the howling wind, the forest closing in around the road like a throat.

He turned off at the sign for *Silverwood Lake Bungalows*—a row of old rental cottages long since abandoned, roofs sagging, windows boarded or half-shattered. He'd been here once as a kid. Summer camp. Bonfires. Laughing until sunrise. The memory felt like it belonged to someone else.

Now, everything was silent. It was like the storm decided to hold its breath, anticipating what would happen next.

He slowed, scanning the line of dark cabins. His headlights washed over endless piles of pine needles, a broken bench, a fallen sign. Then— light.

One window, glowing faint yellow through the storm.

A car parked crooked in front.

He killed the engine and stepped out. The cold hit instantly, slicing through his coat. He didn't feel it. His focus tunneled on the cabin door. He tested the doorknob.

Locked.

Footprints led from the porch toward the shed on the edge of the woods. Firewood scattered just past the steps. Slade followed the tracks to the shed, his boots crunching softly.

Inside, a shadow moved.

His pulse spiked.

Then the door jerked open.

Beau stood there, arms full of another pile of logs, startled for a heartbeat before his face twisted. "What the hell—"

Slade didn't let him finish.

His fist connected hard enough to knock the wood from his arms. The logs hit the floor and rolled, one thunking against the wall. Beau stumbled back, caught himself, and swung wildly.

The hit grazed Slade's jaw. He barely felt it.

"Where is she?" Slade barked.

Beau lunged again. Slade ducked, shoved him into the wall, his forearm across Beau's chest. "Where the hell is she?" he roared again.

"She's fine," Beau gasped, straining against him. "You don't—"

Slade's voice dropped, cold and steady. "You touch her again, and you'll regret breathing."

For a second, Beau froze—rage flickering into something like fear. Then he shoved back, scrambling for an escape.

"Coward," Slade muttered.

Beau ducked under another swing from Slade's fist, then there was just the crunch of his boots running into the trees. He was gone.

Slade didn't chase him. He turned back to the cabin, breath coming hard. He pounded up the porch steps and threw all his force into the thin wood door, splintering it to pieces. He dove inside.

"Noelle?"

A muffled sound answered from the corner. He crossed the room in three steps. She was on the floor, rope tied around her wrists and ankles, eyes wide when she saw him.

He dropped to his knees and pulled her against him before she could speak. She was shaking so hard it felt like her bones might rattle apart.

"You're okay," he said, though his voice barely held together. "I've got you."

Her breath hitched against his chest. "He was—he said—"

"He's gone." He smoothed her hair back, his hands still trembling. "You did good. You got the message out."

"I didn't think it would send."

"Well I thank God that it did." He pulled back just enough to see her face—tear-streaked, pale, alive. "You did everything right. I just wish I had remembered Life360 sooner."

Outside, sirens began to rise in the distance, faint through the storm that had picked back up.

Slade exhaled, the first full breath he'd taken since finding her shattered window.

He didn't let go until the flashing lights reached the edge of the trees.

The sirens grew louder, the sound warping as it bounced between the trees. Red and blue flashed across the tattered curtains, cutting through the dark like a pulse.

Noelle flinched when the lights hit the windows. Slade tightened his hold around her. "It's okay. The police are here."

She nodded, barely.

Two officers burst through the door a few seconds later, guns drawn until they saw her. One of them lowered his firearm immediately, stepping forward. "Miss—are you hurt?"

Noelle shook her head. "I'm okay. He's gone."

Slade stood, his voice rough. "He went north. On foot."

The officers exchanged a look, one of them radioing for backup while the other approached with a blanket. Slade helped her stand, his arm steady at her waist, then settled the blanket around her shoulders.

"Let's get you out of here," the officer said quietly.

Outside, the scene was chaos in the trees—patrol cars half-buried, doors open, radios crackling. Scarlett's car slid in just behind them. She jumped out before it even stopped moving, her hair whipping in the wind.

"Noelle!"

Noelle turned just in time to catch her as Scarlett wrapped her up, shaking and swearing under her breath.

Slade stepped back, giving them space. His hands felt useless now that she wasn't in danger. He flexed them, realizing for the first time how badly they were shaking.

An officer approached him. "You said he ran north?"

"Yeah. About five minutes ago. Dark jacket, gray hood."

The cop nodded. "We'll find him."

Slade didn't say what he was thinking—that Beau would probably make it far enough to vanish into the trees before they did. He just nodded and continued to answer the officer's questions about what he knew.

Noelle was also being questioned for details about how she came to be in this predicament. Once they were done, Scarlett walked her away from the ominous cabin and flashing lights, wrapping the blanket tighter around her shoulders.

After whispering again to Noelle that she was safe now, Scarlett turned to Slade who wasn't far behind. "They're suggesting that she needs to go to the hospital to get checked out."

"I'll take her," Slade said with authority, leaving no doubt that Noelle wouldn't be let out of his sight. Not for a while anyway.

Scarlett didn't argue.

They loaded Noelle into his truck, the heat on full blast. She looked up when he climbed in beside her, her hand finding his automatically. Her fingers were ice-cold.

"Thank you for saving me," she said quietly.

"I would never hesitate to do it again."

Her mouth trembled, but she nodded.

The ride down the mountain was slow, the roads thick with fallen branches and rivulets of rain. Noelle leaned against him on the cab's bench seat, eyes closing. He kept his right arm around her shoulders, every muscle still tight, every heartbeat reminding him she was alive.

At the hospital, Slade refused to leave the hallway outside the exam room.

When the nurse finally let him in, Noelle was sitting on the edge of the bed, a bandage around her wrist and a Styrofoam cup of water in her hands. She looked up, a small smile tugging at the corner of her mouth.

"They say I'm fine," she said. "Just bruises and scrapes from the broken window."

He exhaled, the tension finally breaking. "You scared me half to death."

"I was scared myself." Her voice was small but steady.

He crossed the room and crouched in front of her, taking the cup from her shaking hands. "You did everything right. You kept your head. You saved yourself."

She looked at him for a long moment, eyes shining. "I don't know if that would have happened if you hadn't come."

"Always would."

For a second, neither of them said anything. The only sound was the buzz of the fluorescent lights and the muffled conversation outside the door.

Then she reached out, fingers brushing the edge of his sleeve. "I don't want to go home alone tonight."

He nodded once. "You won't."

Scarlett appeared in the doorway, arms crossed but eyes soft. "Hey girl, I had to make sure you're alright. Everything okay now?"

Noelle slid off the bed, still pale but steadier now and nodded, exhausted. Slade helped her with her coat, his hand brushing hers just long enough to say what words couldn't.

Outside, dawn was creeping over the parking lot. The rain had stopped, leaving everything washed in silver light.

Scarlett stropped at her car which was parked in the spot next to Slade's truck. "You sure you're okay?"

"I will be," Noelle said. Then she looked at Slade. "Thanks to him."

Scarlett smiled faintly. "Good, looks like your knight in shining armor has things covered here. Call me later."

Slade held the passenger door open for her, waiting until she was settled before walking around to the driver's side. He reached over, took her hand, and held it until the city lights came back into view.

Chapter Thirty-Six

The drive back to his apartment was silent. Noelle sat with her head against the window, face pale against the dark glass. When they reached his building, she didn't move at first. Just watched her breath fog up the window.

"We're here," Slade said quietly and they made their way to his doorstep.

He unlocked the door and stepped aside. The apartment was warm, the air faintly coffee-scented, the hall light low. Noelle stood just inside the doorway—then a bark sounded from the bedroom. Maple bounded down the hall, nails clicking against the wood floor.

Her hand flew to her mouth. "Oh my goodness—"

She barely had time to drop to her knees before Maple launched herself forward, paws thumping against her chest, tail wagging so hard her whole body wiggled.

She laughed through the rush of it, arms wrapping around the dog's neck as Maple's face crowded into her shoulder. "Hey—hi—oh, I'm so happy you're okay," she breathed into her fur.

Maple let out a happy huff and pressed herself closer, solid and warm.

Slade shut the door, locking both the handle as well as the dead bolt. "Scarlett brought her over earlier," he said. "Figured you'd want her here when we got you back safely."

Noelle nodded, still buried in Maple's fur. "Thank you."

"Don't thank me," he said. "She's the one who thought of it."

He moved through the apartment on autopilot—checking windows, flipping the blinds closed, turning on the lamp by the couch. When he turned back, she was standing now, a little unsteady, rubbing at her temple. "You okay?"

"Headache," she murmured. "I think the adrenaline's wearing off."

He frowned. "That's been happening a lot lately."

"It's fine. I wasn't really over that flu I had," she said. "Guess my body's just catching up. Stress and all that."

"You sure it's just that?"

She gave a tired half-smile. "Pretty sure. I've just been running on fumes."

He didn't push, only gently suggested, "You should sit down."

She did. Maple climbed up beside her, curling into her side like she belonged there. Slade filled a glass of water and set it in front of her.

"Drink."

"I'm not thirsty."

"Doesn't matter."

Her lips twitched, the closest thing to a smile since they left the cabin. She drank half before setting it down again. He watched her over the rim of his own glass. She looked smaller somehow. Shoulders curved in. Pale skin against the collar of his sweatshirt. The stubborn little crease between her eyebrows that only appeared when she was trying not to cry.

"Thank you for letting me stay here," she said quietly.

"Of course," he said, "There is nowhere else I want you to be other than here with me where I know you're safe."

The quiet that followed wasn't awkward—it was heavy, familiar. Like they'd used up all their words hours ago and neither one had any to spare.

When she started to nod off against the couch cushion, he said, "Come on. Bed."

"I can't sleep."

"Let's just try."

He led her down the short hall. She hesitated at his doorway, clutching the blanket around her shoulders.

He didn't undress, didn't reach for her. Just pulled the covers back. She climbed in, careful, curling toward him with the blanket still tight around her. Maple thumped down on the rug near the bed, sighing.

Slade laid on his back, one arm resting at her shoulder but not pressing, not holding. He let her come closer when she wanted to. Her breathing was shallow at first, uneven. Then it steadied. Every few minutes she twitched, a small sound in her throat, and his hand would tighten reflexively before easing again.

Outside, the city was starting to stir. Tires hissed on wet gravel. Somewhere down the street, a bus grumbled to life.

Noelle shifted closer, her forehead against his chest. "Sorry," she murmured. "For everything."

He brushed his thumb along her shoulder. "You don't owe me an apology for anything."

"I keep saying I'm fine," she said softly. "But I'm not."

"I know but you will be."

That earned him the faintest chuckle—barely a sound, but real. Her body relaxed against him, fingers still curled in his shirt. He looked down at her, brushed a strand of hair from her face.

"You're safe now," he whispered. "I've got you."

She didn't answer. She was already asleep.

The nightmare attacked suddenly and without warning.

There was the sound of glass shattering.

The familiar scent of whiskey, metal, and his cologne—cedarwood, sharp and suffocating.

"Miss me?" His voice was a low rasp against her ear, warm and venomous.

Beau.

She thrashed, nails scraping against his skin, but he only laughed. The room blurred. The floor tilted. Her vision smeared into streaks of color and shadow as he dragged her toward the broken window.

Cold night air slammed into her face.

Then everything snapped to black.

She woke up bound with ropes on the floor.

She knew this place.

The cabin.

The rope bit into her wrists, rough fibers grinding into her skin. Her ankles were bound so tightly she could feel her pulse throbbing against the restraints. The air was freezing, sharp enough to sting her lungs when she breathed.

Her breath trembled out of her in short, panicked bursts. The room was dim, lit only by a single bulb swinging overhead, casting jittery shadows that crawled across the floor. Wooden boards creaked beneath her slightest movement.

Footsteps sounded.

Slow. Heavy. Deliberate.

Her stomach dropped. Her throat tightened. She pulled against the rope, but it only dug deeper, burning her skin. Her heartbeat pounded so loudly she could barely hear anything else.

He stepped into the light.

That same smile. That same cold, hungry look in his eyes.

"You didn't think I was done with you, did you?"

Her breath stuttered. Her vision blurred. Her fingers went numb. She tried to scream, but her voice cracked, trapped behind terror.

He crouched in front of her, close enough that she could smell the mix of cologne and alcohol radiating off his skin. His hand reached out, brushing her cheek with a touch that made her flinch violently.

"You always come back to me," he whispered.

She jerked away, but the chair rocked dangerously. The rope tightened around her chest, squeezing until she could barely breathe.

"No," she whispered, but the word barely left her throat.

A strangled sound tore free.

Then another.

Then the scream ripped out of her.

It was raw—wrenched from somewhere deep, a sound that didn't belong in the quiet bedroom. Her back arched off the mattress. Her legs kicked violently, sheets tangling around her ankles. Her hands clawed at the air, at her throat, at the phantom rope still burning into her skin.

Her breath came in sharp, broken gasps.

Her chest heaved.

Her face twisted in panic.

She thrashed so hard, she put a dent in the wall plaster.

Her head whipped side to side, hair plastered to her damp forehead. Her lips moved around words she couldn't form—half-sobs, half-pleas, fragments of the nightmare still gripping her.

"No—no—don't—please—Stop—stop—Let me go—"

Her voice cracked on the last word.

Her hands flew upward, trying to tear away the invisible grip around her throat. Her nails scraped against her own skin. Her legs kicked again, harder this time, like she was trying to break free from restraints only she could feel.

Her breathing spiraled into frantic, shallow gasps.

Her pulse hammered visibly at her neck.

Her whole body trembled, trapped between sleep and terror.

And then she screamed again—louder, sharper, a sound that ripped through the room and shattered the silence.

"Slade! Slade! Help—please help me!"

Slade bolted upright, heart slamming into his ribs, confused and disoriented to find that they had slept all day and it was night again, before he saw her—thrashing, choking on air, tears streaking down her cheeks even in sleep.

"Baby—hey—hey!" His voice cracked as he reached for her.

She didn't hear him. She was still in the cabin, still tied to the chair, still smelling his cologne, still feeling the rope cutting into her wrists.

Her body jerked violently when Slade touched her shoulder.

He pulled back instantly, hands open, voice softening. "It's me. It's Slade. You're safe."

She thrashed again, a sob ripping from her chest.

He moved closer, carefully, sliding one hand behind her back and the other to her cheek. "Wake up, sweetheart. Come back to me."

Her breath stuttered. Her eyelids fluttered. Her fingers twitched against his shirt.

Then she gasped—a sharp, broken inhale—and her eyes flew open.

She was still screaming.

Slade pulled her into his arms before she could spiral again, holding her tight enough to anchor her but gentle enough not to frighten her further. Her body shook violently against him, breath ragged, hands clutching at him like she was drowning.

"I've got you," he whispered into her hair. "You're safe. You're home. I'm right here."

Her sobs broke open against his chest, and he held her through every tremor, every gasp, every echo of the nightmare still clawing at her.

It took nearly twenty minutes for her breathing to steady. Even then, she stayed curled against him, fingers tangled in his shirt like she was afraid he'd disappear if she let go.

Her voice was small when she finally spoke. "I don't want to close my eyes."

He tightened his arms around her. "You don't have to. I'll stay awake with you."

She shook her head. "You have practice in the morning."

"I don't care."

She exhaled shakily, her forehead resting against his collarbone. The room felt too quiet now—the kind of quiet that made her ears ring. Her skin still tingled with phantom sensations: the rope, the breath on her cheek, the hands around her throat.

She tried to lie back down, but the moment her head touched the pillow, her pulse spiked. Her chest tightened. Her breath stuttered.

Slade noticed instantly.

He shifted closer, sliding one hand beneath her head and the other around her waist. "Come here," he murmured, guiding her to lie on top of him, her cheek against his chest. "Listen to my heartbeat."

She did.

It was steady. Warm. Real.

She focused on the rise and fall of his breathing, the slow rhythm of his fingers tracing patterns on her back. The nightmare still clung to her, but his warmth pushed it back, inch by inch.

Her eyelids grew heavy.

"Sleep," he whispered. "I'm right here and won't leave you for anything.

The SILVERWOOD SCOOP

Local Sports & Community News

Local Shocker: Hockey Player Beau Abbott Arrested After Kidnapping of Noelle Hayes

Samantha Romano, Silverwood Snipers' Media Correspondent

You heard it here first, Silverwood—this story has everything: scandal, suspense, and a fall from grace that's left the whole town talking.

Beau Abbott, 24, former Vancouver Vultures forward and ex-boyfriend of Silverwood sweetheart Noelle Hayes, was taken into custody late last night after a tense standoff in the woods outside Silverwood.

Authorities confirmed that Abbott allegedly abducted Hayes earlier this week, holding her at a remote cabin for nearly twenty-four hours before she was rescued.

Sources close to the Silverwood PD tell *The Scoop* that Hayes is now "safe and recovering" and that the quick response of officers—and a certain hometown hockey hero, Slade Fisher—helped bring her home. Fisher reportedly arrived on scene just as police closed in, though both have declined to comment.

Abbott is being held without bond at the Cumberland County Jail and faces multiple charges, including kidnapping, unlawful restraint, and assault. His arraignment is scheduled for next week.

As for Hayes, friends say she's keeping a low profile, focusing on recovery, and leaning on her inner circle—including Fisher and his sister Scarlett. One close source told *The Scoop*, "She's been through hell, but she's tougher than people think."

No word yet on whether this ordeal will affect Fisher's performance on the ice—but given Silverwood's penchant for comebacks, we're betting this story's not over yet.

Stay tuned, Silverwood. *The Scoop's* watching—because around here, nothing stays secret for long.

Chapter Thirty-Seven

The spring air followed Noelle into the café, chilly but fresh as it filled her lungs. Inside, the heater blasted too high, making her dizzy. Maybe it was the heat. Maybe it was the headache that had lingered for days. Maybe it was the sleepless nights—the ones where she woke with her heart racing, Beau's voice still echoing somewhere in the dark.

Scarlett waved from a corner table. "Hey! Over here."

Noelle forced a smile and wove through the crowd. The smell of espresso and cinnamon turned her stomach, and she pressed a hand low against it before anyone could notice.

"You don't look so good," Scarlett said softly as she sat down.

"Thanks," Noelle said, managing a faint laugh, "but according to social protocol, you're supposed to say I look great."

Scarlett gave her a look. "You don't. You look like someone who hasn't slept in a week."

"Try two." Noelle stirred her tea but didn't drink it. "It's just been… a lot. I keep telling myself I'm okay, but my body's not buying it."

Scarlett reached across the table, squeezing her hand. "Nightmares?"

"Every night." Noelle's voice cracked, quiet. "Sometimes I wake up and swear I still hear him outside. It's stupid."

"It's not stupid."

Noelle nodded, eyes dropping to the table. "Slade keeps saying I'm safe now, and I believe him. I do. But my brain hasn't gotten the memo."

They sat like that for a while, steam curling between them. Outside, light snow drifted past the window in lazy flakes.

Scarlett tilted her head. "You sure you're okay being out? You look pale."

"I needed to get out of the apartment," Noelle said. "Fresh air. Coffee. Pretend I'm normal again." She smiled weakly. "Besides, if I stayed home one more day, Maple would start giving me therapy dog lectures."

Scarlett grinned. "He's not wrong."

Noelle lifted her cup again, but her hand shook. The motion made her vision blur. Her stomach turned over hard.

Scarlett's smile faded. "Noelle?"

The room tilted.

"I just need a sec," Noelle said, gripping the table edge. "I think—"

A voice came from beside her, low and concerned. "Hey, easy."

Hunter had been in line, now suddenly at her side, steadying her before she could hit the floor.

Scarlett jumped up. "She's been sick since...everything. Headaches, nausea, won't see a doctor."

"I'm fine," Noelle muttered, but her voice was slurred with exhaustion. "Just that annoying flu bug still hanging on. And stress, I'm sure. I didn't really...recover."

Hunter frowned. "You're shaking. You should sit."

"Thanks Hunter, I'm fine, really. There is no need to worry about me," she said weakly, even as her knees gave out again. He caught her, guiding her back into the chair and exchanged a worried look with Scarlett.

Scarlett crouched beside her. "You need to go home. I'll call Slade—"

"No!" Noelle's protest came out soft, panicked. "He'll worry."

"Exactly," Scarlett said.

"I don't want him to see me like this."

Hunter glanced between them, phone in hand. "He'd rather see you like this than hear you passed out in public."

Noelle leaned forward, pressing a hand to her temple. "Please. Just a ride home. That's all."

Scarlett looked at Hunter, then back at her. "Okay. Here's what's happening. Hunter is going to go to practice, which is where Slade is now, I'm guessing. I'm taking you home and we're ordering takeout from Veranda Thai because you need real food and comfort noodles. After practice the guys will meet us back at your place for whatever Thai food we have left over for them and to hang out."

A weak laugh escaped her. "Comfort noodles?"

"Yes. Comfort noodles. Pad Thai that fixes your soul. Your favorite orange chicken. Plus those crispy spring rolls you inhale every time."

Noelle shook her head, but her eyes stung. "You don't have to stay with me."

Scarlett arched a brow. "Oh, I absolutely do. You're not spending the rest of today alone. We're going to eat, watch something stupid, and you're going to rest. I'm not leaving you until Slade is home. Deal?"

Noelle nodded faintly, swallowing hard. "Deal."

Scarlett grabbed her coat and looped an arm around her shoulders, steering her toward the door. The cold air hit, and Noelle swayed again, vision flickering. Scarlett tightened her grip.

"You're okay," Scarlett said quietly. "I'm right here."

Noelle nodded, though she didn't feel okay at all. The street blurred around them, and an unfamiliar tightness lingered beneath her ribs, subtle but insistent—something she couldn't yet name.

Slade tugged off his jersey, the post-practice exhaustion settling into his muscles. He sat on the locker room bench, barely paying attention as Hunter dropped beside him, stretching his arms behind his head.

Hunter glanced over. "How's Noelle doing?"

Slade's hands stilled briefly before he resumed tugging at his laces. He hadn't expected the question, and something about the way

Hunter asked it made his stomach tighten—not suspicion, exactly, but dread.

"Why are you asking?" Slade shot back, his voice more guarded than it should have been with his friend. His need to protect her was nearly all-consuming.

Hunter shrugged, rolling his shoulders. "Saw her at the café earlier with Scarlett. She looked awful."

Slade narrowed his eyes. "Awful how?"

Hunter hesitated, then sighed. "She nearly fainted. I caught her arm just before she hit the floor."

His pulse kicked against his ribs, hard, fast. His grip tightened on the laces, his brain working too slow for the words that had just hit him.

"She what?" Slade demanded, his voice sharper than he intended.

Hunter held up a hand. "Scarlett says she's been feeling awful for a while. Thinks it's the flu, but—" He shook his head. "I don't know, man. It didn't look like the flu."

A sharp heat spread through Slade's chest — fear first, then something darker.

"And no one thought to tell me?" he asked.

Hunter frowned. "I figured she would've already. Or Scarlett would've."

Slade stood abruptly, the bench scraping behind him, frustration snapping through him, clean and brutal — not at Hunter, not even at Noelle, but at himself.

He should have noticed.

Scarlett had noticed. Hunter had noticed. Seemingly everyone but him.

Without another word, he yanked his coat from the hook.

"Hey," Hunter said. "Where are you going?"

Slade didn't answer. He was already halfway to the door, heart pounding, one thought eclipsing everything else.

He had to get to Noelle.

Now.

By the time Slade reached Noelle's building, he barely remembered the drive. Every red light felt like a personal insult.

He took the stairs two at a time, heart hammering. The hallway smelled like someone's burned toast, the radiator knocking in the walls. He didn't bother knocking softly—just rapped once, hard.

It opened almost immediately.

Scarlett stood there, takeout container in one hand, concern etched deep between her brows. Relief flickered across her face when she saw him.

"Thank God," she said quietly. "She's on the couch."

Slade didn't waste time responding. He stepped past her, eyes already locked on the living room.

Noelle sat curled into the corner of the couch beneath a fleece blanket, a half-finished container of Thai noodles balanced on the coffee table. The TV was still on, some movie paused mid-scene. She looked up at the sound of his boots, surprise flickering across her face.

"Slade?" Her voice was soft. Fragile in a way that made his chest tighten.

She looked pale. Too pale. Her sweatshirt hung loose at the collar, hair messy, eyes glassy with exhaustion.

"Why didn't you tell me you almost passed out in public?" The words came out sharper than he meant.

Her brow furrowed. "Hunter told you."

"Damn right he did."

She sighed, rubbing her temple. "Please don't be mad. Scarlett already lectured me. I'm fine. Hunter had no right to—"

"He absolutely did," Slade cut in, stepping fully into the room. "You scared the hell out of everyone."

Scarlett set the food down with a soft clatter. "Okay," she said calmly. "Tone. Let's bring it down a notch."

Slade dragged a hand through his hair, exhaling hard. "I'm not mad," he said, forcing himself to slow. "I'm—" He stopped, searching for the right word. "Worried."

Noelle's shoulders sagged a fraction.

Scarlett crossed her arms. "She got dizzy at the café. Lost color fast. I insisted on bringing her home." She shot Noelle a look. "And feeding her."

Noelle muttered, "I ate."

"Three bites," Scarlett corrected.

Slade stepped closer, his voice softer now. "Noelle... you don't look fine."

"Wow," she muttered. "You really know how to comfort a girl."

"I'm not trying to comfort you," he said gently. "I'm trying to figure out why you're still upright."

She leaned back against the cushions, eyes closing. "It's just the flu. I've had it forever. I'll get over it."

"Flu doesn't last forever," he said.

She gave a weak shrug. "Guess I'm an overachiever."

Slade crouched in front of her, one hand braced on the coffee table. "You've been getting headaches. Dizzy. Nauseous." His gaze stayed on her face. "Since before the cabin?"

Her eyes opened slowly.

She hesitated — just a beat — then nodded. "I thought it would go away. And then everything happened and I just... didn't have time to think much about it."

Scarlett's expression softened, worry replacing the edge. "You don't get to put your body on pause forever."

"Damn it, Noelle. That means you've been sick like this for nearly a month." His jaw flexed. "You should've said something."

"I didn't want to worry you."

He laughed once, dry and disbelieving. "Mission failed."

Her mouth twitched, but the humor didn't reach her eyes. She looked exhausted, shadows smudged beneath them. Her fingers trembled when she tried to tuck her hair behind her ear.

Scarlett noticed. "Okay," she said gently. "That's enough. You're not fine, and we all know it."

Slade stood abruptly, grabbing her coat off the back of the chair. "Come on. We're going to the ER."

"Slade—"

"I'm not arguing about this."

"It's expensive," she said quietly. "I can't—"

"Easy solution," he cut in, "I'll pay. End of story."

Scarlett lifted a hand before Noelle could protest again. "Let him," she said softly. "This isn't about money. This is about you and your safety."

She opened her mouth again, then stopped when she saw the look on his face.

"Slade," she said softly. "You don't have to—"

"I do," he said, voice rough. "Because you won't take care of yourself, and somebody has to. I want to be that somebody so please just let me."

Scarlett reached for her purse. "I'm calling ahead to the ER," she said, already moving. "I'll meet you there if you want—"

Slade shook his head. "I've got her."

Scarlett paused at the door, eyes soft but serious. "Text me," she said to Noelle. Then, quieter, to Slade, "Don't let her talk her way out of this."

"Wouldn't dream of it."

She gave Noelle one last look—an unspoken promise—then stepped out, pulling the door shut behind her.

She blinked hard, looking away. For a moment, neither of them moved. Then her breath caught, sharp and sudden—another wave of nausea.

He was there before she could stand, steadying her. "Hey. Easy."

Her head dropped forward, one hand gripping his sleeve. "Just dizzy. Happens sometimes."

He swallowed the surge of panic threatening to crawl up his throat. "Not anymore it doesn't."

"Slade—"

"Coat. Shoes. Now."

Something in his tone must've broken through her stubbornness because she didn't argue again. She just moved slowly, every motion careful, deliberate. He helped her with the zipper when her hands shook too much to catch it.

When they reached the door, she swayed again. He caught her, steadying her against his chest.

"You're burning up," he murmured.

"I'm fine," she said again, her voice thin.

"Stop saying that," he said quietly. "You're not."

He guided her into the hallway, keeping one arm firm around her waist as they made their way down the stairs. Outside, the breeze tugged at their coats.

"You're going to be okay," he said, helping her into the passenger seat.

She nodded faintly. "You keep saying that."

"And I'll keep saying it," he murmured, brushing her hair back from her forehead before closing the door.

He circled around to the driver's side, started the car, and pulled into the street without another word—jaw set, knuckles white on the steering wheel.

Whatever was going on, he wasn't letting her face it alone.

The hospital room was too bright. Too white. It made Noelle feel like she didn't belong there—like her bruises, her exhaustion, her everything were too messy for the clean walls and quiet machines.

She sat on the exam table, fingers twisted in the blanket, trying to ignore the drip of the IV beside her. Slade stood by the door, still in his jacket, watching her with that unreadable look he got when he was trying not to worry out loud.

When the doctor came in, Noelle's chest tightened.

"Miss Hayes," she said, scanning the chart, "you're mildly anemic and dehydrated. Nothing serious. But your hCG levels came back elevated, which means you're pregnant—about six weeks."

The words turned her hearing to static.

Noelle blinked once. Then again. "I'm sorry, *what*?"

The doctor's expression softened. "Congratulations, your little bundle of joy should arrive around Christmas," she said gently. "We'll get you set up with a referral for follow-up."

And just like that, she was gone, leaving the air too thick to breathe.

Noelle stared straight ahead. "No," she said quietly. "That can't be right."

Slade didn't speak.

"I can't be pregnant," she went on, shaking her head. "I mean, I could be, obviously, but... not now. Not after—" She broke off. "Slade, I can't afford this. I can't even afford to take a sick day, and now I'm supposed to..." Her voice trailed. "I can't do this."

He stepped closer. "You won't be doing it alone."

She looked up at him, her eyes rimmed red but dry. "You don't understand. My life doesn't have a safety net. If something goes wrong, there's no one to call. There's just me."

"I get it, but you do have a safety net now," he said quietly.

"You mean you?"

"Yeah." He hesitated, rubbing the back of his neck. "And I want this."

That made her look at him. Really look. "You... *want* it?"

He nodded. "Yeah. I didn't expect it, and maybe the timing isn't perfect, but when the doctor said it, I didn't feel scared. I just—knew."

"Knew what?"

"That I'm not going anywhere," he said.

Noelle swallowed hard. "You don't have to say that."

"I'm not saying it because I have to." His voice was steady, no bravado, no charm. "I'm saying it because it's true."

Her throat worked, trying to form words that wouldn't come. "Slade..."

He reached out then—slow, careful—and took her hand. It wasn't some grand gesture. Just solid, grounding. "I know it's a lot," he said. "I know you're scared. But we'll figure it out. One thing at a time."

She let out a shaky breath that wasn't quite a laugh. "You make it sound simple."

"It's not," he said. "But we have each other and it's real."

For a long moment, neither of them spoke. The monitor ticked softly beside her, steady and constant.

And even though nothing about this felt certain, for the first time in weeks, Noelle didn't feel like the ground was about to give way.

The automatic doors hissed open, letting in a gust of cold air that flushed her cheeks. The world outside felt muted—a misting rain fell lightly under the orange glow of the streetlights.

Slade kept one hand hovering near her back as they walked, not quite touching, but close enough that she could feel the warmth.

"You sure you're okay to walk?" he asked.

"I'm fine," she said automatically, then added, quieter, "or I will be."

He didn't press. Just nodded and unlocked the truck.

The heater kicked in with a low hum as they climbed inside. Noelle sank into the seat, her hospital bracelet catching the light when she rubbed her palms together. The city outside was half asleep, everything washed in silvery raindrops.

Neither of them spoke for a while. The kind of silence that isn't awkward—just heavy.

Finally, she said, "I don't even know what I'm supposed to feel right now."

"Whatever you're feeling's allowed," Slade said, eyes on the road.

She watched the snow blur past the windshield. "It just doesn't feel real yet."

He gave a small nod. "It will."

She glanced over at him. His jaw was still tight, but his hands were steady on the wheel. He looked focused—calm in a way that made her chest ache.

"You're being weirdly calm about all this," she said.

"Trying to keep the truck on the road," he said, a flicker of a smile pulling at the corner of his mouth.

"Seriously."

He sighed. "Would you rather I panic?"

"No. I just..." She trailed off. "I don't know how to do this."

"We don't have to figure it all out tonight." His voice softened. "You've had enough for one day."

Noelle let out a breath that fogged the window. "I keep thinking I'm going to wake up, and it'll all be some messed-up dream."

He glanced at her then, eyes soft in the dim light. "You're wide awake."

The words sat between them, simple and solid.

When they reached her building, he put the truck in park but didn't move to open his door. The rain was falling harder now, whispering against the windshield.

"You don't have to come up," she said quietly.

"Oh, I'm not leaving you alone tonight," he replied. "Not after everything."

She didn't argue. Couldn't.

Inside, the apartment was dark except for the soft glow of the lamp she'd forgotten to turn off. Maple's tags jingled as she bounded over, tail wagging like she'd been waiting for hours. Noelle dropped to her knees, burying her face in her fur.

Slade set her coat on the hook, giving her that small, private moment.

When she finally stood, eyes glassy but calm, she looked at him and something unspoken passed between them—something neither of them was ready to name. But there was an undertone of growing happiness.

"So, you're spending the night?" she asked almost timidly.

"As long as you'll have me." Slade responded in kind.

Noelle nodded, wordless. She moved toward the couch, exhaustion tugging her down. Slade followed quietly, grabbing the blanket off the backrest and tucking it around her shoulders before sitting too.

She watched him for a moment, too tired to speak.

"Get some sleep," he murmured.

The heater clicked on, Maple settled at her feet, and for the first time in weeks, Noelle let her body fully rest. Outside, the rain continued to patter on the windows, soft enough to blur the edges of the world. For days and then weeks, Noelle and Slade had moved through a quiet rhythm of shared silences, lukewarm leftovers, late-night movies watched half-asleep, Maple snoring between them like a living peace treaty.

Slade slipped effortlessly into her space without crowding it.

He walked the dog before practice.

He carried in groceries she forgot she'd ordered.

He sat beside her when she stared at nothing and didn't demand she look anywhere else.

It was terrifying how gentle it all felt.

Chapter Thirty-Eight

Summer was in full swing with dazzling fireworks lighting up the night sky as they sat on a blanket in the town square lawn on the Fourth of July. Slade paused as he looked over at her—something in his face softening, something settling.

"Noelle?" he said quietly.

She looked up at him. "Yeah?"

"We should talk."

Her stomach dipped. "Okay…"

He scooted closer to her, close enough to feel her pulse stutter through the space between them as he clasped her dainty hand in his.

He took a breath, like he was steadying himself.

"These last few weeks," he began, "I've realized I needed to say something I haven't said in a long time."

Her fingers tightened over the blanket. "Slade…"

"I need to say this, need to remind you," he murmured, covering her hand with his. "I love you."

It landed louder than any firework could be.

Her breath caught.

"I know everything's messy. But loving you feels… true."

Tears prickled behind her eyes, uninvited.

"And I want a future with you," he added, quieter than before.

"Slade, there's something I have to ask you," she whispered. "And I hate how it's going to sound."

"Ask me," he said immediately.

Her voice cracked. "Are you doing this—staying with me and saying you love me—because I'm pregnant?"

He stilled as if he'd been body-checked in a place that mattered.

She rushed on, words stumbling over each other. "Because you're good—you're so good to me—and I can see you trying to be steady, and I can see you trying to help, but I don't want to be something you fix. I don't want to be an obligation. I don't want you choosing me because you feel you're supposed to—"

"Noelle." His voice cut through her panic, calm but firm. He cupped her face in both hands, brushing away a stray tear with his thumb. "I'm not thinking about a future with you because of the baby," he said softly. "I'm thinking about it *despite* the baby. If you weren't pregnant, I'd still be right here telling you I love you. I'd still want a life with you."

Her eyes closed as another tear slipped free.

"And you're not something to fix," he added, brushing her cheek with his thumb. "You're someone I want. In every version of the future I can picture."

Her chin trembled. "But what if I can't be enough?"

"You already are," he murmured. "You always have been." He took a breath then, steadying himself. The kind of breath a man takes right before stepping into something irreversible.

"Noelle... What I'm trying to say is that I want to build something with you. Something real. Something long-term. Something permanent."

Something inside her opened, sparked to life.

Slade reached into the pocket of his hoodie and pulled out something wrapped in cloth, holding it the way someone clings to something when they're trying to work up courage.

He unwrapped it.

The lamplight from the street and fireworks in the sky caught on the delicate band, simple and beautiful.

He held it out with steady hands.

"Noelle Faith Hayes… will you marry me?"

A quiet, shattering sound left her—half sob, half relief.

"Slade," she whispered, "I'm scared."

"I know," he murmured, leaning in so their foreheads touched. "I am too. But loving you? That's the part I'm sure of."

Her breath trembled. His thumb brushed her cheek again.

"And this baby is part of our story," he continued, voice low and steady, "I want them to know they came from love. Not from panic. Not from pressure. But from love."

She opened her eyes, flooded with something fragile and fierce.

Then she nodded.

"Yes," she breathed. "Yes, Slade. It'll always be yes."

He exhaled like he'd been underwater too long. Gently, he slid the ring onto her trembling hand and pulled her into him. She curled against his chest, her fingers fisting in his shirt, his arms wrapping around her like something sacred.

Above them, the sky exploded with the grand finale of fireworks—they kissed, slow, certain, full of the promise they'd both been too afraid to admit.

"Happy Independence Day," she whispered.

He smiled into her mouth.

"Best one I've ever had; never felt so free."

SLADES OF GLORY: Silverwood's Most Eligible Bachelor is off the Market

Samantha Romano, Silverwood Snipers' Media Correspondent

In news that has sent shockwaves through Silverwood faster than a puck off Slade Fisher's stick, our star forward is officially engaged.

Yes, you read that correctly.

Slade. Fisher. Proposed.

Noelle Hayes is the local sweetheart who stole his heart—and, if rumors are to be believed, she's also carrying the couple's biggest surprise yet.

Whispers around Silverwood suggest the couple may also be preparing for another major life change with a little addition, though no official confirmation has been made. Friends close to Noelle describe her as "glowing" and say the pair has been focused on keeping things private for now.

While the couple has not released an official statement, a teammate who asked to remain anonymous said: "He's been head over heels for her for a while. We all saw it coming—except him."

It's no secret that Slade and Noelle's relationship hasn't exactly been smooth skating—rumors of her kidnapping and her ex Beau's arrest still hover around them like fog over Silver Lake.

But from all accounts, the two have been inseparable the last few months. Slade has been spotted walking Noelle's dog before practice, buying groceries with her, and reportedly turning down extra ice time to make it home for dinner.

No wedding date—or due date—has been announced, but stay tuned, Silverwood. With a ring on her finger and a baby on the way, this may just be the sweetest news of the summer.

Chapter Thirty-Nine

The Cozy Cup smelled like coffee, syrup, warm bread, and morning sweetness. Noelle slid her sunglasses to the top of her head and spotted Slade in a booth by the window. He was already watching her with that easy, unguarded smile he'd adopted since the proposal, like looking at her was a habit that came naturally now.

She slid into the booth across from him, careful not to bump the table with her belly which had recently started to show.

"Morning," she said.

"Morning," he echoed.

The waitress and one of Noelle's friends, Nicolette, dropped off a cinnamon hot chocolate without needing to ask. "Hope the baby loves hot chocolate as much as you do," she said, with a nod to Noelle's tummy before bustling off again.

Slade lifted a brow. "You've got her trained," he said, nudging her foot with his under the table. Noelle just laughed lightly.

For a moment, they just sat and took in the warmth, the clatter of plates, the comfort of being together without anything pressing at them. Noelle rested one hand lightly on her stomach. Slade noticed the gesture but didn't call attention to it.

He set his coffee down. "I was thinking," he said.

Her lips twitched. "Should I be concerned?"

"Probably," he deadpanned. Then he smiled. "Just kidding."

She waited, curious.

"We're engaged," he said, finishing the sentence like he was still getting used to the fact. "And we've got a baby on the way...." He trailed off for a second, rubbing the back of his neck with a shy grin. "Feels like it's time we stop pretending we don't already live together."

Warmth unfurled low in her chest.

"Oh," she said softly. "You want to move in together."

"I do." His voice didn't waver. "If you want that too."

Noelle let the words settle as her heart soared.

There was no panic. No breath catching. Just... rightness.

"I thought you'd never ask," she said.

Slade's smile widened, almost boyish.

"So that's a yes?" he asked.

"That's a yes," she said, her tone certain now. "Let's do it."

He let out a quiet breath, one he didn't seem to realize he'd been holding. "Good. Because going home without you has felt... wrong...for a while now."

Her cheeks warmed. "So," she said, "your place or mine?"

He didn't hesitate. "I was kind of thinking we could start somewhere fresh and with more room for the baby," he said with a grin, adding, "I hear they need a lot of stuff."

She laughed, not loud, but hearty and real.

Slade looked at her hand resting on her stomach again, then back at her. "It'll be good," he said quietly. "Somewhere to make our own special family memories without shadows of our past lurking around any corners." The words landed gently, and settled over them.

Noelle reached across the table and laced her fingers through his. "Yeah," she said. "I think so too."

Outside, the morning sun was almost as dazzling as the smiles they had plastered on their faces. Inside, *The Cozy Cup* hummed with chatter and the clink of mugs and plates, but none of it touched the happiness blooming in their booth.

They had a plan now. They had a home to find to make their own.

And for the first time in a long time, Noelle felt the future shift into place.

Two months, twelve showings, three rejected offers, and one almost-disastrous bidding war later, they were busy settling into the place that felt like theirs from the first step inside.

The white clapboard exterior still gleamed under the pale Maine sun, deep-blue shutters framing the windows like something pulled straight from a postcard. The wraparound porch creaked softly beneath their boots—wide enough for reading in rocking chairs, for slow summer nights, for watching snow fall in December without feeling alone.

Slade shoulder-checked the door open, a duffel slung over one arm, a cardboard box wedged under the other.

"This is deeply concerning," Scarlett announced behind him, maneuvering around a stack of labeled moving boxes. She carried a plant she'd bought ten minutes ago because every new home needed oxygen. "You packed your entire life in athletic bags."

Slade shot her a flat look over his shoulder. "There's actual furniture pieces coming later when the guys can help."

"Mmm," she hummed skeptically. "I'll believe it when I see something that isn't stitched with your last name."

Inside, the spacious living room opened up around them—original wide-plank pine floors stretching toward a stone fireplace that anchored the far wall. The hearth was empty for now, but Noelle could already envision the family photos propped up and stockings hanging there. Christmases that didn't hurt.

Maple trotted over and immediately sat on the nearest duffel as if she'd been waiting to claim it. Noelle laughed under her breath from the kitchen, a soft sound that tugged at something steady inside Slade.

"You made it back," Noelle called from near the kitchen sink. It had a window above it, sunlight pouring in behind her. The view overlooked a generous backyard, wide and open, edged by tall pines. Plenty of room for Maple to run. Plenty of room for a swing set one day without crowding the lawn.

"I was afraid the second trip would end with one of you stranded on the side of the road."

Scarlett brushed past him with the plant. "Where does this go?"

"Anywhere with light," Noelle said. "We still don't have curtains."

"Perfect," Scarlett replied, setting it on the kitchen counter anyway. "It lives here now."

The house still smelled faintly of fresh paint and sawdust — new keys, new beginnings. A mudroom sat just off the side entrance, already half-filled with boots and a hockey bag, built for Maine winters and messy springs. Slade's gear wouldn't take over the living room here. There was space for all of it. Space for all of them.

And his parents and siblings were just a few streets over in either direction. The arena was less than five minutes away—close enough for early practices, close enough for home to always feel within reach.

Slade carried the duffel into the bedroom—their bedroom—and dropped it onto the bare mattress. The bed frame hadn't arrived yet. Half-assembled nightstands leaned against the wall. Two closets stood open, waiting. A large bathroom stood between the closets.

Down the hall was the other bathroom and three more rooms—one they'd already started calling the nursery, another that would be the office where Noelle could write with a view of the backyard, and the other that would grow into whatever their life needed next.

His things. Her things. No ghosts of old apartments lingering in the corners.

Noelle leaned in the doorway, one hand resting absently over her stomach now. "I can't believe this is actually our house."

"Believe it, babe. *We* have a house." He tossed her a hoodie. "You steal these anyway."

She smiled, small but warm, rubbing the fabric between her fingers before folding it carefully onto *their* dresser.

A heavy thud echoed from the hallway.

"Your hockey equipment should qualify as industrial machinery!" Scarlett called. "I nearly died bringing this in."

Slade sighed and went to retrieve it before she broke something important. She stood in the hall beside the dropped box, breathless and unapologetic.

Scarlett wandered off to find snacks. She'd helped, and now it was time to do what one did in a home...feed everyone.

Slade returned to the bedroom and started putting T-shirts into the top drawer. It stuck halfway in—the old-building charm Noelle always talked about—and he forced it gently instead of wrestling with it.

Noelle was watching him again. There was something soft in her expression, something almost startled by how natural it all felt.

"You okay?" he asked.

She nodded. "Yeah. Just... taking it in."

He crossed the open space and brushed a kiss against her forehead.

"We're good," he said quietly. "This is good."

Noelle leaned into him for a moment, her fingers curling lightly in the fabric of his shirt. "Yeah," she said. "It is."

She slipped an arm around his waist, and he rested his hand over hers without thinking. Maple wandered in and leaned heavily against both their legs.

Noelle looked up at him with a small, certain smile. "I love it here, it already feels like home," she whispered.

"Yeah," he murmured. "Feels like it."

Scarlett reappeared with an open bag of chips. "I vote we take a break till the guys can get here to relieve me."

Chapter Forty

The September breeze was refreshing as they stepped out of the doctor's office.

The envelope felt heavier than it should have. Slade held it between two fingers as they walked to his truck, like it might burst open on its own if he gripped it too tightly. Noelle slipped her hand into his the moment the glass doors closed behind them, her thumb brushing over his knuckles in that grounding way she'd picked up recently—soft, reassuring, real.

"Well," she said lightly; though her eyes were shining. "We survived."

He huffed a quiet laugh. "Barely. I think I stopped breathing when the tech smiled."

Noelle bumped her shoulder into his. "You're so dramatic."

"Only about important things," he said, lifting the envelope slightly. "This definitely qualifies."

They paused beside his truck. For a moment, neither of them moved to open the door. The world felt suspended—no reporters, no teammates, no rumors. Just the two of them and the tiny life they hadn't even met yet.

She tilted her head, studying him. "You sure you're okay with doing this today?"

He smiled, softer than she'd ever seen it. "Best birthday present I could ask for."

Her expression melted. "Good. Because I didn't want to share this day with anyone else."

"Agreed. You, me and our little one," he said, "Old Orchard Beach. No distractions. That's perfect."

She nodded contentedly, "Promise you won't peek?"

He lifted his free hand in surrender. "Scout's honor."

Her smile softened. "You were never a scout."

"Still honorable."

That earned him a laugh, and the tension eased just enough for them to climb into the truck and head north.

Old Orchard Beach greeted them with salt air and sunlight, the boardwalk alive with laughter and music drifting from open storefronts. The ocean stretched wide and blue, endless and steady—exactly what Noelle hoped for.

They kicked off their shoes and walked barefoot along the sand, Slade carrying a small paper bag from a souvenir shop and the still-sealed envelope tucked safely inside it. The breeze tugged at Noelle's hair, and she let it, one hand resting instinctively over her stomach.

Slade noticed. He always did.

"You okay?" he asked softly.

She nodded. "Yeah. Just...thinking about how weird it is that everything has changed so drastically, and yet it still feels like us."

He stopped walking, turning to face her fully. "It is us. Just with a precious addition."

Her throat tightened. She leaned forward, resting her forehead against his chest. "I am so thankful for you. I love you."

His arms wrapped around her without hesitation. "I love you too. Both of you."

They stayed like that for a moment longer, the ocean murmuring around them like a promise.

They found a quiet stretch of beach away from the boardwalk crowds. Slade laid out a blanket then pulled the bag closer, his movements suddenly careful, deliberate.

Inside was a soft teddy bear they bought for the baby to celebrate the occasion alongside the envelope. He swallowed.

"You ready?" he asked.

Noelle took a breath. "As ready as I'll ever be. This is so surreal."

He reached into the bag and pulled out the envelope at last, holding it between them. For a heartbeat, they just stared at it, grinning like kids on Christmas morning.

"Together," she said.

"Always."

Slade tore it open excitedly.

Inside was a single card, folded once. His hands shook as he opened it, and Noelle laughed quietly, nerves bubbling over.

"Well?" she urged.

He looked at the words, then back at her—eyes bright, disbelieving, full.

"We're having a—"

He broke off as Noelle reached for the teddy bear, holding it as if it would help with the sense of suspense. They both laughed, breathless and giddy.

"Okay," she said. "No more stalling."

They looked down at the paper together.

GIRL was written in pink, swirling script.

For a second, the world went silent.

Then Noelle gasped, her hands still holding the teddy bear flying to her mouth. "A little girl!" She squealed in pure excitement.

Slade felt it hit him all at once—the reality, the joy, the fear, the overwhelming love. His chest tightened as he laughed, a broken, happy sound.

"A little girl," he repeated, awe threading every syllable.

Noelle's eyes filled instantly. "She's ours."

He dropped the paper and pulled her up and into his arms, spinning her around before remembering himself and setting her down gently. He cupped her face, pressing his forehead to her again, breathing her in.

"I'm so screwed," he nearly whispered.

"She's going to have you wrapped around her little finger." Noelle said through tears.

He smiled through his own tears. "She already does."

They sat on the blanket afterward, toes buried in warm sand, the teddy bear sitting between them. Slade traced absent circles on Noelle's palm as they talked about names, about tiny jerseys, and bedtime stories and how surreal it felt to be planning a future that finally felt safe.

The September sun dipped lower, casting everything in gold.

Slade leaned in, pressing a kiss to her temple. "Best birthday of my life."

She smiled softly. "Happy birthday, daddy."

As the waves rolled in and out, steady and sure, Slade thought about how far they'd come—how, somehow, the best part of his life hadn't even begun yet.

Chapter Forty-One

The suitcase sat on the bed, still open from the night before, looming like a promise he didn't want to keep—jerseys folded, skates packed, a reminder that another away game had arrived whether Slade was ready for it or not. He stood in front of it, hoodie sleeves pushed up, but he hadn't moved in ten minutes.

Noelle leaned against the doorway, wrapped in a blanket, her face pale but calm.

Slade turned, eyes tired. "I don't want to go."

She walked over slowly, sitting on the edge of the bed. "It's just a few days."

"You've been sick all week. You barely slept last night. What if it gets worse while I'm gone?"

"It's just a little cold and I'll have your family around. Scarlett's going to come hang out and your mom's going to come by with her famous soup," she said before adding playfully, "And I don't know if you remember, but your brother, Callahan, is a doctor and is just around the corner. You really have nothing to worry about."

Slade leaned forward, resting his forehead against hers. "I'll call to check in. Text between periods. If anything feels off, I'm heading straight home."

The hotel room was quiet, lit only by the soft glow of the bedside lamp and the flicker of muted sports highlights on the TV. His gear was scattered across the chair, his duffel half-zipped, but he wasn't thinking about the game anymore.

He was thinking about Noelle who was at home, seven months pregnant.

The video call rang once, then twice—and then Noelle's face filled the screen.

Hair pulled into a loose bun, cheeks flushed, wrapped in one of his old hoodies. She was curled on the couch, legs tucked under her.

"Hey, beautiful," he said, voice softening instantly.

She smiled, tired but radiant. "Hey, hockey man."

Her voice alone eased something tight in his chest. He shifted against the headboard, trying to shake the feeling that the distance between them was bigger than the hours on a bus.

"How's my girl?" he asked.

"Tired," she admitted. "This little acrobat hasn't stopped moving since lunch. I swear she thinks my ribs are drums."

Slade's mouth curved. "Just getting warmed up. She'll be a winger like her daddy."

Noelle rolled her eyes but didn't fight the smile. "Please don't start grooming our little princess for hockey while she's still the size of a cantaloupe."

"Too late. Already picturing her scoring on breakaways. She's gonna skate circles around the boys, I just know it."

She laughed, soft and a little breathless, then winced as she shifted. Slade leaned forward immediately.

"You okay?"

"Yeah," she said quickly. "Just stretching wrong. Everything feels... crowded these days."

He swallowed, worry curling inside him the way it always did when he wasn't home. "You sure you're not overdoing it?"

"Slade," she said gently, "I promise, I'm fine."

He didn't feel fine. He felt useless. He felt like every mile between them made him worse at the job of taking care of her.

"Scarlett's checking on you tomorrow?" he asked.

"Yes," she said. "She already texted me a list of snacks she's bringing. It's mostly pickles and candy."

He exhaled, just a little. "Good."

Noelle tilted her head. "You're doing that thing again."

"What thing?"

"The worry-eyebrow thing."

"I don't have a 'worry-eyebrow'."

"You have at least two," she said sarcastically.

He huffed a laugh, but it didn't stick. "I just... I hate being gone right now."

Her expression softened instantly. "I know. At least you won't be away for long."

"It's different now," he said quietly, rubbing the back of his neck. "I used to travel and it was no big deal. But now I keep thinking, what if you need me? What if something happens? What if I miss something important?"

"You're not missing anything." Her voice gentled even further. "Well, except your daughter reenacting a tap-dancing number on my bladder. But you're lucky to be sitting that one out."

He shook his head, smiling despite himself. "I want to be there. For every bit of it. Even the weird stuff."

"You are here," she said simply. "Every single day, even if you can't physically be for a couple days."

He let the silence settle for a moment, watching the way she tucked a hand over her belly without noticing she was doing it. Then he shifted the phone in his hand, thumb brushing the edge of the case. "Keep your phone on tonight, okay? Call me if you need anything at all. Doesn't matter what time."

"I always do," she said. "And I'll be fine, Slade. Really."

He didn't believe her. Not because she was lying—she never lied. But because *fine* wasn't the point. He wanted her cushioned, supported, held. He wanted to be in the same room, not pixelated on a cheap hotel Wi-Fi connection.

"Hey," Noelle said softly, pulling him back. "Look at me."

He did.

"We're okay," she said. "You've proved you're capable of playing hockey and still being a good partner. You're allowed to go after the life you worked so hard for. And I'm allowed to miss you while you do it."

His throat tightened, he was so grateful for her. "I miss you like crazy."

She smiled, small and sure. "Good. Means we're doing this right."

The warmth of it sank into him, slow and steady.

"Get some sleep," she whispered.

"You too."

She started to pull the phone away, and panic shot through him—not fear, just a deep, stupid longing he couldn't shake.

"Noelle?"

"Yeah?"

"I love you."

Her eyes softened in that way that made him feel hit from the inside out. "I love you too, Slade." The screen went dark. And the room felt even quieter than before.

The next evening, Noelle heard the key in the lock before the door opened. The apartment was dim except for the soft glow of the lamp beside the couch, and she sat curled beneath a blanket, pretending she hadn't been checking the clock every ten minutes.

Slade stepped inside looking worn in that post-game way—hoodie half-zipped, hair flattened under a cap, shoulders tight with travel. But when his eyes found her, the tension loosened all at once.

"You're awake," he said quietly.

"I couldn't sleep."

He crossed the room and dropped beside her, letting out a breath like he'd only just stopped moving. She leaned into him without thinking, and his arm curved around her like it belonged there.

"How was the game?" she asked, tracing the seam on his sleeve.

"You watched it."

"On mute," she said. "Which doesn't really count."

He gave a tired laugh and brushed a kiss against her hairline. "We won."

"I saw."

"Every win means we pull ahead in the standings."

She looked up at him. "Standings...Is that good or...?"

"It's good." He hesitated, the smile faltering just slightly. "It's one step closer to making the playoffs."

Noelle beamed at him, though a faint nervousness fluttered inside her. "Slade, that would be so amazing."

"Yeah," he murmured, rubbing a hand over his jaw. "It is. I mean, I know playoffs are still months away. It's just..."

She waited.

"If we make it, I'll be traveling more." His thumb brushed along her arm. "And the baby will be here by then too, so tiny, and you'll both need me; I don't want to miss a single moment. Just the thought of it is so much harder than I expected."

The baby shifted gently beneath Noelle's palm, a quiet, reassuring roll that grounded her and unsettled her all at once.

"I'll be okay, we are going to be able to make it work," she said, though the words were softer than she meant.

"You say that like you're trying to convince me."

"Maybe I am," she admitted.

He tipped his head back against the couch, eyes closing briefly. "I want that—God, I want that. Playoffs are the dream. But every time I'm away I worry about you."

"There's nothing to worry about," she whispered.

She slid her fingers through his and guided his hand to her stomach. The baby nudged again, and Slade stilled, eyes going soft.

"That," he said quietly, "I don't want to miss that."

"You won't," she whispered. "Even when you're gone, you won't. It will still be happening when you get back."

He let out a slow breath, thumb brushing the curve of her belly like he could memorize it. "I just—this feels so big. All of it."

"It is big." She smiled faintly. "But you still don't have to choose between being a good dad and being a good player."

His jaw tightened. "Feels like someday I might."

She shook her head and pressed her forehead to his cheek. "Not today."

His arm tightened around her, the kind of hold that wasn't desperate—just certain.

"I'm proud of you," she murmured.

Slade swallowed. "Even if I'm not here enough?"

"You're here," she said softly. "Right now, that's all that matters. And I missed you."

He kissed her temple, and held her like he wasn't sure how to let go.

Noelle held him back, feeling something steady take root beneath the nerves, something that would follow them into every month that came after.

The arena was alive in a way Noelle had never felt before. The noise wasn't just loud; it was a roar that shook the walls. She sat several rows behind the bench, one hand wrapped around a cup of ice water, the other resting over her belly as the baby bounced like it wanted to join the crowd.

Scarlett sat beside her, vibrating with nervous energy.

"Okay," Scarlett muttered, "I know you're pregnant and everything, so if you need to scream, I will scream for you."

Noelle laughed. "I'll let you know if I don't think I can handle it."

Down on the ice, Slade cut across the blue line with laser focus. He moved differently tonight. Sharper, quicker, like the ice itself was pushing him forward. Every time he skated close, the crowd surged around her, and she gripped the rail a little tighter, steadying herself against the wave of noise.

The puck hit his stick.

He hesitated just a fraction—reading the defense, lining up the angle.

Noelle held her breath.

Slade stepped into the shot.

A crack of motion.

A blur.

And then the red light snapped to life.

The arena erupted.

Noelle flinched at the sudden roar, her heart slamming, her belly tightening with the force of it. Then relief flooded her so fast she had to blink back tears. Slade didn't celebrate wildly, just a fierce grin and a sharp tap against the glass as he skated past their section.

Right where she sat.

Instinctively, she pressed her hand to the glass in return. Scarlett grabbed her arm.

The last minutes felt endless and frantic. When the final buzzer blared, the arena detonated into cheers.

The Snipers had won again, and they'd be flying to Connecticut next weekend to face off against one of their biggest rivals: the Hartford Whales.

On the ice, players swarmed Slade, shoving and tapping at him, grabbing him in a celebration that looked more like a joyful brawl. His smile was wide now—uncontrolled, boyish, the kind that always made her chest feel too full.

Scarlett nudged her. "Come on. He's gonna want you."

Security waved them through, and Noelle took the stairs carefully, one hand on the rail as the baby rolled under her ribs. The closer she got to the tunnel, the colder the air became—sharp with ice and victory.

Slade spotted her the second she reached the edge of the rubber mat.

His whole expression changed.

He skated toward her, slowing just before he reached the tunnel, pushing his helmet back. He was flushed, breathing hard, eyes bright with adrenaline, and something softer she felt all the way to her core.

"You made it down here," he said, voice rough but warm.

"Yeah, well, the belly helps part the crowd," she murmured.

He leaned in and kissed her. A kiss that tasted like speed and sweat and pure joy. When he pulled back, he looked a little dazed.

Scarlett cleared her throat from behind them. "I'll... be somewhere else. Over there. In a corner. Not watching. Definitely not watching. Maybe I can find Hunter in this crowd."

Slade didn't look away from Noelle.

His gloved hand lifted, resting gently over the curve where the baby was still celebrating, too.

"You okay?" he asked.

She nodded, her throat tight. "Yeah. She's been dancing all over the place."

At the mention of the baby, Slade's breath caught—not a big sound, but enough that she felt it.

"You good?" she asked softly.

"Yeah," he said, the word coming out low, honest. "Just... really glad you were here."

She pressed her hand over his, the cold of his glove seeping into her skin. "Me too."

Behind them, the crowd kept roaring, teammates kept shouting, coaches kept clapping, but all of it blurred into a distant hum.

Slade leaned his forehead against hers for a moment, breath warm in the chill of the tunnel.

And with the bright ice behind them and the warm thump of the baby beneath her hand, Noelle felt a small, deep certainty take root.

Whatever came next—travel, distance, the long stretch of Noelle's third trimester—they were walking straight into it, ready or not.

The morning he had to leave for the game in Hartford came too soon.

Pale gray light filtered through the kitchen curtains, brushing softly against the countertops. Noelle stood barefoot on the cool tile. The house felt emptier already.

Slade stepped out of the bedroom with his duffel over one shoulder, hair still damp, hoodie hanging open. He looked ready for the road in every way except the eyes.

They met in the middle of the kitchen, drawn together like instinct.

Slade touched her face, thumbs brushing along her cheeks, and rested his forehead against hers.

"You sleep at all?" he murmured.

"A little."

He huffed softly. "You're terrible at lying."

"So are you."

His mouth twitched, but only for a second. When he pulled back, his hands drifted down, settling over her belly. The baby pressed upward, a slow stretch beneath his hand, and Slade's thumbs traced the curve like he was absorbing the moment.

"I hate leaving right now," he said quietly. "Every part of me is telling me to stay."

"You're not leaving me," she whispered. "You're just going to play hockey."

"Yeah." His jaw flexed. "I just wish the timing could've lined itself up a little neater."

Her throat tightened. "You want me to tell the baby to schedule herself around the season?"

One corner of his mouth lifted. "If she would listen, I'd take it."

Another slow movement rolled through her stomach, a firmer push this time. She inhaled quietly, steadying herself without making a big show of it. Slade noticed—of course he noticed—and his hand slid to support her.

"That hurt?" he asked softly.

"No," she said. "She's just... strong."

"Like her mom," Slade muttered, but the attempt at levity didn't hide the anxiety threading through his voice.

He wrapped his arms around her then, and Noelle let her eyes close. The scent of his hoodie, the rasp of his stubble against her temple, the solid weight of him: all of it settled something fragile inside her.

"You'll call me?" he asked.

"Of course."

"Noelle." His voice dropped. "If anything feels off. Even a little."

"I will," she insisted.

"And don't talk yourself out of telling me." His hand slipped up her back, palm flattening between her shoulders. "I know you try to be tough. Just... let me come home if you need me. Please."

Her eyes stung. "Okay."

He nodded, swallowing hard like the words cost him.

A horn honked faintly outside.

Slade exhaled through his nose, the sound small and pained. "That's Stryker waiting for me."

Noelle's fingers curled into his hoodie. "Good luck."

He kissed her, slow at first, then deeper, their breaths catching. She held his neck, he held her hips, both of them trying to memorize something they'd only be without for a few days, but somehow that felt enormous.

When he pulled back, he rested his forehead against hers again. "I love you," he whispered.

"I love you too."

He bent, kissed her belly, lingered there.

"See you soon," he murmured to their daughter.

Noelle's eyes burned.

Slade straightened, picked up his bag, hesitated in the doorway like he couldn't make his legs move.

She whispered, "Go," because he needed permission, and she needed to give it.

He stepped into the hall. Turned once. Met her eyes.

Then he was gone.

The door clicked shut, soft and final.

Noelle pressed her hand to her stomach. "We'll be okay," she whispered.

Chapter Forty-Two

The early November wind rattled the windows, carrying the first hints of winter. Noelle sat curled on the couch, her body had felt off since the night before shortly after Slade left for Connecticut—tightness, pressure, a strange ache she couldn't quite name.

At first, she told herself it was just fatigue. She'd been nesting all week, folding tiny onesies and organizing drawers by color and size. But now, a strong cramp grabbed at her abdomen, her breath caught.

The cramps had deepened. They came in waves—sharp, breath-stealing pulses that made her grip the edge of the couch and close her eyes.

When it eased she sank back against the cushions of the couch blinking away the sting in her eyes. "Okay" she whispered to herself. "That was definitely more than a little tightening. More than being tired. Okay, little lady I'm going to call Aunt Scarlett because Daddy is away."

She reached for her phone, hands trembling, and tapped the screen to life. Then she hesitated. Texting felt too slow. Too distant. She needed a voice. She needed Scarlett.

She hit the call button and brought the phone to her ear. It rang twice.

"Hey," Scarlett answered, cheerful and unsuspecting.

Noelle's voice cracked. "Can you come over? Please? I think something's wrong."

Scarlett's tone shifted instantly. "What's happening?"

"I don't know. My back hurts. My belly's tight. It doesn't feel normal, and it's sharp. I feel... off."

"I'm on my way."

Ten minutes later Scarlett walked in to see Noelle sitting on the edge of the couch, doubled over, one hand clutching the couch cushion the other pressed to her belly, tears running down her face as another wave of pain gripped her stomach.

Scarlett crossed the room in two strides. "Hey. Look at me."

Noelle tried—and failed—to straighten.

Scarlett took her face gently but firmly between her hands. "Okay. We're not debating this. We're going to the hospital. Right now."

The arena was electric tonight. The kind of buzzing, restless energy that made the board vibrate and the ice feel alive beneath his skates. Away games had a different edge, a sharper bite. The crowd wasn't cheering for him, they were waiting for him to slip.

Normally he loved that. He thrived on it. But tonight, something felt off. Not physically.

There was a tug in his chest he couldn't shake.

"You good?" Stryker nudged him as they lined up for the faceoff.

"Yeah" he lied tapping his stick twice on the ice. "Let's go."

He knew that Stryker saw through his lie and he would deal with that later.

The puck dropped.

The Snipers won the draw.

Stryker snapped it cleanly back to him, muscle memory taking over before Slade had time to think. He accelerated down the ice, cutting between defenders, the roar of the crowd rising—not in excitement, but anticipation. He could feel them holding their breath, waiting for him to miss.

He didn't.

He lined up the shot and ripped it.

The puck sailed past the goalie's glove and slammed into the back of the net.

The red light flashed.

For a split second, everything went quiet in Slade's head—then the sound crashed back in all at once. Booing. Groans. A few stunned pockets of silence. His teammates swarmed him anyway, sticks banging against his pads, Stryker's grin fierce and proud as he collided into him.

"Atta boy," Garrett and Jayden shouted in unison over the noise.

Slade forced a smile, lifting a hand to acknowledge the moment, but even as adrenaline surged through him, that tight feeling in his chest didn't ease.

The game rolled on—fast, brutal, relentless. Slade played well. Too well. He blocked shots, drove plays, stayed sharp. By the third period, the Snipers had pulled ahead by two, the crowd growing restless, hostile.

When the final buzzer sounded, the win felt solid. Earned.

But the relief he expected never came.

In the locker room, sweat cooling on his skin, Slade reached for his phone the second he sat down. Noelle always texted after games. Always.

There were three missed notifications.

Scarlett.

Scarlett.

Scarlett.

His stomach dropped as his phone rang again.

Scarlett sat in the chair next to Noelle's hospital bed, the lights glowing around them, too bright for the nerves wracking their emotions. Noelle lay curled slightly on her side, one hand resting over her stomach, her face pale but composed in that careful way Scarlett recognized all too well.

The nurse had said it was likely Braxton Hicks. Practice contractions. Common. Normal.

Scarlett still didn't like it.

She pulled out her phone and tapped Slade's name again, fingers moving faster this time. Fourth call.

"Come on," she muttered under her breath.

Finally, the line connected.

"Scarlett? Is it Noelle?" Slade's voice came through strained and breathless, as if he'd been running. "What's happening—is Noelle okay?"

Scarlett cut in before he could continue. "Hey. Don't freak out. Just listen, okay?"

She stood, turning slightly away from the bed, lowering her voice without softening it.

"Noelle had some cramping. She didn't want to bother you during game time. I'm bothering you anyway because she's scared and pretending she's not." She glanced back at Noelle, whose eyes were fixed on the doorway. "You know how she gets."

Scarlett paced once, then stopped.

"I got her to the hospital. They're monitoring her now. The nurse thinks it's Braxton Hicks." She paused, letting that land. "Vitals are stable. Baby's heartbeat is strong. They are saying it's not labor."

His jaw tightened, "Dammit, I knew I shouldn't have left her."

"But Noelle keeps thinking she overreacted, and she didn't. She didn't." Her voice sharpened. "And if one more person says 'false alarm' like this is no big deal, I might throw something very medical and very sharp."

Noelle let out a shaky breath from the bed.

"She's being brave," Scarlett went on, quieter now. "But she keeps looking at the door like she's hoping you'll walk through it."

She exhaled. "I know you're in Connecticut for a game. I just— I know you'd want to know. She needs you. Even if she won't say it."

"I'm with her," Scarlett added. "I'll stay as long as she needs. I promise."

There was silence on the line for half a second too long.

Then—

"I'm coming," Slade said. No hesitation. No discussion.

He immediately changed out of his gear, barely registering the cold air hitting his skin, damp with sweat. His hands shook as he pulled on his sweatpants and a hoodie. He shoved his phone into his pocket and then pulled it out again. He pushed through the back exit of the arena, the night air hitting him in the face.

He dialed the team's travel coordinator as he ran.

"Hey, it's Slade. I need a flight home. Tonight. Now. As soon as possible."

There was a pause "Fisher, what's going on?"

"Noelle is having contractions. Scarlett is with her at the hospital. I have to get back home."

The fluorescent lights buzzed softly overhead. Noelle lay in the hospital bed, monitors strapped to her belly, her heart racing louder than the machines. A nurse moved gently around her, checking vitals, offering water, speaking in calm tones.

"It's not labor," the nurse reminded her kindly. "Just Braxton Hicks. False contractions. Your body's practicing."

Noelle nodded, tears slipping silently down her cheeks. Scarlett sat beside her, holding her hand.

"You did the right thing," Scarlett whispered. "You didn't overreact. You protected yourself. And the baby."

Noelle's phone buzzed. An incoming call from Slade.

She answered on the second ring.

"Noelle?" His voice was tight, breathless. "Scarlett called me. How are you feeling? Are you okay? The baby?"

She swallowed. "It wasn't real labor. Just practice, apparently."

"I'm coming home."

"No, Slade, you have another game tomorrow—"

"I don't care," he said. "I'm not missing this. I need to be with you."

She closed her eyes, letting the sound of his voice settle her. "I was just.. I-I'm scared."

"I know, babe, you don't have to be scared. I'm here" he said. "I'm booking the first flight out. I already talked to Coach Carlson. I'll be there soon. And Noelle, I love you, both of you."

"We love you too," Noelle said, trying to fight the urge to burst into tears.

The sky outside was still a deep, sleepy gray, the kind that lingered just before sunrise. Inside the house, the lights were low, the air quiet except for the hum of the refrigerator and the soft clink of a spoon in a mug.

Scarlett sat at the small kitchen table, one leg tucked beneath her, a hoodie pulled on over yesterday's clothes. A half-empty cup of reheated tea sat in front of her, forgotten. Her eyes were fixed on the couch.

Noelle lay curled beneath a blanket, one hand resting over her belly, the other tucked beneath her cheek. Her eyes were closed, but her breathing was too light for real sleep—hovering in that fragile space between exhaustion and waiting.

Scarlett hadn't left her alone for a second.

The front door clicked open.

Scarlett looked up immediately, heart jumping, and then she exhaled.

Slade stepped inside, duffel bag slung over one shoulder, his hoodie damp from early-morning mist. His eyes went straight to the couch. He dropped the bag carefully by the door, as if even the sound of it might be too much.

Noelle stirred, eyes fluttering open. "Slade?"

He crossed the room in three strides and dropped to his knees beside her, taking her hand like it was instinct, like muscle memory.

"I'm here," he whispered, voice cracking. "I'm here, baby."

Her breath hitched. "I'm really okay. You didn't have to—"

"I did," he said quietly, firm without raising his voice. "I needed to see you. Needed to know."

She shifted, sitting up slowly as the blanket slid from her shoulder. "It wasn't real labor or anything serious. Just a scare."

"I know," he said, brushing his thumb over her knuckles. "Scarlett told me everything. I wish you would have called me like we agreed."

Scarlett stood, already pulling her hoodie tighter around herself, suddenly aware of how tired she was. "She's been stubborn," she said lightly. "Vitals were good. Doctor says it was Braxton Hicks like we told you they suspected it was. She's just supposed to rest."

Slade nodded, gratitude sharp in his eyes. "Thank you."

She waved him off. "That's my job." She bent down and pressed a quick kiss to Noelle's temple. "Text me if you so much as *think* about another cramp."

Noelle smiled faintly. "I will."

Scarlett grabbed her keys, pausing at the door just long enough to look back. Slade had already pulled Noelle against his chest, her forehead tucked beneath his chin like she'd always belonged there.

Good, Scarlett thought.

"I'll check in later," she said quietly, and then she was gone, the door clicking shut behind her.

Slade rested his forehead against Noelle's hair. "You were scared," he murmured. "And I wasn't here. Again."

Noelle leaned into him, forehead resting against his collarbone. "I didn't want to ruin your game. I don't know who Braxton Hicks is but I'd like to give them a piece of my mind."

That made Slade laugh out loud. "You didn't ruin anything, I'm glad it was a false alarm," he said, kissing her then her belly where the baby kicked in response. "You reminded me what matters, nothing is more important than you and our child."

They stayed entwined for a long time—his arms around her, her fingers curled into the fabric of his hoodie, the silence between them warm and full.

Eventually, he pulled back just enough to press a kiss to her temple. "You and this baby are my whole world. Hockey can sit on the sidelines."

Her eyes filled again, but this time with something softer. "I'm so happy you're here."

"I always will be."

The words lingered between them, heavy with promise.

Noelle shifted closer, pushing herself up on the couch despite his instinctive reach to steady her. She cupped his face in both hands, thumbs brushing along his jaw, and kissed him—slow at first, then deeper, more certain.

Slade froze.

Not because he didn't want it.

Because he wanted it *too much*.

"Noelle," he murmured against her lips, pulling back just enough to look at her. His hands stayed careful at her waist, like he was afraid pressure alone might undo her. "You don't have to—"

"I know," she said softly. Then she kissed him again, this time with intent, her fingers sliding into his hair, tugging just enough to make his breath hitch. "I want to."

His forehead dropped to hers. "You scared me earlier."

"I know," she whispered. "But I'm okay now. And I need you."

That need—quiet, sure, unafraid—undid him more than anything else could have.

Slade exhaled slowly, wrestling with himself, his thumb brushing over her hip like he was grounding himself. "I don't want to hurt you," he said. "Or her. Or make things start up again."

Noelle guided his hand down, resting it over the curve of her belly. "She's fine," she said gently. "And so am I. I promise."

He swallowed hard.

When he kissed her again, it was different—hungrier, but still controlled, like he was holding back something wild. Noelle met him there, shifting closer, guiding him to her, her breath catching as his mouth traced along her jaw.

"See?" she whispered, lips nibbling his ear. "Still okay."

Slade groaned softly, the sound low and rough, his grip tightening just enough to make her gasp. He pulled back immediately, searching her face. "That okay?"

Her smile was slow and knowing. "Very."

They moved together carefully, but the want between them crackled —every touch deliberate, every kiss unhurried but charged. Slade followed her lead, letting her set the pace, letting her reassure him with every sigh and soft sound.

In the bedroom, he kept her close, never far, his body a shield more than a force. When Noelle arched into him, fingers digging into his shoulders, he shut his eyes like the trust in that movement was almost too much to carry.

"Slade," she breathed.

"I've got you," he whispered back, reverent. "Always."

After, he stayed wrapped around her, one hand anchored over her belly like it belonged there, the other stroking slow paths along her back. Noelle rested against his chest, warm and boneless, content.

"Still okay?" he asked quietly.

She smiled, eyes closed. "Better than okay."

Slade pressed a kiss into her hair, relief and love tangling in his chest. "Good," he murmured. "Because next time you scare me like that, I might never let you out of my arms again."

She laughed softly. "Deal."

Outside, the sky finally began to lighten—and inside, everything felt steady, warm, and safe.

Chapter Forty-Three

The Fisher and Murphy families had gathered for another Thanksgiving around the long dining table along with Noelle, Willow and Violet. Plates were piled high with turkey, ham, mashed potatoes, cranberry sauce, and warm rolls.

Noelle's belly felt stretched and unsettled, like the baby had shifted into a new position and forgotten to leave room for anything else. Her due date was just around the corner now. Thirty-six weeks and counting. The baby was the size of a melon and had dropped lower.

Slade watched her from across the table, his eyes never straying far. He'd filled her water glass twice, rubbed her back between bites, and leaned in to whisper, "You okay?" more than once.

She nodded each time. But now, as the meal wound down and the conversation turned to pie and football, Noelle felt the need to move. To stretch. To breathe.

"I think I'll stand for a minute," she said softly, pushing her chair back.

Willow looked up from her plate. "You feeling okay there, mama?"

"Yeah, I'm good, I think. I just feel like I need to move around a little."

She walked slowly, one hand on her belly, the other trailing along the edge of the table. She meandered around until she reached the doorway to the living room, where the fire crackled softly and the couch waited like a promise.

She sank into it with a humph. It didn't take much to make her feel worn out these days.

Willow brought her some ginger ale without being prompted. "I bet all that heavy food has you feeling extra cramped in there," she said with a light-hearted giggle as she handed the drink to Noelle.

"Thanks, hopefully this settles my little acrobat down so I can digest that feast." The bubbles fizzed as she took a sip and her stomach eased. It was comforting knowing her friend was a nurse. Willow had put her mind at rest so many times throughout this journey and Noelle was more than grateful for her.

Slade came in hurriedly with that worry-eyebrow of his in full effect. "Hey, are you sure you're okay? What do you need? What can I do?"

"Oh you worry-wart, everything is fine, I promise. It's just hard to fit a baby and a full Thanksgiving meal in my tiny 5'2" frame all at once. Willow brought me a ginger ale though and I'll just need to walk some of that delicious meal off in a little bit." Noelle assured him with a warm smile.

Slade grinned breathing a sigh of relief, "Well okay, as long as you're sure, that's good. We need to keep that bun in your oven for a few weeks longer."

"Hopefully she joins us in time for the next big family meal on Christmas."

"That would be the best gift ever." Slade replied as his chest filled with happiness.

The Winter Walk wrapped Silverwood in festive, twinkling lights that sparkled down on them as they walked around it to celebrate Noelle's birthday. Christmas Eve felt like it held more magic than possible this year.

Every tree lining the town square shimmered with white and gold, strands of bulbs draped like constellations between lampposts. Storefront windows glowed from within, fogged slightly from the cold, while the air carried the sweet bite of pine, sugar, and roasted chestnuts. Somewhere near the gazebo, a quartet sang *Joy to the World*, their voices floating through the crowd like a benediction.

Noelle slowed her steps, taking it all in.

"I don't think it ever gets old," she said softly.

Slade glanced down at her, his breath visible between them. "And it never will, especially since we get your birthday, Christmas and our little girl any day now."

She was bundled in her long coat, scarf wrapped twice around her neck, one gloved hand tucked into his pocket, the other resting low on her belly. Slade's arm stayed snug around her shoulders, protective without realizing it, like instinct had already begun rewriting him.

"Happy birthday," he murmured, pressing a kiss into her hair.

She smiled up at him. "Best one yet."

They moved with the slow rhythm of the crowd, past vendor stalls where mugs of hot cocoa steamed and paper cones of warm chestnuts were passed from hand to mittened hand. A child darted by clutching a candy cane nearly as tall as she was, laughter echoing behind her.

Slade stopped at one booth and bought a cocoa, handing it to Noelle before taking his own. She wrapped both hands around the warm mug, sighing contentedly.

"Almost as perfect as mine," she said contentedly. "I swear, Winter Walk should be prescribed."

"For what?"

"For everything."

They giggled, then grew quiet again as the carol shifted to *The First Noel*. The bells in the nearby church tower chimed the hour, deep and steady.

Noelle inhaled slowly—and then paused.

Slade felt it immediately. "Hey. You okay?"

She nodded, eyes thoughtful rather than worried. "Yeah. I think so. Just... that felt different."

He didn't panic. He simply waited.

A few seconds passed. Then she exhaled, a smile tugging at her lips. "Okay. That one definitely counted."

His brows lifted. "Counted how?"

She looked up at him, eyes bright, almost amused. "I think our little girl decided my birthday party needs a plus-one."

The world seemed to soften around them. Slade stared at her for a heartbeat, then let out a slow, disbelieving laugh.

"Tonight?"

"Not *right* this second," she said, squeezing his hand. "But yeah. I think she's about to make her debut."

Another carol swelled, the crowd humming along, unaware that anything extraordinary had just begun. Snow started to fall—light, lazy flakes that caught in Noelle's hair.

Slade leaned in, resting his forehead against hers. "You're calm."

She shrugged gently. "I'm excited. She picked Christmas. She picked now. I feel so blessed."

His throat tightened. "The biggest blessing I could possibly imagine."

They turned toward the edge of the square, walking cautiously now, stopping when Noelle needed to. Each contraction came like a quiet wave—noticeable, manageable, almost welcome. Slade counted under his breath, steady as a metronome, his hand warm and sure at her back.

At the edge of Winter Walk, she paused again, laughing softly.

"What?" he asked.

"She's dramatic," Noelle said. "All that buildup. Just like you."

He grinned. "I feel attacked."

They made it to the truck just as the snow thickened, the lights behind them blurring into something dreamlike. Slade helped her in, then sat for a moment before starting the engine, just holding her hand.

"Happy birthday," he said again, voice rough now.

She squeezed his fingers as he pulled out and pointed in the direction of Silverwood General.

"Best gift ever."

The drive to the hospital passed in a blur of falling snow and steady breaths. Slade kept one hand on the wheel, the other firmly wrapped around Noelle's, grounding himself in the rise and fall of her chest.

"You're doing great," he murmured, even as another contraction tightened her grip around his fingers.

She smiled through it. "You keep saying that."

"Because it's true."

At the hospital, everything moved quickly but smoothly. Willow was on shift and guided Noelle back, Slade never once leaving her side. He helped her change, helped her breathe, helped her laugh when she made a joke about timing her contractions to Christmas music playing faintly down the hall.

When they were finally settled, Slade brushed a kiss to Noelle's forehead then pulled his phone from his pocket with his free hand and opened the family group chat.

SLADE:

> Noelle's in labor. Real labor. We're at Silverwood General now. She's calm. I'm trying to be calm. Our baby girl is on her way!!

The replies rolled in almost instantaneously.

MOM:

> Oh my heart. Praying hard for all three of you. Tell Noelle we love her so much. I can't wait to hold my grandbaby!

DAD:

> You've got this son. We're on our way.

SCARLETT:

> I KNEW she would pick Christmas! Do you need anything? I can bring snacks. How's Noelle?

CALLAHAN:

> Amazing news brother! Any idea how far
> along she is yet? I'm not on duty right now
> but I'm heading that way.

STRYKER: *You're really trying to outdo me for Christmas gifts this year, huh? Tell my niece to take it easy on her entrance.*
Slade snorted quietly, earning a weak but amused smile from Noelle.
JULIETTE:

> I can't believe my baby brother is about to
> be a daddy! So happy for you both and can't
> wait for my next visit so I can cuddle the little
> love!

BENNETT:

> Sending good vibes, prayers, and
> structurally sound thoughts from NM where
> it is NOT snowing!

SCARLETT:

> Did you just architect-bless the baby?

BENNETT:

> Absolutely. Solid foundation. Open-concept
> future. Tell that little girl of yours her uncle
> can't wait to meet her for his summer visit
> when the weather isn't frightful.

STRYKER:

> Since I'm two minutes older, I call dibs on
> teaching her to skate first.

SLADE:

You're all ridiculous. She's doing great but
has a ways to go I think. I'll update you when
I can. Love you guys.

The waiting room quickly and steadily filled with members of the Fisher family.

Slade slipped out of the delivery room to give them a quick update on Noelle's progress. His parents were the first ones he saw, his mother's eyes already shining, his father's hand firm and grounding on Slade's shoulder. Callahan came over from chatting with a nurse and clapped him on the shoulder with a proud smile. Stryker crushed him in a bear hug. Then Scarlett swooped in with Violet, breathless and flushed from the cold, wrapping her arms around her brother, speechless for once.

As all of their animated questions and chatter bombarded his ears, he raised his hands, "Okay, okay, I know you're all excited and we're so thankful you're here. I just wanted to let you know both her and the baby are doing great. Now, I'm going to get back in there before I miss my daughter entering the world."

He dashed off before another moment could keep him from the two most important girls in his world.

Chapter Forty-Four

Hours blurred together in soft lights and whispered encouragement. Slade counted breaths, pressed cool cloths to her forehead, let her grip his hand until his knuckles ached. He told her stories—silly ones, sweet ones—anything to keep her grounded.

Noelle squeezed his hand so hard he lost feeling in three fingers. He didn't care.

He hated every sound of pain she made.

Every cry.

Every wince.

Every whispered "Slade, I can't—"

"Yes you can," he whispered back, forehead pressed to hers. "You are. You're doing it right now."

He tried to be calm for her.

He felt anything but calm on the inside.

Every contraction felt like watching the person he loved most fight a battle he couldn't help with. It gutted him. Ripped him apart in slow, relentless pieces.

But then—then something shifted.

Her breathing changed.

Her grip adjusted.

Her whole body shifted into some primal gear he didn't recognize.

The doctor stepped closer. "It's time to push."

Slade's heart almost stopped. Willow was there giving reassurances as she assisted the doctor and supported Noelle in ways Slade didn't know how.

"Okay," he whispered, kissing her temple. "Okay, baby, I've got you."

She pushed.

And he held her steady.

She sobbed.

And he wiped her tears.

She shook.

And he braced her shoulders.

She told him she couldn't do it.

And he whispered, "You're the strongest person I've ever known."

He meant it with every atom he had.

When it was finally time, Slade stayed right where she needed him—close, steady, awe-struck. He whispered her name like a prayer, felt tears blur his vision when he heard the first sharp, perfect cry.

The room seemed to exhale.

"She's here," Willow announced, beaming at her friends.

Slade's entire world imploded. He had never heard a more beautiful sound.

The doctor lifted a tiny, wriggling, furious little girl into the air. "Congratulations. She's perfect."

Slade's hand flew to his mouth.

"Oh wow," he said, voice cracking. "Oh my—"

They placed the baby on Noelle's chest, warm and small and pink, and Slade leaned over them with tears he didn't even try to stop.

Holly Faith Fisher was born just after dawn on Christmas morning.

Noelle swallowed, her heart bursting with a love she didn't know was possible. "Holly Faith," she whispered to the baby. "Welcome to the world."

The world beyond the hospital window was pale and quiet, snow blanketing the town like a promise kept.

"Noelle," he whispered, his voice wrecked. "Look at her. Look at her —she's... she's ours."

She cried.

He cried harder.

The baby wailed like she had opinions about everything already.

Slade kissed her hair, her forehead, her shaking fingers.

"You're incredible," he whispered. "You're... I can't even—Noelle, you did it."

Snow drifted softly outside the hospital windows, the flakes taking their time as though they wanted to look in and witness the tiny little miracle themselves.

Slade's nerves were all over the place and he bumped into the side table by the hospital bed. Their daughter startled at the sound, then nestled in again.

Slade placed a trembling hand on the baby's back.

"Hi, princess," he whispered. "Welcome to the world."

For the first time since losing Jess in the fire, Slade Fisher truly felt a future expand in front of him so wide it stole the breath right from his lungs.

And he knew he would spend every day of that future loving these two with everything he had.

The hospital room was quieter now.

Morning light spilled in pale and slow through the window, catching on the soft curls of Holly's chestnut hair as she slept against Noelle's chest. The machines hummed low and steady, a gentle reminder that time was still moving, even though it felt—just for a moment—like the world had paused.

Slade sat in the chair beside the bed, one hand resting lightly on Noelle's knee, the other curled protectively around Holly's tiny foot. He hadn't slept. He didn't care. Every time he closed his eyes, he saw the same thing: Noelle's strength, her courage, the way she had looked at him when it was over—exhausted and radiant and utterly unbreakable.

A soft knock came at the door before it opened a crack.

Scarlett slipped in first, carrying two coffees and wearing a smile that was equal parts joy and awe. "I brought fuel," she whispered. "And I swear I won't cry."

Behind her came Genevieve, already teary eyed, followed by Daniel, Callahan and Stryker who was carrying a teddy bear dressed like a hockey player.

They didn't rush the bed.

They didn't crowd.

They gathered gently, like people who understood this was sacred ground.

Genevieve reached Noelle first, smoothing a hand over her hair. "You are incredible, sweetheart," she said softly. "I hope you know that. I'll never be able to thank you enough for giving me my first grandbaby, she's so precious. How are you feeling? Do you need anything?"

Noelle shook her head as her throat tightened in overwhelming gratitude. She may have just become a mother for the first time but receiving this maternal support from her future mother-in-law made her heart swell in ways she hadn't felt since she was a child herself.

Callahan stepped forward next, his doctor's instincts subdued by something far more personal. He glanced at the monitors out of habit, then smiled. "Everyone looks perfect," he said. "And for the record—I wasn't worried for a second."

"That's a lie," Stryker muttered. "You texted me 'she's fully dilated' in all caps."

Callahan shot him a look. "That was... professional urgency."

Scarlett leaned closer to the bed, eyes shining as she looked at Holly. "She's real," she whispered. "Like... actually real."

Slade watched Noelle absorb it all—the warmth, the attention, the easy way they made space for her. Something settled deep in his chest as he realized this wasn't just support.

This was family.

Noelle shifted slightly, careful of the baby, and finally looked up at all of them. "Thank you," she said quietly. "For being here."

Genevieve smiled at her like the words meant more than she knew. "There's nowhere else we'd be, you're our family."

Two days later, when they were finally home as a family of three, Slade helped Noelle ease back against the pillows of their bed. Holly stirred between them, her tiny mouth forming a soft, indignant pout before relaxing again.

Slade brushed a thumb over her cheek, overwhelmed in a way that felt steady instead of terrifying now.

"Noelle," he said softly.

She looked at him. "Yeah?"

He swallowed. "You know you're never going to be abandoned again, right?"

Her eyes softened. "I know."

"You have us," he continued. "Me, my family, all of us. And I—" His voice caught. "I'm not going anywhere. Ever."

She reached for his hand, lacing their fingers together. "I know that too."

Holly let out a small sigh, her body warm and heavy between them, as if she already understood the promise being made.

Slade leaned down, pressing his forehead to Noelle's. "We're going to be okay," he whispered.

Noelle smiled, tired and sure. "We already are."

Outside, snow began to fall again—quiet and unhurried—blanketing the town in white as if sealing the moment in place.

And for the first time, Noelle didn't feel like she was bracing for what came next.

She was home.

The SILVERWOOD SCOOP

Local Sports & Community News

Silverwood Welcomes Its Newest Little Star

Samantha Romano, Silverwood Snipers' Media Correspondent

Silverwood has a new reason to celebrate — and this time, it's not a goal horn.

Slade Fisher and Noelle Hayes have officially welcomed their baby girl, Holly Faith Fisher, into the world, and sources confirm that both mom and baby are happy, healthy, and already completely adored.

Born on Christmas Day, Holly Faith arrived with a full head of chestnut hair and a set of lungs that made her presence immediately known. "She let everyone know she was here," one insider shared with a laugh. "Very on-brand for a Fisher."

The proud new parents have kept things quiet since the birth, opting for family time over press statements, but those close to them say Slade hasn't stopped smiling since the moment he held his daughter.

Noelle, described as glowing despite the exhaustion, is reportedly a natural when it comes to motherhood.

From high-profile games to very personal challenges, their road hasn't always been smooth — but if this moment proves anything, it's that they've arrived exactly where they're meant to be.

No word yet on whether Holly Faith will grow up on skates or prefer the stands, but one thing is certain: she's already the tiniest MVP in town.

From all of us at *The Silverwood Scoop*, congratulations to the Fisher family. Silverwood is lucky to have you—and your newest little miracle.

Epilogue

One year later

Snow drifted past the chapel windows in slow, silvery spirals, catching on the candlelight that lined the aisle. Evergreen garland and twinkle lights wrapped the beams overhead, softening the wood in a warm, golden glow. The whole place felt like winter had paused for them—like the world outside had agreed to be quiet and gentle for one night.

Noelle stood in the small bridal room, smoothing a hand over the satin of her dress. It fit differently now—softer in places, a little more forgiving in others—but she liked the way it moved with her. After everything her body had done this year, she wore it with a kind of quiet pride.

Scarlett held the baby on her hip, rocking her lightly. "Okay," she whispered, "you look ridiculously beautiful. Like, criminally so."

Noelle snorted. "It's just the dress."

"No. It's you," Scarlett said simply, then leaned in. "Also, prepare yourself. Slade's probably vibrating out of his suit."

A knock sounded.

Genevieve peeked in, cheeks pink from the cold. "Oh you look stunning, sweetheart. I have just one more thing to add to complete your look if you'll allow me?" she asked as she presented Noelle with a gold locket dangling from a delicate chain.

"Wow, that's gorgeous, are you sure?" Noelle asked, a bit breathtaken by the surprise.

"More than sure. This was my mother's and I decided a long time ago that each of my girls would receive a special piece from her collection on their wedding day. I'm so blessed to have you as my bonus daughter." Genevieve told her lovingly.

Noelle could hardly speak as she welled up with love. "I'm speechless, this means so much to me, thank you, Genevieve. I will cherish it forever and save it for Holly."

"I'm so thrilled that you like it." Genevieve said as she hugged her. "Now, are you ready, darling?"

Noelle breathed out, slow and steady. "Yeah. I think I am."

Genevieve adjusted the veil with gentle hands. "He keeps looking at the door," she murmured in amusement. "Every thirty seconds, like clockwork."

Holly let out a soft coo, and Noelle bent to kiss her tiny cheek. "Be good for Aunt Scarlett, okay?"

"She will," Scarlett said. "She's perfect. I'm... slightly less perfect, but I'll manage."

Daniel stood outside the door waiting to walk Noelle down the aisle to his son. "Wow, kid, you look amazing. Thank you for doing me the honor of walking you down the aisle, we can't wait for you to officially be a Fisher," he said, his eyes shining a bit.

Noelle thanked him, trying not to cry, as she looped her hand into the crook of his arm. She counted her lucky stars to not only be gaining a husband today, but the loving family she always wished she could have.

The chapel doors opened.

Music rose—soft piano, simple and warm—and every guest stood. Noelle stepped into the aisle, her heart thudding beneath the lace bodice, her bouquet of winter roses and holly trembling just slightly in her hands.

And then Slade turned.

His breath caught audibly, shoulders dropping as if someone had untied something inside him. His eyes softened, steady and full in a way that made her knees wobble just enough that she tightened her grip on the flowers.

Before she made it all the way down the aisle, he moved—just a step, just close enough to offer his hand, unable to wait the full distance. His father handed Noelle's hand to him with a proud smile beaming at both of them.

"Hi," he whispered when she reached him, voice roughened with emotion.

"Hi," she whispered back.

"You look..." He exhaled like the right word didn't exist. "You look like home."

Heat rushed to her cheeks. "You do too."

He squeezed her hand once, anchoring them both, and together they faced the officiant.

The ceremony was simple, quiet, and soft around the edges. When it came time for vows, Slade swallowed, glancing for a heartbeat toward the baby in Scarlett's arms before looking back at Noelle with a trembling smile.

"I loved you before I knew what I was doing," he said, voice low. "But now I know. Loving you means choosing you. Every day. Especially the hard ones. And that's all I want. A whole life of choosing you."

Her eyes burned. When she spoke, her voice was unsteady but sure. "You made me feel safe when I didn't know how to be. You made me brave when I didn't feel brave at all. You love every version of me—even the ones I'm still getting used to. I want all of it with you, Slade. Every day we have."

Scarlett let out a single very loud sniff behind them, and someone—probably one of his brothers—snorted quietly.

The rings slid into place.

The kiss was soft and certain.

The room erupted into applause.

Slade rested his forehead against hers, laughing under his breath. "We did it."

"We did," she whispered.

Outside, lanterns glowed against the snowbank edges as they stepped into the cold. Scarlett followed with the baby bundled in a tiny red hat and mittens, proudly announcing, "Here she is—the actual headliner of tonight's event."

Slade took his daughter in his arms. "Hey, little lady," he whispered. "Guess what? Your mom and I made it official."

The baby blinked, then reached for Slade's bow tie with determined little fingers.

Noelle leaned into Slade's side, slipping an arm around both of them. He kissed the top of her head, voice low enough only she could hear.

"Perfect night."

"It is," she said softly.

Noelle leaned back and watched them, her heart folding into something warm and full and entirely new. Last Christmas, they were welcoming the birth of their sweet little Holly. This Christmas, they were ushering in the next chapter as an established, happy family—hand in hand with the man she loved, their baby safe between them, a life finally taking shape on a firm foundation—steady, chosen, and whole.

And it felt like forever beginning.

At the reception, Noelle stood with Holly perched on her hip and Slade by her side at the head table, ready for the cake cutting ceremony. In lieu of a traditional wedding cake, they had decided to make it a birthday cake for Holly to celebrate her first birthday with all of their family and friends. Holly's bright blue eyes lit up as the colorful cake in the shape of a Christmas tree with little holly berries drawn out of frosting was placed before them. Everyone sang a very boisterous round of *Happy Birthday* to Holly and they all toasted to the happy couple.

Holly enthusiastically dug her little fist into the rich frosting and had it smeared across her rosy cheeks in an instant. Giggling and clearly pleased with herself, she scooped another fistful of the cake and presented it to her parents like a prize. Slade and Noelle looked at each other playfully and nodded in silent agreement, smushing both of their faces into their daughter's tiny hand covered in cake, causing everyone to laugh and clap.

Slade leaned close, brushing a messy kiss against Noelle's jaw. "You look beautiful," he murmured, his voice low enough for only her. "I can't believe you're mine."

Noelle smiled as she wiped the cake from hers and Holly's faces. She kissed Holly's head, then handed her off to Genevieve.

It was time for their first dance.

Nerves fluttering, Noelle took Slade's hand, threading her fingers through his as he began to swirl her around the dance floor, all eyes on them. Quietly, she said, "There's something I need to tell you."

His brows lifted, curious. "What is it?"

She pressed his palm gently against her stomach. "We're not just starting our marriage tonight, Slade. We're growing our family again."

For a heartbeat, he stared at her, uncomprehending. Then his eyes widened, shimmering with sudden light. "You mean—"

She nodded, tears pricking her lashes. "I'm pregnant. Our second little miracle."

Slade stopped dancing immediately and scooped her up fully in his arms with an excited *whoop* and they both began laughing.

Holly squealed at the sound of her parents' laughter, as if she understood. Slade gathered his daughter from his mother and into his arms along with Noelle, holding them tight, his forehead pressed against Noelle's. "Noelle.... You've given me everything. Everything."

Around them, the family and guests began to catch on, voices rising in joyful confusion. The room erupted in cheers.

Slade barely heard any of it. His world had narrowed to the two girls in his arms—the woman he'd just vowed forever to, the daughter who had already changed his life, and now the promise of another child. He kissed Noelle, slow and reverent, as if sealing every vow all over again.

Outside, the bells of the chapel rang, mingling with the sound of carols and the laughter of their family. Snow fell heavier now, blanketing the world in white, as if heaven itself had chosen to bless their beginning.

Noelle whispered against his lips, "Merry Christmas, husband."

Slade's smile trembled, fierce and full—the kind that came from surviving what once tried to break him. He kissed Holly's cheek, then Noelle's.

"Merry Christmas, my girls." Then he bent, pressing a reverent kiss to Noelle's belly. "And Merry Christmas to our new little one."

The bells continued to ring as he drew them both closer, holding his whole world in his arms.

Christmas finally didn't feel like something he had survived.

It felt like something he had been given.

And he knew beyond a shadow of a doubt, he was never letting go.

Not Ready To Say Goodbye Yet

Thank you for stepping onto the ice with the Silverwood Snipers in their small hometown of Silverwood, Maine.

If you're not ready to say goodbye to them yet... good!

Stryker Fisher, is the captain of the team.

Focused. Unshakable. The steady twin. The one who kept everyone else together.

But life has a way of checking even the strongest players into the boards.

And when a certain sharp-tongued, soft-hearted nurse crosses his path, Stryker's carefully controlled world tilts.

He's not looking for love.

He's definitely not looking for *her*.

Every time they are around each other she looks at him like she sees the man beneath the captain... and it makes him fall a little harder.

He just doesn't know it yet.

Lace up.

The Snipers' fearless captain is next to find his happily ever after.

Book 2 *Face-Offs & Fresh Starts* is Stryker & Willow's story

About the Author

Ashley Malinowski is a wife, mother, and author.

In her free time, she can be found with her nose in a book or writing out pages of details for an upcoming story that will one day be available to the world.

She resides in Bristol, Connecticut with her husband (Matthew), two daughters (Daisy and Lily), and German Shepherd (Buttercup).

Available on:
Facebook
Instagram
Tik Tok
Amazon
Goodreads
Booksprout